Sel

By TL Clark

Published in the United Kingdom by:

Steamy Kettle Publishing

First published in electronic format and in
print in 2018.

ISBN: 978-0-9956117-1-9

Acknowledgements

Cover design by Robin Ludwig Design Inc.
www.gobookcoverdesign.com

Owen of Little Lillies was my consultant florist for this
novel. Thank you ever so much for your insights into
your world.

This story is inspired by, but not based on my own
slimming journey. I lost two and a half stone; a drop in
the ocean compared to Molly's target. But the struggle
was still real.

Thank you ever so muchly to my alpha, beta, proof and
ARC readers. I really do appreciate your hard work and
support.

Thanks as ever, must go to my supportive husband. I
couldn't be any luckier. You are my soul mate. I
couldn't do this without you. Thank you. I love you.

And last but by no means least, thank you,
dear reader. Without you I am silent. I hope you enjoy
reading this book as much as I enjoyed writing it.

Table of Contents

Chapter	Page No.

Chapter 1 – The Wedding

The bride looks resplendent as she wafts down the aisle like a drifting cloud, but a stone plummets into the deep well of my stomach.

No, I'm not the bride, I'm over here. Cooee! See me waving my hand? No, back further, in the…1, 2, 3…17th row on the bride's side.

I'm sandwiched between two very fat people. Really, I'm big myself, but I expect other fatties to have respect for one another's parameters. Too many parts of our bodies are touching, and I'm really not comfortable with that.

Yes, here I am. Hello, my name's Molly. Pleased to meet you. I'm sorry it's not under better circumstances.

'But you're at a wedding,' I hear you cry, 'Surely this is a time of merriment and celebration?' Well, not this one. Before I launch into vitriol, I'd like to point out that I'm not normally this bitter. But today's one massive ordeal, and we've not even got to the vows yet.

This bridezilla really takes the biscuit. She, who also answers to the name Amelia, contacted me a mere two weeks ago to call in a favour, as her florist let her down. Those were her words. But having worked on this wedding, I think the woman in white stamped her foot once too often and the florist quite rightly decided it simply wasn't worth it.

I'm not even sure which favour Amelia thought I owed her. It's not like she's ever done anything for me. We worked together when I had an office job. She thought she ruled the roost even then, despite the fact we were on the same pay grade.

Anyway, stupid gullible me felt some sort of obligation to help out an old…acquaintance. God, I can't even bring myself to call her a friend. Why did I do this?

I'm a florist. My business is still being built up, but it's doing OK. I suppose I hoped a big wedding like this might help promote me a bit more. Oh, that sounds horrible, doesn't it? But really, if she was as great a friend as she insinuated, wouldn't she have hired me from the outset?

But no, she walked into my little house, armed with her mother. Yes, my business is run from home at the moment. Amelia oozed charm and implored me to come to her aid. What was I to do? I couldn't say no. Maybe I should've, but I couldn't.

Amelia, who had at best, disregarded my presence before, managed to enlist my services at mates' rates. Her mother glared icy daggers at me the whole time, daring me to say no. I firmly believe she was disappointed that I didn't give her an excuse to launch into a torrent of verbal abuse.

Looking around the church I can see just how conned I was. I'm getting virtually nothing for all this work, and yet they don't seem short of a bob or two. Nothing has been spared anywhere else. That dress alone must have a price tag in the thousands.

That's not even the worst thing. Do you want to know the most deplorable part of this whole sorry saga? Gyp! She demanded bloody gypsophila in her bouquet. You may know it as baby's breath. The tiny white fluffy, ridiculous flowers are nothing but fillers used by lazy florists, or ones stuck in the eighties. It's hideous and smells like cat pee.

I had tried to keep it to a minimum in the bouquet, and hid it as much as possible, but Amelia has only gone and bloody teased it out, so it's sticking in all directions now. This is my professional reputation here. I'm spitting feathers.

The bridal bouquet contains as many peonies as my limited budget would allow, along with some hydrangeas, sweet peas, and roses; all in white. All designed to disguise the appearance and smell of the gyp.

The bridesmaids' bouquets have the addition of dusky pink roses for a subtle splash of colour and a touch of elegance. I actually managed to convince Bridezilla that gyp should be in her flowers only, as it would emphasise hers as the important one.

Phew, I'm a sweltering mess here. I daren't look, but suspect there are pit stains on my dress. My hair is clinging to my face. I tried to sweep my long red hair up into a chignon, but strands have escaped already. It can't be a good look.

Today is astonishingly hot. Who would have thought that Wiltshire in good old England could produce this on a June day? Maybe Amelia's parents paid someone so the sun shone down on their precious daughter? Oh now, that really is too bitchy. I apologise. I'm hot, tired and grumpy.

A piece of toast and a cup of coffee has been the gross sum of my fuel as I dashed around like the proverbial fly. It's beyond lunchtime, and hunger is making itself known with embarrassingly loud moans and groans. My arm is pressed against my stomach in an attempt to hush it.

Oh hang on, we're rising to our feet like good parishioners to sing a wholesome hymn. What a joke. I doubt Amelia's been in a church since she was christened. If you're not religious you shouldn't get married in a church. It just seems rude, doesn't it?

My mouth silently opens and closes like I'm some sort of fish. My singing tends to hurt people's ears, and I find hymns particularly challenging. Why are they all written in an odd key, which seems more suited to dolphins? I'm miming out of respect and compassion for the people around to me, who clearly don't share my good manners.

I really hope there's canapés upon arrival at the reception. Passing out seems increasingly likely in this heat if I don't manage to eat something soon.

Pardon? Oh, why am I attending the wedding? Well, obviously I wouldn't usually. But Amelia claimed acquaintance, and begrudgingly offered. She thought she was being polite, fulfilling the social obligation in return for putting someone out. But she had drilled my prices down so much, and raised my hackles to such high levels that I actually accepted.

To my shame, I'm here for the free food. I wanted to get some sort of return on my investment. And yes, I thought I may hand out some business cards too. Does this make me a bad person? Don't answer that. I'm really not coming across well here.

I'll be honest. I'm also hurting for other reasons. A plus one was supposed to be accompanying me today, but Nigel the wanker dumped me yesterday. Who does that? He actually dumped me the day before we were supposed to attend a wedding. What a cock!

So, my eyes are all red and puffy after I sobbed my heart out yesterday, whilst trying to create flower arrangements for happy brides. I'm sure that's not a good omen for the couples today. Having 'jilted person tears' on their flowers can't be good, can it? I really hope I haven't unwittingly cursed them.

Nigel and I had been dating for a few months, and I thought it was going well. He was certainly coming round to my little house quite frequently. My house used to belong to my grandmother, by the way. I'm the only grandchild, and as my parents already have a house she left hers to me in her will. I really miss her, and would happily swap my house for her return.

Oh, now I'm sad about my grandmother **and** my breakup. Happy thoughts, happy thoughts, quick…summer meadows, bees, butterflies. Lalala.

My body is getting squished and jostled as we all try to take our seats again. The happy couple are certainly popular. The church is bursting with people. It's not a big church, but it's still impressively full. You'd be forgiven for thinking it was a society wedding. It's very fancy, and the guests all seem well-heeled. Apart from me, obviously.

Amelia really does look beautiful; the perfect bride. The long flowing gown, complete with lace detail which compliments her alabaster skin. Her long blonde hair is perfectly quaffed and supports her cathedral length veil effortlessly. Her train drapes behind her like a silky cascade as she turns to her equally beautiful almost-husband.

He looks like he was on the rowing team. He is incredibly tall, well-built and has the tan and blond hair that you can only get by being outside a lot. Perhaps he's a sailor? Owns his own yacht, or something.

What a gorgeous young pair they make, still in their twenties, in the prime of life. Their children will be beautiful too. And they'll all live happily ever after in the perfect house. A happy sigh escapes my mouth as I dream of their happy future. See, I can be nice.

I have to confess I'm more than a little jealous. They've got it all made. They're there. They've won at the game of life. Me? I'm all alone again, back to square one. I must've landed on a snake whilst they rolled a six and landed on a ladder. It's not their fault. I don't blame them. Of course I don't. I just wish it was me standing at that altar.

Each year seems to be flying past at breakneck speed. Thirty-four has crept up on me by stealth. How am I not married yet? Most of my old friends are, and have children too. I say old friends, as they seem to drift off once they give birth. I suppose there's a camaraderie between new mums. They seek each other out, desperate to find someone else who is struggling to cope with motherhood. It makes sense.

Aww, they're saying their "I do's". Tears prick the corners of my eyes as the couple gaze at each other lovingly.

"I, Amelia Wilson, take thee Richard Tomkinson to be my lawful wedded husband," she parrots the priest.

Priest? Vicar? I don't know. I told you I'm not religious. Anyway, the bloke in robes standing up the front is saying words and she's repeating them. It's very traditional and very sweet.

The choir bursts into action again as the important people gather round to sign the register. The singers are really very good, and their melody is softly hypnotic. My tension may actually be being soothed. My shoulders are starting to shrink away from my earlobes.

As others begin to crowd round the newlyweds with their cameras and phones, I take the opportunity to stroll towards the door.

"Are you alright?" a rather lovely usher asks me.

"Oh, I'm fine. Just getting a bit of fresh air."

"It is a bit stifling, isn't it? Mind if I join you?"

"It's a free country." Honestly, I'm smiling as I say this. I'm being cheeky, not rude.

We stroll through the arched door and into blazing, bright sunlight. The usher leads the way to a lovely bit of shade under a large tree.

"Mind if I smoke?" he asks.

"Not if you throw one my way," I reply, rather saucily.

What? I've had a very stressful day.

I'm liking this chap. He may be a little young for me, but he's quite pleasing on the eye and has lovely manners. He's poked a cigarette out of the packet, and freely offers it up.

Oh, my heart skips a beat as he leans in to light it for me. I get just enough time to inhale his fresh, clean smell before the lit cigarette's smoke takes over. I hope to hell that my body odour didn't reach his nose in exchange.

Our gazes do not lock, the choir inside cannot be heard from here and so they do not serenade us. He's average height, dark hair, nice looking and slightly tubby, but still miles out of my league. He's simply being nice, humouring me.

My back leans against the tree trunk as I inhale deeply and puff out smoke, like the dragon I am. Well, I am a fiery redhead.

"I'm Luke by the way," the usher says on an exhale, interrupting the silence I was enjoying.

"Hi. I'm Molly. Thanks for this. I needed it after my morning."

"It's been a busy day."

"It really has. I've been rushing around like the proverbial fly. I apologise if I look a complete state."

My rather dull conversation is interrupted by the church organ piping up.

"Oops, duty calls," Luke half apologises, as he walks briskly back inside.

I'm quite happy to remain under this tree. It's cooler, and I can still see the bride as she comes out. It's not like she wants me spoiling her photos anyway. They're all posing in groups outside the picturesque church.

Nobody bothers me. I doubt they even notice. They're all preoccupied with jostling into family units and smiling for the camera. It's organised chaos, but Amelia is smiling like a cat who's got the cream. I suppose she has.

It's such a happy scene. There's elbow nudging, people rushing round, the photographer shouting orders, and it's all wrapped up in laughter. Just as a wedding should be.

Sneaking across to my van, I make my getaway, wanting to check on the table arrangements before everyone arrives at the reception.

Chapter 2 – The Drinks Reception

Would you just look at this place? Stunning long driveway, leading up to a gorgeous old building. It's the stuff dream weddings are made of. I don't know what it is about them, but old manor houses somehow lend themselves to romanticism.

Checking in, I smile at the receptionist as she hands me the room key. I've not got time to take my overnight bag to my room, so it stays in my van. I stow the key in my clutch bag, which narrowly still manages to close.

Instead of going to my room, I head to the one where we'll all be eating in the hopefully not too distant future. It's sumptuous, and the flowers compliment it beautifully. The heady reds of the walls are contrasted by the white flowers on the tables. It's all very elegant and opulent.

The blooms are lasting well, but I can't resist a little zhush here and there, just to be sure. Perfectionist much? Well, maybe. But I take pride in my work.

Right, I'm going to run to the toilets, and freshen up a bit before everyone arrives. Bear with.

***

Phew, there was an old fashioned hand dryer in there. I told you I had pit stains. I knew it. Serves me right for wearing a close fitting pale grey dress, I suppose. How embarrassing. Oh well, all dried now. Just the visible rolls of blubber to brave out.

After a bit of mopping up, hair brushing and retying, as well as a retouch of makeup I'm feeling less like a sack of potatoes. And just in the nick of time.

The bride and groom are pulling up outside in their Rolls Royce. Well, they had to have a posh car bring them to this posh place, didn't they?

The photographer is already lined up and taking more photos as I hide away, peeking from behind the curtains in the hotel's reception. The wedding co-ordinator goes out to greet the couple, armed with champagne. She's all smiles and politeness.

Amelia must be as famished as me, but is taking a rather large gulp of that bubbly. She may regret that later.

The co-ordinator gently yet firmly leads them inside. She's used to taking control. Her welcoming outstretched arm to show the way in shows her openness, yet seems authoritative. She's standing very upright, like an army major, or something. I'd say she's used to directing rogue brides. This is backed up by her confident strides as she leads the way in. Eek, I duck behind a pillar, not wanting to be seen.

As they're escorted past I sigh in relief. It would be bad form to be seen arriving before the happy couple. They're yet to inspect the rooms they've hired.

Cars are starting to fill the car park as the wedding guests arrive in dribs and drabs. Some had arrived already, and are milling around, clearly waiting for friends.

As they all start filing in, I subtly join the queue of people being led through to the rear terrace. In this heat it's a bit of a suntrap, but at least rain's not spoiling the big day. But then I suppose we'd be in a room inside in the event of a downpour.

Waiters are on hand with trays. Champagne flutes filled with bubbles and a raspberry are served to grateful recipients, including me. Other servers are carrying trays of canapés, thank heavens. Now all I need to do is manoeuvre myself in their direction. It's quite crowded, so this will be easier said than done.

Come on people, move. You don't want to get between me and food. I didn't have time for lunch, as I'm sure you all did. Come along now, beep beep. Of course, these are merely thoughts in my head, I wouldn't dream of saying it out loud.

"Pardon me," escapes my mouth, politely.

Hmm, too politely. Nobody seems to be moving. Please let me get to the canapés before they run out and I pass out. Please. I could kill for a vol-au-vent, or even one of those salmon and cream cheese wheel things. I can't see what's on offer from here, just that there are trays of food.

"Oh hi, Molly."

I try ever so hard not to let my shoulders slump as I hear a once familiar voice hail me. I plaster a smile on my face as I glance over my shoulder.

"Hello Paul."

Yes, it's Paul. He's an ex work colleague. He thinks he's wonderful, but really isn't. Sure, he's tall, dark and handsome, but he knows it. And right now he's even more annoying, as he's hampering my desperate search of snacks.

"The office hasn't been the same without you," he tells me.

Yeah, like he's even noticed I'm gone. It's been two years and he's never once contacted me. We used to be friendly enough. We'd chat by the coffee machine, exchange pleasantries by the printer, that sort of thing. We weren't exactly bosom buddies. I didn't expect him to contact me. But please don't lie and pretend you miss me.

"I'm sure," I manage to respond, noncommittally.

"No, no, I mean it. It's a much duller place without your presence."

"You're not about to call me a ray of sunshine, are you?"

"More like a breath of fresh air," he says with a smile, gazing upwards.

"Oh dear, how many of those have you had?" I ask, nodding at his empty glass.

"Just the one," he says with a smirk.

I look over at the beautiful gardens.

"It's a stunning setting, isn't it?"

Spot the rapid change of subject.

"Very romantic," he admires.

Spot the epic fail.

"And Amelia looks beautiful. She always does, of course. But even more so."

"Yeah, I suppose, but looks aren't everything. Inner beauty is important too." His smile is sickly sweet, and turns my stomach.

Seriously? What has happened to him? Why's he being so weird? He was never like this before. He's starting to creep me out.

Happily, a waiter finally emerges with a tray of goodies. I quickly grab a few. I don't wish to appear greedy, but there's no telling when or even if they'll manage to circumnavigate the throng of people again. And have I mentioned how hungry I am?

A bit of crème fraiche squirts out as I bite into a smoked salmon canapé. Why do these things always happen to me? I manage to catch it with my hand before it drops off my chin.

Paul chuckles and offers me his napkin, forcing me to offer an embarrassed thank you.

I stuff the rest of the smoked salmon into my mouth before any further disasters can ensue. This is immediately followed by a parma ham lollipop. Delicious! And not messy. Happily, I took two of those, so the other one gets pigged down.

I become aware of Paul who's still standing there and appears to be grinning at me.

"I'm sorry. That wasn't terribly lady-like, was it? It's just I missed lunch."

"There's no need for you to explain."

That hurts enough to cause a wince. Yes, there is a need for an explanation. I may be fat, but I'm not a glutton. He shouldn't accept my hurried eating blindly, as if he expected it. It's not normal behaviour for me. And he should know me better than that.

A bit of pride gets swallowed down along with the sip of bubbly. Sighing, I gaze across the gardens, contentment filling my system now it's been slightly mollified by some nibbles. The happy couple are posing in the grounds.

"Poor people. Their mouths must hurt by now," Paul mutters beside me.

"What makes you say that?"

"Their day has been filled with smiling for that camera. It takes its toll."

"You sound as if you know."

"Well, I was once there myself."

I inwardly kick myself. He got divorced a while ago. I'd learned as much from our work kitchen chats.

"I'm sorry. Of course. That was thoughtless."

"It's fine. These things always bring back memories, you know?"

"I suppose they must. But hopefully happy memories."

"Oh yes. The wedding day was everything that's expected of it. We were happy then." Sadness furrows his brow as he speaks.

I struggle to think of something comforting to say, but all I can think of are meaningless platitudes. Oh, I know.

"I'm surprised Becky's not with you."

"We broke up last year."

Nice one, Molly. Just kick the man whilst he's down. I should have realised by the fact she wasn't there. Becky was his girlfriend I'd heard about. I had sort of hoped she was freshening up, or something, and I'd simply not seen her.

"I'm sorry to hear that."

"Just one of those things. In the end we were too different. Maybe we always were."

"If it makes you feel any better, my latest ended our relationship yesterday."

"Oh, I am sorry."

An awkward silence ensues. I start looking around to see if any other former colleagues are nearby, anyone who may be able to salvage this wreck of a conversation. But no such luck.

I merely feel even more self-conscious. Many of the other guests seem refined, and their posh tones carry through the air like sirens, warning the lower ranks not to come near. I shift from foot to foot.

The harpist is playing, but it's difficult to hear from here, over the din of chatter. I'm actually glad to be outside. Small spaces and the hubbub of people talking hurts my ears and makes me feel claustrophobic. However, I'm getting worried about sunburn. Having the 'English Rose' complexion isn't compatible with extended periods in the sun.

"Well, it was very nice catching up, but I'm afraid I need to find some shade," I apologise, excusing myself.

Paul lets me battle my way through the crowd. I think he's as happy to end our conversation as I was. It was terribly awkward.

It's sad that we hadn't kept in touch. I know I said we weren't bosom buddies, but we were friends of sorts. It's difficult to be friends outside of work though. I mean, for people of the opposite sex. He had a girlfriend, and it felt like I'd be accused of trying to steal him.

Whilst I'm re-assessing things, I suppose I have to admit Paul probably doesn't think as much of himself as he appears either. He just gives off this…aura of confidence. Of over confidence. But I think maybe it's masking the opposite; that he's really quite unsure of himself.

Isn't it marvellous what a small amount of food and alcohol can do to improve one's mood? My happiness levels are still on the up as I squeeze closer to the building, and stand under the veranda.

The harpist is very close, and I can now fully enjoy her pleasing music. My eyes close as the melody washes over me. There's always something a little sorrowful about harps, but it's lovely at the same time.

When the song ends I clap, but am aware how few others join in the applause. The poor lady. She's playing until her fingers virtually bleed, but people are barely noticing. I smile appreciatively at her, letting her know that at least one person values her music. She gives a little smile back. She got the message. Good.

I sip the last drop of my champagne, and realise that's the last drop. Well, that's going to leave me a bit squiffy. There will be more during the meal, I'm sure, when we have the obligatory toasts. Plus the wine with the meal. It's a good job I'm staying over.

As the next piece of music starts it plucks at my heartstrings. "O Mio Babbino Caro" always has that effect on me, but today it serves to remind me of my loss. I've been trying desperately to keep Nigel from my mind. The ratbag. Oh no, tears are pricking my eyes, and there's no drink left in my glass to wash away the lump in my throat.

At last, a bit of good luck falls my way, and a kind waitress has a tray of champers. I swap my empty for a full glass, and gratefully gulp some down.

Oh no, please not "A Thousand Years". Oh you cruel harpist, you have betrayed my gratitude. No amount of champagne will rescue me from this. This was our song. A harsh reminder of yet another failed relationship, of Nigel's rejection. I quickly walk inside and hide myself in a toilet cubicle so some tears can escape in privacy. Fine, so it's a lot of tears and some sobs.

I sit down on the closed loo, and fall to pieces. All alone. What is so wrong with me? Why can't I find lasting love? Why does nobody want to marry me? Why can't I find my happy ever after? I just want to be loved.

I'm panicking and need to stop. I'm at a wedding, for crying out loud, and cannot fall apart like this now.

Taking some deep breaths, a few sobs pop out of my mouth. More deep breaths. I can do this. I pull up my imaginary big girl pants and creep out of the cubicle, after blowing my nose and flushing the evidence away.

Cool water splashes on my eyes, and I glance up at the mirror. What a state. I run to get some more toilet tissue, and wipe away the panda eyes. I'm so glad I remembered to put my makeup in my bag. It gets fished out, and once more, the cosmetic mask gets put back in place. My eyes remain obstinately red and puffy, but apart from that I'll pass muster.

A few more deep breaths and I'm ready to face the world, or at least a room of wedding guests. I grit my teeth a little as I hold my head up and try my best to look confident as I walk somewhat unsteadily back into the daylight.

Standing near the traitorous harpist seems unwise, so I risk the sunshine, and look down at the gardens again. Happy thoughts, happy thoughts. Aren't the flowers colourful? How blessed are we in this world, to have such natural beauty?

Who am I kidding? There's not too many flowers visible from here. And the ones which are visible are mainly marigolds and roses, if I'm being honest. Now, if I owned a property like this I'd plant…Saved by the bell. Or gong. The wedding breakfast is announced, and we guests all start pouring in to the allotted room.

There's something close to being a rugby scrum as we all try to see the seating plan. I'm short, so it's a nigh on impossible challenge. My progress is agonisingly slow as I wait, shuffling towards the front.

"Come on, Molly, we're this way," a gentle voice calls, as a hand is placed on my elbow.

I involuntarily recoil at the unexpected touch, but smile gratefully at Paul. He's tall and has located the 'work' table. This could be fun. Let's see who has turned up.

Chapter 3 – The Unpalatable Wedding Breakfast

We reach the table and I find the little card with my name on it. I expect to find Nigel's name next to mine, with an empty seat waiting for the guest who will never arrive. The dreaded moment is upon me. I don't want to have to explain to the whole table that I've just been dumped.

My excuse is ready; he's been called into work. It's possible. No big drama. Completely reasonable.

But Nigel's name isn't on the card next to mine. I check the other side of the setting, but that says Wayne. I look back to the place on my right and double check. No, it definitely says Paul. I had texted Amelia through my tears last night, hoping there was time to tell the caterers. I didn't want them to cook food only for it to go to waste.

She must've got the hotel to change the settings too. Bless her, that was really thoughtful. I didn't expect her to go to that much trouble. I'm sure she had far more important things to worry about the day before she got married. Guilt washes over me, as I realise what a nuisance I am. Maybe she didn't fully deserve all my bad thoughts earlier.

It dawns on me that Paul is standing by my back, holding my chair out. Steady, it's not as if we're on a date. Still, it's a nice gesture.

Cue a failed attempt at being elegant. My huge arse somehow almost misses the chair as I sit, and Paul has to quickly shove it further forward. I fall more than sit down. I'm just lucky it didn't break from the shock of my sudden weight.

My cheeks are burning as the blush fills my entire face. I don't need to look in a mirror to know it's there.

My gaze is fixed firmly at the tablecloth as I feel Paul take his seat next to me. I'm mortified. Thankfully, not many of the others are at the table yet.

The room is beginning to fill, and former colleagues are emerging at our table. I stand excitedly and hug Sharon as she approaches.

"Sharon, it's so good to see you," I tell her honestly.

"Molly, it's been too long. We really must meet up for lunch or something. I'm terrible. I get so distracted by life."

"I know the feeling."

Sharon is scooched along as others come to take their seats, but she's not too far away from me. Hopefully we can manage a conversation over the meal. I've missed her. I really don't know why I've not made more of an effort to see her. Silly really.

Wayne bends down to kiss my cheeks, telling me not to get back up as he finds his place. I'm secretly glad to be sitting next to him. He was the 'funny one' in the office, and made the otherwise stressful environment bearable.

Sharon catches my attention again. "This is Lisa. She's the new you."

I swallow down my surprise. I left of my own free will, and they were always going to have to recruit someone else to fill my role. I just never expected to come face-to-face with that person.

"Oh hello," I greet her, attempting to smile.

We're too far apart to shake hands, so we merely wave awkwardly at one another. She's on the opposite side of the large circular table, an empty chair next to her. Is it wrong to feel grateful she's mostly obscured by my flower arrangement? I can't help it. Jealousy is a nasty thing, and doesn't always shut up, even when you point out it's being childish and completely unreasonable.

More lovely waiters, or maybe the same ones as earlier, come around with more filled champagne flutes, which they place on the tables.

"Ladies and gentlemen, please be upstanding for your bride and groom, Mr and Mrs Tomkinson," a very official person calls out loudly from beside the room entrance.

The doors open and in comes a beaming Amelia and her husband. Bless them, they're still walking on air. Happiness just radiates from and around them.

They make their way to the top table, and we all toast them with a sip of champagne, or non-alcoholic alternative for some which I now wish I'd asked for. Initial toast done, we all take our seats again.

As if he has no thought or feeling for our rumbling bellies, the father-of-the-bride stands up. Those little canapés have run their course, and my hunger is nagging again.

"Ladies and gentlemen, thank you all for coming today. It is the best of days and the worst of days, as I have had to give away my darling, beautiful daughter, Amelia. But I couldn't have given her to anyone more deserving."

Other gushing things escaped the man's mouth, but I shan't bore you with the whole thing. It ran along the lines of him being grateful and honoured to have a daughter like Amelia.

It occurs to me that every bride is automatically appointed sainthood status. They're never terrible tearaways, are they? No, they're perfect angels. It's the same when anyone dies. You see people on the television, decreeing the deceased's impeccable life. I suppose there's times when the truth is unforgivable; marriage and death being amongst them.

Anyway, he's finally shut up, and it's a huge relief to see the starters being brought in. Of course, being amongst the lowest ranking guests, our table is the farthest away, so we're served last. I swear I can see some main courses being brought in before our starters arrive. Did that sound irritable? There's a reason for that.

The beef carpaccio is tasty, to give the venue credit where it's due. And it takes the edge off my hunger enough to enable more pleasing conversation with my companions. To my shame, I was rather silent until the food arrived.

It's not easy seeing the people you used to work with, you know. You exited the building, and they may have grieved for the loss of you in a way. I seriously doubt it in my case, but there is a sort of grief when team members leave. There's this empty space where they used to sit and an unsettling feeling of the group no longer being whole.

If only Nigel hadn't been such a total wanker he would have been here, talking to me, and bigging me up. But instead, I'm left feeling awkward. There's a strange distance between me and these people. Damn my pig-headedness. I should've turned down the invitation.

My knife and fork almost drop onto my plate as Wayne suddenly strikes up a conversation, which appears to be directed at me.

"So, how's business going? I must say you're very brave starting up on your own the way you did. But you've not come crawling back so I assume it's going well."

"Yes, I—"

"It's a pity. I really thought Amelia would've asked you to do the flowers for today."

"Well—"

"But I suppose it would've been too awkward when you're a guest, eh? Never mind. I'm sure you would've done a far better job of things."

"Well actually —"

"What's that? Oh, don't insult poor Molly by talking about the flowers. That bouquet was far inferior to anything she'd ever create," interjects Sharon.

"I —"

Sadly she continues, "Did you see Amelia's bouquet? Quite a mess. It looked like it had been pulled through a hedge backwards. She really should have called upon you."

I give up.

"The bridesmaids' bouquets were lovely though," I say, trying to raise people's opinions, feeling like a spy in their midst now.

"Oh, they were OK. But then I heard it wasn't the original florist. I can't say I'm surprised. Amelia turned into quite the bridezilla. It was obvious even to us in the office. No wonder the poor florist flounced off," Sharon added.

"Yes, I suppose you have to allow for having to do things at short notice. But really, any florist should be able to provide better than that garbage poor Amelia had to carry," Lisa says from behind my unappreciated display.

That does it. I can't stand it. I shouldn't have to sit here and listen to these people insult me. I clear my throat, and try to raise my voice loud enough to be heard.

"I can assure you that bouquet didn't start the day off that way," I tell them just a little too loudly.

Not only did the people on our table fall silent, but the people on the next one did too. Fortunately, I don't think it reached any farther than that. For once, it's a good thing to have loud chattering in a room.

I purse my lips and try to regain my composure. This is quite difficult to do when heat rises back up to your cheeks.

Sharon looks mortified.

"Molly," is all she can get out.

I testily grab my phone out of my bag, which I'd plonked under my chair. Some contortion is required to reach it, but Paul kindly moves slightly.

"Here. Look. It was beautiful this morning," I tell them, almost crying as I hold up my phone.

I pass it around the table so they can all witness that I am in fact a good florist.

"You wouldn't believe the budget she landed me with, either. I had precious little to work with. *And* she insisted on bloody gyp. I tried to dissuade her. Who wants to smell like cat pee on their big day? But she wouldn't listen. I tried to work it in nicely."

"Oh I can see," Sharon admires, as the phone is finally passed to her.

"Oh that was beautiful. What on earth did she do to it?" Lisa wonders out loud.

She's beginning to grow on me.

As the phone makes its way back to me, murmurs of admiration and astonishment also make the rounds. They're slowly realising it wasn't my fault, and are becoming annoyed at the bride and her disrespectful treatment of my flowers.

The main courses are served just in time to stop any escalation of all this negativity.

Regard, the fatty is only having halibut. It's a low fat, healthier option. My subtle message is being sent out to my fellow diners. I know I've put on weight since they last saw me, and it bothers me. But nothing seems to work. So the best I can do is to show them I'm trying.

But that pork looks good on Paul's plate. I lick my lips between bites as I cast a furtive glance in its direction.

"How's the fish?" Paul asks.

Oops, was it obvious I was staring longingly at his food?

"Delicious. How's the pork?" ˄

"Very good. Would you like to try some?" he asks, loading his fork with both pork and black pudding.

What a wonderful man. I could kiss his feet. But I manage to meekly nod and stretch my neck forwards to bite off the porky offering.

"Mmm…that really is good."

"Would you like to swap?"

Oh I could kiss him for asking.

"That's very kind, but honestly, the fish is lovely too. Here, try," I offer.

"It's nice, but I'll stick with the pork," he says with a cheeky wink.

The others around the table seem to be staring.

"How's the lamb, Sharon?" I call over.

"Oh, lovely, thank you," she replies, her eyes flitting at me then back to her plate.

What's up with her? I shrug and carry on devouring my fish.

Amelia bashing seems to be the new theme of conversation as the meal progresses. It sounds like she's been a nightmare to everyone. I'm sort of relieved to hear this, as at least it means it's nothing personal. But we're at her wedding, show some decorum, people.

Anne from Accounts has started chipping in now.

"She even upset one of her best friends. She's a bridesmaid short."

"Really?" I ask, astonished, as I'm sure all my bouquets have been utilised.

Curiosity got the better of me. The question was out before I could stop it.

"Oh yes, three weeks ago they had a massive argument, and they've not spoken since. Her room here was all paid for and everything."

I feel as if someone's punched me in the face. How could I have fallen for her tripe?

Amelia told me she'd managed to get me a room as an extra thank you for being so wonderful and stepping in at the last minute. I had hoped she was beginning to actually show me signs of potential friendship. It'd be nice to have someone else to call my friend. A little bit of kindness is all I want. But no, she was just making sure she got her money's worth, and probably protecting her group discount.

Another sip of this delicious chardonnay will cover the shocked look on my face, I hope. The glass seems to be bottomless. I'm sure I've not topped it up, but it's lasting a long time, and that warm fuzzy feeling is creeping along my veins.

Have you ever been to a function and really wish you hadn't bothered? Today has been one big ball of stress. From running around delivering flowers, to being squashed in a hot sweaty line in the church, the embarrassing flood of tears, the insults, the pretending to be happy when all I want to do is sob about being dumped, and witnessing someone else's extreme happiness in stark contrast to my own feelings.

Oh, you're probably telling me to shut up, and stop whinging. There's worse things that happen at sea. There's plenty of people worse off than me. You're right. Sorry.

The desserts arrive, and I'm grateful I opted for the tart. I can almost feel its sticky comforting goodness already.

"How are you bearing up?" Paul whispers at my side.

"Oh, you know, fine," I try to respond with a smile.

His hand briefly squeezes mine under the table. It's a nice gesture, but overly familiar.

We manage to get through dessert with no further faux pas. And oh dear, more champagne is poured into our glasses. This can only mean the start of the speeches. And I really don't think I should have any more alcohol yet. It must be the heat earlier which has increased the wine's effect on me. My head is swimming.

The speeches are a mixture of boring to hilarious. The best man is very funny. But my mind's a little fuzzy. Just note that with each speaker came a toast, so too much champagne was consumed. I'm quite thankful for the black coffee, with the obligatory mint.

Chapter 4 – Getting Jiggy With It

The bride and groom cut the cake, and yes, many photos are taken, and I'm one of the people snapping away. What? It's a gorgeous cake and a lovely moment.

As I make my wobbly way back to my seat one of the women on the adjacent table beckons me over.

"I hear you did the flowers. They're simply marvellous."

"Thank you," I acknowledge bashfully.

"My daughter is getting married next year."

I cheekily pass her a card from my bag with a smile. Some others around the table take a card too. This boosts my ego a bit. At least today wasn't a complete disaster. It's been saved by a few kind people. Hoorah!

News travels fast, and a few more cards are handed out as we all make our way to the room where the real party is about to start. I'd been expecting a string quartet, given the style of the rest of the day, but happily a DJ is present. There's nothing wrong with sophisticated elegance, but one really does like a good dance to celebrate nuptials.

My part is over; there are no flowers here. It's all long forgotten and I finally begin to relax.

We all crowd round to observe the First Dance. John Legend's honeyed voice begins to softly sing "All of Me", and the happy couple begin their beautifully sweet dance. Her long gown sways and swishes behind her as they sweep around the dance floor. It's quite possibly the most romantic thing I've ever seen, and tears begin to prick my eyes.

Other couples are caught up in the moment and join the bride and groom once they're invited to. I can only gaze on, longingly. Nigel should be spinning me around now. Sadness creeps into my heart again as I feel the loss and separation. How could he do this?

"Come on," Paul insists, once more at my side.

"No, I can't. You're not my boyfriend."

"We can pretend, can't we?"

"Can we?"

Sparks fly between us, a tension that never existed before as he grasps my hand.

"Come on, just for fun."

I must be more drunk than I thought, as I find myself being pulled into the throng.

Paul is very respectful, and holds me in a natural dance grip, not bringing his body too close. There's a bit of a gap. We begin to sway side to side and I let myself get swept into the moment. It's nice to be held by someone, even if it's not Nigel. What am I saying? Especially if it's not Nigel.

But as soon as I get comfy in his arms the music changes, and it's time to get lively. I brush it off and pretend I'm relieved.

"Oh thank goodness," I comment.

For a moment, Paul looks hurt, but it's a fleeting emotion which passes his face in a matter of seconds. We start to get crazy on the dance floor, arms and legs flying around as the tempo of the music increases.

Age is not a good friend, and I'm getting breathless already. But "Come on Eileen" starts up, and my body is forced to participate in the iconic dance. If you've never experienced it, you must find an opportunity soon. The British consider it a staple of our dance repertoire.

After much fist pumping, clapping and foot stomping which built into a crescendo, I'm pooped. I need to go and get some fresh air.

Paul has become my shadow, and accompanies me outside. I suppose he's taken pity on me, and has made himself my welfare watcher. My hand dives into my bag and pulls out my cigarette case and lighter. Once I've lit up I offer my new minder a smoke too, which he surprisingly accepts.

I don't remember him ever smoking, and tell him as much with an oh-so-original, "Since when did you start smoking?"

"I restarted after the Becky thing."

"Oh, sorry."

"It's old news, stop apologising. To be honest, and I'm only telling you so you know you're not alone, my last relationship ended last week."

"Oh, Paul. I'm so sorry."

I have no idea why I feel I should keep apologising for things which are clearly not my fault. It just seems like the right thing to say.

He takes a long drag on his cigarette before he responds. "It wasn't anything serious. We'd only been dating for a month. We weren't right for each other. But it makes you reflect on your life, doesn't it? I've got a failed marriage and a few ex-girlfriends in my wake. I don't know where my life is going."

"Wow, I didn't know men thought like that."

"Of course we do. We just don't let on as we're expected to know what we're doing."

"Sometimes life feels like one big test. It's like someone up there's asking how much pain and torment I can endure. I have to tell them, I don't think it's much more."

I inhale on my cigarette steadily to help control my breathing which had become erratic.

Paul breaks the silence. "Hey, we're a couple of gloomy pusses. We're here at a wedding, and should be happy. It's a day of celebration. Let's say we forget all the doubt and worry and let our hair down?"

"Sounds like a good plan," I tell him with a genuine grin.

I don't get out much these days, and a bit of mindless fun sounds like just the tonic. I'm on my way to being drunk already, might as well finish the job.

Once we finish our cigarettes we go up to the bar and order shots, which we recklessly down before heading back onto the dance floor.

I abandon my usual self; she's been hung up on a coat hook somewhere. I'm 'fun Molly' as I jig around like a thing possessed. There's regular breaks for drinks, mostly alcoholic. It's not like I suddenly developed super powers; it's still exhausting. But I'm definitely having a great time.

My neck scarf is drooping loosely around my shoulders, and I swirl it frivolously as I dance around.

All too soon the tempo slows. Time has lost all meaning, but it must be late. The slow songs are being played.

Paul pulls me close as José Gonzales sings "Heartbeats". I close my eyes and pretend he's my boyfriend, as he suggested earlier.

My cheek rests on his chest as we shuffle around to the song. His chin is touching the top of my head. We're super close, and it feels super nice. I know him and he knows me. The familiarity is comforting. It's easy to let myself believe the lie.

As the song ends I find Paul's lips on mine and his hand on my arse. I jump at the intimate contact. I'm stunned for a moment.

Sensing a few pairs of eyes on us, mainly from my former colleagues, I want the ground to open up and swallow me whole. What just happened? We were only *pretending* to be a couple, weren't we?

Too embarrassed to know how to handle this, I run from the room, escaping into the cool night air. I'm trying to get to my cigarettes, but my intoxicated fingers are fumbling with the clasp on my bag. Damn it!

A packet is shoved under my nose.

"Here, have one of mine."

Well, Paul's persistent, you have to give him that. But I'm in no mood to even look at him.

"Please leave me alone," I bark.

"Molly, I'm sorry."

He's still holding out the packet, so I snatch the proffered cigarette and take the lighter from him.

"You groped me," I state, glowering.

"I'm sorry. I didn't mean to upset you. I got carried away."

"Well you did upset me," I tell him, sparking up the cigarette, and inhaling its heady toxins.

"I know. I'm sorry. I guess I was mistaken. I thought it's what you wanted. I'm sorry." His hands ruffle his hair as he speaks.

I scrunch my face before exhaling up to the dark sky. "I don't know. Maybe I'm overreacting. You caught me by surprise. And everyone was looking."

40

"Again, sorry," he says, drawing nearer to where I'm leaning against the wall.

"I need to clear my head," I tell him, stepping back a pace to lengthen his encroaching presence.

"Please don't overthink this. We were having fun, right?"

"Fun is a far cry from what just happened, Paul."

"It was just a kiss. I already said sorry."

Just a kiss? Well, I suppose it was. And a grope, don't forget that. But we're adults. Adults kiss. Was it really that bad? I did like it until I noticed the people watching us.

"No, you're right. I'm sorry. I'm such a mess," I tell him, pinching the bridge of my nose, fighting back tears.

"Hey, come here."

He opens his arms out for a hug and I accept, needing the reassurance. OK, it's probably a stupid idea. But I'm hurting and I want a hug, even if it is from the man who may have overstepped the mark. But this is Paul. I can trust him. I think.

As I let the tears fall down my cheeks I hold onto him tightly, and think about the evening. If I'm honest, upon reflection, I've probably been flirting with him all day. It felt good to have someone pay attention to me. It boosted my ego. There, I said it. I was flattered. It went right to my head along with all those bubbles.

Paul's being quiet. Bless him, he's been letting me cry on his nice shirt.

"OK, enough tears. He's not worth it," he finally tells me.

"Pardon me?"

"I assume you're wasting tears on the idiot who left you."

"Well, yes."

"Well, stop. The man's a fool if he can't see what a wonderful person you are and what he's thrown away."

"Oh please."

"I mean it."

"Yeah, you were just chasing me around the office."

"If I'd not been with someone I would've been."

My breath sticks in my throat. He looks shy as he looks down at me. He must be telling the truth. I can't believe it. He never showed any sign of fancying me before. I blamed his behaviour tonight on being drunk.

A shiver runs through me, and only now do I realise how cold it is out here. Paul gallantly pulls his jacket around my shoulders.

"Thanks," I remark shyly.

We're both acting like a pair of guilty teenagers. I try to remind myself we're both adults. Two lonely, slightly inebriated adults, with needs.

My eyes travel up and down Paul's tall self. It's as if I'm truly seeing him for the first time. He's good looking in a plain sort of way. Short dark hair and brown eyes, with a tall, slightly tubby frame. I thought he was out of my league, but he's always been nice to me. He was one of the first to welcome me to the office.

Today he's shown me nothing but courtesy, up until the ill-judged groping kissing bit, of course. I'm still trying to absorb the impact of his words. He hinted he's always fancied me. It makes sense; in his head he can see the former me, and he's still chasing that idea.

Smoke swirls in the night air between us, as we both silently contemplate what's happening. I turn and start to pace. I don't know what to make of all this.

"Molly, we have an opportunity here. Aren't you curious what we'd be like together?"

It hadn't really occurred to me before today, but I have to admit that I am now. I turn back to look at him again as I nod slowly.

"We don't have to do anything you don't want to do. I don't want to be pushy. But can we try that kiss again?"

My curiosity is getting the better of me. And it would be nice not to be alone tonight. It's good to be wanted. Paul is not a stranger. He's not some random one-night-stand. I'm not like that, I wouldn't do it. But with someone I know and trust, could I?

Tingles run down my spine again. I stub out my cigarette with my foot. He does the same. My feet are taking me towards him. My stomach feels fluttery as I approach.

Before I really know what I'm doing I'm leaning in for his kiss, silently giving permission this time. He tentatively leans in. This is going to happen. Is this really a good idea?

Too late to back out now, Paul's lips are on mine, and they feel good. I begin kissing him back. My hands slide up to his shoulders, drawing me up. I don't want to stop. I want to go further.

He wraps his arms around my back. My body is pulled closer to his. Oh, this feels really good. What was I moaning about? He was right to kiss me. Kiss me more, Paul.

Just as desire starts pulsing through me he stops. I feel deserted. Did I do something wrong? Maybe he didn't like it as much as I did? Perhaps he's realised he was being an idiot?

"Molly, I don't want to sound like an arsehole, but it's getting late. I need to call for a taxi."

"Oh right, of course," I tell him, unable to hide my disappointment.

"Would you let me finish? I need to call for a taxi if you want to call it a night. Unlike you, I don't have a room here. So, it's up to you."

"This is all happening so fast."

"I know. This is not how I wanted this to happen."

I have to make a choice. My head is saying to let him go, but my heart, or my groin at least, is telling me to drag him back to my room and ravage him. That kiss has me all fired up. And heaven knows I need this.

I'm craving some sort of reassurance that men won't be repulsed by me, that there is life after Nigel. I need to feel the comfort of a body next to mine. And my body is telling me that the body I need is Paul's.

"You'd better come with me then," I say over my shoulder as I start walking.

He is following close behind as we make our way around the outside of the building in the darkness. I stumble a little as we make our way along the path and over to my room.

That damn clasp on my bag is still playing silly beggars and it takes me longer than it should to free my room key from its grasp. My fingers fumble as I try to insert it into its slot, and unlock the door. My whole hand is shaking as I try the door handle and finally open the door to a dark room.

Paul is still right behind me as I switch the light on. It seems to shine a spotlight on our situation, and it suddenly feels weird again. This is Paul! What am I doing?

"Are you sure you want to do this?" he asks me.

I was all ready to tell him I wasn't sure, but his velvety voice is drawing me in.

"Kiss me," I request, hoping it will settle my mind.

"Don't overthink this," he whispers before finding my mouth with his.

Well, that's quite convincing. His kiss is deep and heated, and oh so sensual. I can feel the wetness pooling between my legs.

"Yes."

"Yes?"

"Yes," I practically moan.

I back up to the light switch and turn the brightness off. He stays right with me, nipping at my lips and cheek, and oh my neck. Do me now!

His jacket slips from my shoulders into a heap on the floor. I begin to unzip my dress, before panic strikes.

"Hang on a sec. I'll be back," I squeal as I run to the bathroom.

I shimmy out of my dress under the bright light of the bathroom, before wrestling with my figure shaping underwear. Thank goodness I remembered in time. They are a real passion killer. Bloody things! My fingernail scratches my waist as I peel the elasticated fabric away from me. I almost topple over as I wriggle my way free and my flab sags out.

I avoid the mirror as much as possible. I don't need that painful reminder, and I'm in a hurry. Paul will wonder where I am if I'm much longer in here.

Switching the light off, I peer out of the bathroom and make my way shakily to the bed. Paul is already there.

"Oh, I don't have any protection," I cry.

"Already prepared," he confirms.

I collapse down next to him, expecting him to jump my bones. But he rolls onto his side and begins kissing me again. This is both lovely and annoying at once. It's great he's being respectful, but I kind of want him to just get on with it.

"You're beautiful," he whispers.

"Please don't."

"Don't what?"

"No platitudes. We both know what I am."

He grunts, but sensibly holds his tongue. I don't want sweet nothings.

"I want you." Did I just say that out loud?

His finger sliding down my slit makes me jump. I hadn't been aware of his hand travelling down. We both moan at the contact, and my knees fall open for him.

"Please, I need you," I beg.

I groan as he mounts and deftly slides into me. Ahhh, it feels wonderful. He slowly moves in and out, and the world falls away. This was the correct decision. This feels so right.

But as we being to move, my head starts to swim. I've had too much alcohol for this. Panic grips my sloshing stomach.

His hand grips onto my fleshy side, and I cringe at what he must be thinking.

Gritting my teeth, I try to get my head back into the moment. Sexy thoughts, sexy thoughts.

I grind my hips, and force him into a slower rhythm. That's better.

Riding the rippling waves, I relax a bit. I give in to the sensations, the building friction. It increases until it makes me cry out as my soul is plunged into a dark abyss and I'm sent to oblivion.

Paul grunts after a few more thrusts, and collapses next to me.

I pull the covers up, and hazily surrender to exhaustion.

Chapter 5 – The Morning After

Bleurgh, I wake up not knowing where I am for a moment. As I sit up in the semi darkness of the room and look down at the sleeping form by my side, it all comes flooding back to me. I did something stupid last night.

Paul, having shown me some attention won me over. It's not like he was a stranger, but one night stands aren't exactly my thing. And I can't believe this would ever develop into anything more. Like I said, he's out of my league. Last night was two lonely people working off their frustrations. It's embarrassing. Maybe it would've been easier if he'd been a stranger, after all.

"Is that any way for a nice young lady to behave?" my mother's voice shrills in my head.

Oh, she'd have a field day with this. I've cheapened myself by being easy.

What have I done? This is no way to get a husband. Call me old fashioned, but I would like a husband first, children after. But here I am, just sleeping around. Why? Comfort, I suppose. Or is it in the sad little hope Paul will give me more? That he will become Mr Right?

Creeping to the bathroom, I relieve my bladder. I had way too much to drink yesterday. Looking at the crumpled dress on the floor, I realise my overnight bag is still in the van. The shaping underwear is too much for me to handle at this time of day, so have to go commando under the rumpled dress.

Paul is stirring.

"Can I borrow your jacket as I nip outside?" I whisper.

"Meurgh, sure."

He's clearly feeling as foggy as I do. Shrugging on his jacket, I grab my clutch bag. The room key gets shoved hastily into the jacket pocket.

Despite his jacket, the morning air is still chilly as I make my way to my van as quickly as a sore head will allow. No time is wasted as I hurl my bag out of the back. Eurgh, wrong choice of words. My acid reflux gets stifled.

Gingerly, I tread back up the path back to my room. My hand reaches into the jacket pocket for the key. As I pull it out, a piece of card falls to the ground. My head complains as I bend down to pick it up.

I stagger back in shock as I read the name 'Nigel' on the card. Oh my God, this was his place card. But what? Why? What?

Amelia had rearranged the table, hadn't she? A gong sounds in my head as the penny drops. No, she clearly hadn't. Well, that's just about right. It makes more sense than her being overly concerned about me. I'm relieved I didn't put her to any trouble, and also that my feelings about her were right all along.

But if she didn't change the settings then…the hangover fog in my head begins to clear a little. Paul did.

The cogs begin to turn and flashes of the day pass through my mind. I'd seen but not truly noticed some important things. Paul was the one who'd shown me to my seat. He'd been the one who kept topping up my wine glass during the meal. He was the one who kept inserting himself into my presence. He'd instigated the 'fun'. He'd bought the shots.

Oh love a duck, how could I have been so stupid? He'd planned it all. He had imposed himself upon me, gotten me drunk and had pretended it was all good fun. What a...a...git! He manipulated me.

I thrust the key into the lock and throw the door open.

"Time to go," I storm at him.

"What?" he asks, with the audacity to sound shocked.

"The game's up," I shout, holding up the incriminating card.

"What? I changed seats to sit next you."

"I don't want to hear it. I just want you to leave."

I chuck his jacket at him, emphasising my point.

He's sitting in bed, looking dumbfounded.

"Now," I add, hoping to stir him into motion.

"I don't understand what I've done that's so wrong."

"And that's even more reason for you to go."

He rubs his hand down his face and shakes his head, but gets up. He still looks confused as he pulls his trousers on.

"Quick as you like, Paul."

I want him out of my presence. I can't bear to look at him. He betrayed my trust, lured me into his clutches. And like a fish, I swam right up and hooked myself up. Gargh, how naive?

"You're making a mistake," he tries to tell me as he shrugs on his shirt.

"No, I made a mistake last night. But it won't happen again."

I stand by the other side of the bed and herd him towards the door.

"I refuse to regret what happened," he tells me as he finally crosses the threshold.

I slam the door behind him. Refuses to regret it? What an arsehole. I'm sure he doesn't. He certainly got what he wanted didn't he? Gargh, I was so easy. I just jumped into bed, didn't I? My instincts tried to warn me, but I had to follow my hormones. Argh!

My throat is dry and my head hurts. I shove the little kettle underneath the bathroom tap to fill it. Plonking it back onto its stand and hitting the on switch, I wait, in desperate need of coffee.

Packets rustle too loudly as I rummage through the biscuit selection. Custard Creams are unwrapped and shoved into my gob as tears break through the dam of anger.

The kettle rumbles and rattles before eventually clicking off. Boiling water is poured over the contents of a coffee sachet in a little cup. It'll be ages before it cools enough, so I take the opportunity of grabbing a shower.

Ordinarily I'd luxuriate in the awesome power of the jets pouring over me, but I'm far too het up. I scrub at myself, using the free bottle of shower gel. I need to wash away all the remnants of my foolishness. The combination of my scrubbing and the very hot water turns my usual pasty white skin a vivid red.

Having shampooed my long red hair, I towel myself off, feeling even more hot and bothered than when I began. Little Pauls have been dancing in my head. What was once a cheeky smile has morphed into a smarmy smirk in my imagination, as he gloats at his victory over stupid little me. I let him do this. My desperation and emptiness was taken advantage of.

Wearing only a hotel robe, I flop onto the bed and gulp my now lukewarm coffee. The shower took longer than I intended. But it's still a welcome reviver, as is another packet of biscuits.

The lure of the breakfast room is a big draw, but can I face going? Other guests will be there, looking at me. They'll probably know what an idiot I am. They'll sit there with their judgemental eyes, staring at the trollop. No, it's not something I wish to go through. But my rumbling stomach demands more than the meagre biscuits.

A brush gets dragged through my hair as I start to dry it with the dryer on the wall. It's taking too long, so my hair remains damp as I climb into my jeans and sweatshirt. I need to escape this room. It knows what happened in that bed as well as I do. The evidence of my stupidity is staring me in the face.

With a quick check round, I gather my things, stuffing yesterday's laundry into my bag as I beat a hasty retreat.

"This will never happen again," I promise the room as I leave.

I've had enough of people taking advantage of me. It happens time and time again.

I dump my bag in my van on my way to breakfast, and check that Paul's car isn't there.

Two ratbags in as many days, I'm doing well. Walking past, I try to smile at the good looking male receptionist, wondering if I could make it three. Of course I have no intention of doing anything; it's only my bitter self being snide.

Hurrying past, I find the breakfast room, and wait to get seated. Many eyes stare as I enter, my head held low in shame.

"Mummy, that lady," a young girl starts, but her mother quickly hushes her.

My eyes glance towards the source of the exclamation.

"Shh, it's rude to point," she admonishes, lowering the girl's raised arm.

"But mummy…"

"Shh, eat your fruit, Chelsea."

Forcing my eyes back to the ground whilst still following the waitress, I shuffle towards my table. I order a cooked breakfast and coffee, so I don't have to stand next to people at the buffet for the continental version.

I sit here, all alone at a too-large table, with people staring. What? Are adults not allowed to have fun? Promiscuity isn't exactly that uncommon now. Come on, people. Get on with your meal, there's nothing to see here.

My coffee mercifully arrives, and I fiddle with the cup as the liquid cools to a drinkable temperature. Murmured conversations buzz all around me, but I can't make any of them out, which is probably for the best. All my attention is focussed on the cup and table linen.

A delicious plate of hot food gets placed in front of me, which I devour as quickly as possible, anxious to satisfy my hunger and to expedite my departure. I shouldn't have come in here. I feel like a sore thumb, sticking out all too obviously.

As soon as I'm finished I get up and return to reception.

"Did you have a nice stay?" the handsome chap asks as I check out.

He sounds deliciously Italian. Doesn't that just cheer me up a little?

"Mm, yes thank you," I tell him with a tight-lipped smile.

"Err, your top, it is," he says, pointing.

I look down, and actually gasp as I see a label pointing up at me. Not only have I managed to put my top on inside out, but back-to-front too. Blushing wildly, I offer my thanks and make my escape, covering the offending label with my hand as if that'll make it less obvious. Could this day get any worse?

My steps are hurried as I seek the safety of my van, and subsequently speed down the driveway. Perhaps my foot is a little heavier than it should be on the accelerator as I get onto the main road.

The sun is shining right into my eyes, which makes my headache worse. Two sunny days in a row? What's going on? Have the Powers forgotten it's the English summer here? I scrabble around in my glovebox for my sunglasses.

My thoughts revert to Paul as I travel onwards, making my way home. Smarmy git, fooling me that way. Why am I so stupid? Gullible, that's what my mother calls me. And as always, she's right.

Self-loathing consumes me all the way home, through my door, and up the stairs. The overnight bag is abandoned on my bedroom floor as I face-plant the bed. How did I end up in this mess? I know I only really have myself to blame, but that doesn't make it any easier.

One of Nigel's sweatshirts leers at me from the chair, where it too was dumped. You know, one of those boyfriend sweaters that they let you wear because it's comfy, and you like to have his smell nearby. But now it's a harsh reminder of my single status.

Oh Nigel. You were supposed to be the dependable one. Nobody ever expects to get dumped by a Nigel, do they? It's a good, strong, normal name. Slightly geeky. You can rely on a Nigel. They certainly don't dump their girlfriends by text.

But oh yes, yes they do. It turns out you can't rely on them either. I mean, what's the world coming to when you can't even depend on a Nigel? It's gone mad. There's no reliability to be had anywhere.

My head still hurts, and my lie-down isn't helping. Tea will help. After changing into a T-shirt, I plod downstairs again, feeling zombie-like as I seek out more caffeine. Whilst waiting for the kettle to boil, I discover some chocolate biscuits.

I can't be bothered to climb the stairs again, so opt for my sofa. Pulling the throw up over my knees, I hug the teacup to me. No, it's not cold, but I need to feel cosy. Anything to make me feel something other than utter rejection.

Rejection; it's a horrible word. Rejected by Nigel. Eurgh, so depressing. As I sip my tea, it slowly dawns on me that maybe it's the rejection that I'm sad about more than the loss of Nigel himself. Yes, he was nice company, but he wasn't exactly the love of my life. He made me feel wanted. Am I really that desperate? Oh crumbs.

The answer has to be yes, if I judge myself on last night's activities, which I do. So shameless. I let myself be lured into bed because I was so needy. I went willingly. Didn't I only think about my need as I went? Yes. I wanted to be comforted.

Did Paul really do anything so bad? It's not like he dragged me kicking and screaming back to my room. He's no Neanderthal. All he had to do was show me some consideration and suck up to me a bit. And I got what I wanted didn't I?

So, the sex wasn't the greatest, but it did the job. For one night I felt wanted. There were no promises of a happy ever after. It was all in the name of fun. Fine. So pouting and sulking really isn't warranted. Fine.

It's taken me a whole cup of tea and a packet of biscuits to reach this conclusion, but there it is. I'm a sad lonely thirty-four year old woman who wants to be loved. Last night was just a bit of fun, but real life is here again now. I need to get on with it.

Chapter 6 - What Friends Are For

Didn't I sound healthy by the end of yesterday? I came to all sorts of adult conclusions. Well, it was all a load of bunkum. I'm still sad and lonely. I don't want to be on my own.

"You should be married with children by now. You're going to be left on the shelf unless you do better," my mother's voice admonishes my inner self.

The doorbell chimes and I haul my arse up out of bed, throw on my dressing gown and go to see who's on my doorstep at this hour. What time is it anyway?

"Oh, I'd say good morning, but that seems inappropriate," my very good friend Wendy greets me.

My lovely, quirky friend with her crazy brown hair tamed back in a plait. Her hazel eyes are looking down at me from under a frown. She's a bit taller than me, which isn't difficult.

Damn, I forgot that we'd arranged for her to come round. I'd phoned her the other night and bawled down the phone after Nigel callously discarded me. Bless her, she'd wanted to come around straight away, but it was getting late and I didn't want to drag her out. Then there was the wedding to attend, and she had to work yesterday. So this is the first chance she has to be a dutiful friend.

She'd obviously been expecting something a little above the level of creature from the black lagoon to answer the door. But that's what she gets.

"Morning," I groan, leaving out the 'good', and leading the way to the lounge.

I blush as I make a path through the detritus.

"I'm sorry," I apologise, picking up discarded tissues, wrappers and a large pizza box.

I may have been more upset last night than I let on. OK, my mood seriously nose-dived. I'd started thinking sensibly, but then my loathing came crashing in and tore down the walls of 'grown up'. I didn't want you to see the carnage, but Wendy's here witnessing it, so there's no avoiding it now.

Poor Wendy manages to find a spot on the sofa with guidance, as I take an armful of rubbish to the kitchen and dispose of it. You know, the way normal people dispose of rubbish when they're not fat lazy hippos.

At least the kitchen's tidy. Having been out Saturday and thanks to my takeaway yesterday, there's not been much washing up to attend to, thank goodness.

"Go on, I'll finish making the tea. You go up and have a shower, and make yourself human," Wendy says, encouraging in her own way.

I thought she was sitting down in the other room, and I hadn't heard her come into the kitchen. I don't deserve a friend like her. Why she sticks around is beyond me.

There's no arguing with Wendy when she has 'the tone', so I have a quick shower. It feels a bit weird, showering with someone else in the house, so I make it quick. But I still take a moment to let the hot water rain down on my forehead, easing the ache.

I chuck on the first clothes my hands fall upon, and roughly brush my hair. It'll frizz up again as I've not put any products on, but Wendy won't mind. She's seen worse.

"That's better," my friend tells me as I re-enter the lounge.

She pours tea from the pot, and I spy a plate of Jaffa Cakes on the coffee table. I'm sure I would've scoffed those yesterday if they'd been in my cupboard, so she must've brought them with her. Have I mentioned what a good friend she is?

She pats the sofa next to her. "Come on, come and tell me all about it."

"I don't even know where to start," I tell her through a mouthful of Jaffa Cake.

"Whilst there's coherent words, why don't you tell me what the text said?"

Oh right, she's still focussed only on the Nigel thing.

"Err, there's more dung for the heap. Um, I sort of hooked up at the wedding."

"At the wedding? Oh my God. Who?"

She sounds a little too excited by this news.

"Do you remember me telling you about Paul, who I used to work with?"

"Not him?"

"Yeah. He was nice to me."

"And you're in the habit of sleeping with every man who's nice to you?" she asks with raised eyebrows.

Wendy knows how untrue this is. But she is leading me to explain, so I do. I tell her all about the smarm trap I fell into.

"Are you sorry?" she asks once I'm done.

I'm stunned for a moment, but then realise something.

"No."

"Then what are you moaning about?"

"I don't know really," I say with a wince and a shrug.

Her tough love really does hammer through my outer crap.

"He wanted sex. You wanted sex. You both got what you wanted," she explains, turning each palm up in turn.

"I suppose so."

"And there's no strings? It doesn't sound like either of you were after a long lasting relationship. You weren't, were you?"

"Eww, with Paul? No, that would be weird. We were work friends, that's all."

"So does it matter how you got into bed? The result was what you wanted, wasn't it?"

"Yes, Wendy," I answer like a child replying to an authority figure.

This is why I phone her in times of trouble. She makes me realise how stupid I'm being. And I can clearly see my stupidity here. I caught a glimpse of it yesterday before I decided to beat myself up. Maybe that's why I did? I don't know.

"And Nigel?" she asks, pouring more tea.

"Oh, I realised yesterday that it's more the *idea* of Nigel that I'm upset about. He was nice, and everything, but when I was at the wedding I couldn't envisage him and me standing at the altar."

"That sounds healthy."

"Yes, but I'm still upset. Isn't that stupid?"

"Molly, a relationship has ended. You are allowed to be upset, you know. No matter how boring that relationship was."

That earns her a grin. She's right, I had complained he was boring. Why am I upset about not having a boring boyfriend?

"But he was *my* boring boyfriend," I tell her, as a tear trickles down my cheek.

"I know. But there will be others. Boyfriends, I mean. And hopefully the next one won't be boring."

"I seem to keep attracting them, though. Is it me? Am I boring? Am I putting out a dull vibe?"

"Molly, you could never be boring."

Somehow this doesn't make me feel better. It feels like a dig.

"Just look at me. I'm fat and ugly. What lovely guy is ever going to fancy this?" My hands splay out and indicate the mounds of flab.

"You are not fat, and you are definitely not ugly."

"I know what I am, Wendy. I've put on so much weight. I hate it. And Mother won't let me forget it."

"Ignore her. But if you're not happy with how you look do something about it."

"I've tried. I really have. But I always end up putting on what I lost, and a bit more."

I really have tried. My weight battle is more of an ongoing war. But I really should do something more positive about it. Maybe then I'd be able to get Mr Right? Is that why he's in hiding? He's seen me, and decided not to go for the whale look. But having tried and failed so many diets, where do I begin?

Wendy interrupts my thoughts. "I don't know what to tell you. I hate seeing you like this. You're so sad, and I don't know why. Look at what you've done. I could never do what you did. You're a successful business woman. You're doing your own thing."

"Well, I'm not exactly making money yet. The business is still growing."

"But it *is* growing."

"Slowly. Anyway, enough about me. What's going on with you?"

Wendy proceeded to tell me some gory details about her nursing job, which I'm quite sure you don't want to hear. I find her tales fascinating, but appreciate I may be the odd one out in this.

***

Right, I wasted my day yesterday, and although it was lovely seeing my friend this morning, she's gone now and I need to get a move on. I need to go to my flower 'creation station' and tidy up. It's carnage in there. I had a 3am start on Saturday, and bits and pieces went flying in my frenzy to get all the orders delivered. Plus, if I don't get the remaining flowers delivered soon they'll wilt beyond respectable display.

Not many people know this, but sometimes I have spare flowers left at the end of an order. I gather all the offcuts, the not quite good enough for a bridal bouquet bits and spares, and create little displays for a local children's hospice. It's the least I can do. They do such wonderful work there. I know, I've seen it with my own eyes.

One of my friends, Beth, gave birth to a beautiful baby girl, but she was born with a life-limiting heart condition. It's a long story, but my friend and her husband were at breaking point. They were constantly in and out of hospital with baby Rachel, and were severely sleep deprived, stressed, worried beyond belief and suffering. I truly think their marriage was ending.

They found the hospice, and they mercifully helped the family through what became Rachel's end of days. It was terrible watching them go through those dark times. And I know they were grateful for all the support they received.

They sadly ended up moving away. There were too many memories here for them. I've not seen Beth for years, but I hear they're doing OK. We stay in touch online. They've got a gorgeous little boy, and I think he's brought them joy.

Anyway, after seeing all that, I wanted to do something to help. And this is what I can do.

It may not be much, but the flowers help cheer the place up a bit. And when parents get referred to me, having to do what no parent should ever have to do, I give them the lowest rates possible. What they're doing is hard enough without me trying to take money from them. Some of those coffins are so small. But I'm making myself cry. Enough.

I finish off the little vases and take them to their new home to spread some happiness.

**

The very next day, I find myself at Wendy's house. She sent me a distress message, so I've come armed with chip shop chips, curry sauce and beer.

Bless her, she's sobbing in my arms as we sit on the sofa. Death is a frequent visitor to her world, as she works in the Intensive Care Unit. Most of the time she copes amazingly well, but not today.

"She'd been with us for a couple of weeks," Wendy says, wiping at her eyes, "Thirty-two is no age. She was a little younger than us, Molly. How can someone our age have a stroke? It seems so unfair."

"These things happen. We know this," I tell her whilst rubbing her back in circular motions.

"I know, but they shouldn't, should they? She'd been showing signs of improvement, and her family were all excited. Then wham, another stroke struck. Lights out. Her family witnessed everything. It was horrible."

"At least they were there with her at the end."

"I know, but they didn't need to see that. It wasn't pretty. I didn't want their last memories of her being like that."

"It was out of your control."

And that's part of the problem. Wendy walks that line every day at work, trying to keep people alive. Sometimes she feels she's winning the fight, and she can control death. Then something like this happens.

It hits harder when the patient is your own age, I guess. It's a stark reminder of our own mortality. There is no rhyme or reason, and that can be hard to accept.

We talk it out whilst munching our way through the steaming chips and sauce. Carbs are great at times like this. A comforting reminder of the good things in life, they soothe the soul.

By the time the evening's over, we've put the world to rights. The conversation naturally progressed onto larger problems in the world, including governments and their politics. Sometimes it's good to talk, to just get all this stuff off your chest.

Satisfied that Wendy is recovered from her shock and feeling much better, I make my move to leave and we hug goodbye.

Chapter 7 – Busy Little Bee

I forgot to eat lunch today, and I don't think the remaining Jaffa Cakes really count as food. But by the time I'm back home from my delivery it's getting late, and close to dinner time. I'm famished and in a hurry.

Cooking for one is really miserable and I can't face it. I don't have time anyway. So a ready meal gets bunged into the microwave. My meal is ready in minutes, and gets washed down nicely with a can of cola.

The TV is on, but it doesn't quite hide the emptiness echoing around my house. I'm all alone. And the despair creeps in. I try to shut it out with meaningless drivel on the box, but it's not distraction enough.

My thoughts start picking at my failed relationship with Nigel. What did I do wrong? I need to know. I need to be better. I'm far from perfect, that much is clear. Even a boring man doesn't want me.

"Who's going to take you if you can't even keep hold of him?" Yeah, that voice is in my head again.

Normal people manage to find lasting relationships. Even Amelia. She's married now, despite being a hoity-toity cow. Oh, she is. I'm sorry, but I will call a spade a spade. Not to her face, of course. But she is not a nice person.

They must be on their honeymoon now, making happy memories, starting their married life in bliss. And I'll be damned if the likes of her can have that and not me. I'm a good person. This must be achievable.

My career isn't exactly suited to finding Mr Right though. My clients are mostly excited, happy brides, and visit with their overbearing mothers. No men folk. I get a few orders for funeral arrangements, but that's really not an opportunity now, is it? How inappropriate.

Besides, maybe I need a break from men for a while. I've only just got out of one relationship and shagged someone else. That's probably enough action for me for a good few months. Well, maybe not that long. But I'm not ready for the next disaster yet.

It's a busy time of year anyway; peak wedding season. There are many brides requiring my attention. Their mothers are ready with their demands.

When is it going to be my turn? I so desperately want to get married. Amelia's wedding was so beautiful. It may be selfish, but I want to have that. That one perfect day of happiness. Which leads me back to trying to find Mr Right.

The enormity of my problem looms large. Who am I going to attract looking like this? I thought I was lucky to have found Nigel. He was nice looking, and not just after one thing. And he didn't arrive with kids included. That's getting harder to find the older I get. I don't want to be a cuckoo to someone else's, I want to have my own children. My ovaries don't have an everlasting supply. I need to get a move on.

Hello hopelessness and panic. My heart is in a vice and a belt is tightening around my stomach. How much time do I have left, exactly?

***

Apologies. I disappeared into a puddle of tears last night. I was better off left to my own devices, and only dolphins would've understood my squeaks of attempted communication. Tissues are on my shopping list; they seem to be disappearing at a rate of knots. As is ice cream. There weren't any biscuits or Jaffa Cakes left, so I raided the freezer.

I've just polished off a bowl of cornflakes and a glass of orange juice. My stomach has been filled with junk, so I'm trying to start the day off healthily.

And as much as I didn't feel like it, I've had a shower and got dressed. It's delivery day, and I don't think the handsome chap from the Dutch wholesaler needs to see my wobbly bits masked by only a dressing gown.

Don't get any ideas. Yes, he's lovely on the eye, but too young and miles out of my league. He simply delivers the flowers and goes. He's a busy boy.

Oh, that must be him now. The doorbell's ringing. He's early.

"Oh, hello Mother," I say breezily, feeling anything but.

Why the hell's she here? She's supposed to give me warning before she graces me with her presence. I've told her many times that it's not always convenient, that I may be in a consultation, and it wouldn't be the done thing to have my mother appear mid-conflab. This is true, but really I need a chance to get myself and the house looking vaguely respectable.

She's one of those; you know, the type that never thinks anything's ever good enough. I can't think of a single word of praise ever coming out of her mouth, at least not in my direction. Mind you, she'll run it off no end when one of her friend's daughters does something commendable.

Thank goodness I have some makeup on. Only enough to cover the most hideous craters in my face. I wasn't trying to look good for the delivery driver. What? I wasn't. I just didn't want to scare him.

I've escaped into the kitchen to put the kettle on for the unwelcome, unexpected visitor. One must have manners, mustn't one?

"Darling, have you seen the state of this place? I know you must be feeling upset, but there's no excuse to let your standards drop," she calls out.

Really "the place" is not that bad. There's no tissues or pizza boxes littering the lounge. Crumbs, I'm thankful she didn't drop in yesterday. Mother would've had a cardiac arrest.

I pretend not to hear as I pour water into the nice white teapot. No novelty one for Mother. And I'm using the nice cups and saucers; absolutely no mugs. As far as she's concerned I don't own any, so shh, don't tell her.

I carry the tea tray into the virtually spotless room and lay it down on the clean coffee table. It really is a puzzle what could've possibly offended her delicate sense of propriety. Perhaps a cushion hadn't been fully plumped? Or a speck of dust did a jig on the mantelpiece?

"Not that I'm not delighted to see you, Mother, but is there a particular reason for this unexpected visit?"

Spot the veiled hint that she hadn't informed me of her intentions to see me.

"Do I need a reason to see my own daughter?"

"No, of course not."

"But I had heard from Fiona that you'd been put aside again, so I thought I'd come and check how you are."

"How did Fiona know?"

Mother grapevines are long and complicated, but I hadn't expected it to have picked up on this news yet. I only found out myself on Friday.

"Really, that's not important. What did you do this time?"

It's always my fault. "I don't really know."

"Didn't you ask him?"

"Of course, but he only sent me a text message on Friday."

"And what did that say?"

"Would you like to see it?"

"There's no need to take that tone, young lady, I'm only trying to help. What can you learn for next time? You really must try harder. You're not getting any younger, and you should've learned how to keep hold of a man by now. But then, you always were a slow learner."

The doorbell chimes and I offer up silent thanks for the intervention.

I excuse myself and go to answer it. This time it is Jan from the wholesaler. I tell him to start unloading in the usual place, and hurry back to my mother.

"It's the delivery driver. I'm terribly sorry, but I really need to get these flowers in. It may take a while."

Hint hint.

"Can't he come back later?"

"No, mother. He has many deliveries to make, and a route to follow."

Rolling one's eyes is not proper, and my mother would never stoop so low. But there must have been a fly on the ceiling, as her orbs pointed that way momentarily.

"Oh, very well. It's most inconvenient."

"This is why I ask you to call first."

"Yes, yes, but this was an emergency. I came to visit in your hour of need."

"And I thank you very much, I do. It was very good of you. But I really am very busy."

My mother reluctantly gets shooed out of my house, but she does manage to fit in a parting blow.

"Have you tried going on a diet? I'm sure that would help."

I close the door firmly behind her, and lean my back against it, huffing out a relieved sigh. With mothers like her who needs enemies? I have no idea how my father puts up with her. He deserves a medal.

Right, now to see to the wonderful Jan. No, it's not a girl's name. He's Dutch. It's pronounced *Yahn*.

I go out of the back door and open up the 'creation station'. This was formerly a garage at the end of my garden. Jan's at the garage door as I open it up. It really is very handy for deliveries. Vehicles can drive up and it's a few short steps to offload.

The weather is still hot, making the process a little slower. We seem to be having a heatwave, and despite being in the shade, I've still worked up a bit of a sweat by the time the flowers are all safely ensconced in my workshop. Not terribly attractive.

I offer Jan some tea. My mother hadn't had time to touch it. It's probably cold by now, I realise too late. But Jan fortunately declines the offer anyway. See; drop and go. He's not one to loiter. Busy, busy, busy.

Waving Jan off, I close the door to keep the heat out, and go to admire the flowers which will be used for this week's brides. There's five of them this week. I'm so pleased my business is finally getting off the ground. It's been flipping hard work.

I surprised even myself with my bold career change. Mother was none too pleased. Apparently, floristry is not a highbrow career choice, and she expected more of me. It may be the first time in my life I stood up to her properly.

Working in an office was sucking my soul away. It had never felt right, but the intense pressure was steadily getting to me. Between you and me, I think I was close to a full-on breakdown.

When my grandmother died I was devastated. She was my father's mother, and I had always been close to her. She'd shown me the kind of love a mother should. I lapped it up. When she passed I felt bereft. It was like the sun had been taken away from my life, plunging me into darkness.

But she left me this house. I feel close to her here, and I would never think of selling it. She also left me a little money. She quite rightly left most of her investments to my father. When I added my inheritance to my savings I saw a golden opportunity to pursue my heart.

I wash out and bleach my containers before filling them with water and some flower food. As I'm happily trimming stems on the newly arrived flowers, a bumble bee buzzes near. It must have come in with Jan.

The bee hovers near me, but I don't flinch. I have flowers in my hand, which are far more attractive to it. But oddly it's sort of looking at me more. I slowly and carefully go to the door to the garden to help encourage it out where it belongs. Of course it doesn't take the hint, and lands on one of the floral bunches on my workbench.

I'm mindful of not upsetting it by making any sudden movements as I continue to prepare the flowers for cold storage. It must be collecting some yummy pollen.

Only when I've finished, does the bee take flight to follow me outside. It hovers momentarily before flying off as I go back into the house. It felt quite nice having a little friend whilst I was working.

Time for a quick cup of tea, I think. I bung the kettle on and collect the abandoned tray from the lounge. My nose scrunches as I tip out cold tea from the pot and retrieve the cold teabags, which get deposited into my bin. The teapot and now empty milk jug get relegated to the dishwasher. Such a waste!

I'm really hungry, and manage to find a chocolate bar in my emergency supplies, which gets munched as I wait for my tea to cool. Wiping my fingers first, I paw through my folder for Friday's weddings. There's two this Friday, with three on Saturday.

Sighing deeply, I allow myself to feel a brief sensation of happiness. The weddings this week are all exciting, and it feels good to be able to play with some beautiful designs.

There's no rest for the wicked. My phone is ringing, interrupting the moment.

"Hello, is that Holly Molly?" someone asks before I have a chance to say a word.

Hearing my business name brings a smile to my face. Doesn't it just say Molly is a florist with a difference?

"Hello, yes, this is Molly. How can I help?"

The young lady on the end of the phone sounds excited. Brides often do at this stage. They're only starting to enter the world of wedding arrangements. It's not until later that the stress has turned them into nervous wrecks. Not all turn into bridezillas, but there is always an element of stress as the day approaches.

It's also helped me realise that I'm not the only one with an overbearing mother. I've seen heated arguments erupt in front of my eyes between mother and daughter. Some girls speak to their mothers so disrespectfully that I struggle to believe my ears.

It seems there's a conflict of interest between the two generations. The mothers push hard for the perfect wedding according to their ideals. It's as if it's their big day. Whilst the daughters struggle to demonstrate that times have moved on and they don't have to have carnations as buttonholes etc.

Somehow, I have to appease both parties. I fight to fulfil the bride's wishes, whilst trying to please the mother. It's a fine balancing act, and my skills of diplomacy are definitely improving. I may end up being worthy of a role in the UN.

By the time this particular phone call ends it's dangerously close to lunch time, and I need to head out to the shops. I haven't got time for a big shop, so I'll just have to pop up the road. It's a nice day for a walk.

As biscuits and ready-made sandwiches are being piled into my shopping basket, my phone pings with a text alert. After rummaging in my bag, I locate said phone, and see a message from Sharon from my old work. I'm pleasantly surprised to see her name.

"What happened with Paul? He's been miserable all week. You spoke to him a lot at the wedding. Was he OK? Did he say anything to you?"

Of course, silly me. She's not chasing the long promised lunch with me, or asking after my health, no 'it was lovely to see you Saturday'. She's asking because the idiot is making a nuisance of his sorry self.

What to tell her? Should I tell her the truth? Or just deny all knowledge? I don't really want my error in judgement to become public knowledge. They'd have a field day with that in the office.

"Sorry, no idea," I respond.

Well, he could be upset about anything. It's not necessarily because he got caught out in his scheming ways, or that I was a disappointing lay. He may be sulking in general, ruminating on the state of the world. How am I supposed to know?

The remaining items on my list get shoved more forcefully into my basket, along with some extra biscuits and chocolate. Ooh, that's a nice looking bottle of white wine. Yoink, in it goes. Oh, and that big bag of crisps would go really nicely with my sandwiches. Peanuts for the wine? Don't mind if I do.

On the way back, I regret my choice to walk. I have a few bags of heavy shopping, and it's really too warm to be playing the part of overladened donkey. Eww, I'm all hot and sticky.

My heart sinks a little more as I pass a school. The children are laughing and screaming in the playground. Tears prick my eyes as I hurry past. I can't begin to tell you how much I want one of my own to join them. I have so much love to give.

Despondency has set in by the time I reach my door. My bags fall to the floor as I try to find my keys and shove them into the lock. Once inside, the contents of those bags are flung into cupboards and I rip the sandwich packet open.

The sweet and salty taste of bacon, lettuce and tomato hits my tastebuds, helping to halt the bitter taste of despair. The malted bread makes me feel like I've made a healthy choice, and there's lettuce and tomatoes. I ignore the handfuls of crisps and can of cola. I'm sure it's all balanced, and I had a healthy breakfast of cereal.

There's still a question ringing in my head though. Where is my life going? I can't keep going on like this.

Chapter 8 - Plans

I try really hard to get stuck back into my work, but my head's not in it. Someone's coming for a consultation tomorrow, which should be exciting. I love talking to new brides, the buzz of excitement in that first meeting. But my heart is broken, and excitement is beyond my reach. A black cloud is hovering over my head.

My mother's words still ring in my ears and pierce my soul. Have I tried to diet? Oh, why didn't I think of that? Oh, that's right, I did. I've tried so many diets it's almost a hobby of mine. But nothing works.

The worse one was the cabbage soup diet. It's a good job I have easy access to flowers, is all I can say. Lilies have a great scent to help fill rooms, covering more sinister odours.

The more sensible plans have been attempted too; the diet milkshakes, the cereal, the cutting carbs. Done, done and failed. The more I diet the hungrier I seem to get.

In today's day and age, it shouldn't matter what I look like anyway. Aren't we all supposed to love our bodies? We shouldn't fat shame. We should love ourselves the way we are. So why do I hate myself?

The temptation to look at the evidence is overwhelming. My mother's constant critique heads the list. Even when I was slim she'd point out every bit which didn't conform to her high standards. It's been that way my entire life. Ask Wendy, she'll tell you. She's witnessed some of it.

Wendy and I have been friends since school. We found solace in each other, I think. Her mum is also critical, but not quite in the same league as mine. Once we'd discovered that, a bond was formed; a sisterhood out of torment. She's never criticised my appearance. She knows only too well how much that hurts.

But it's not all my mother's fault. There's also the string of boyfriends past. Maybe some of them have helped raise my confidence, but then dashed it on the rocks of desertion. Any good they ever did got washed away in the tide of tears which followed their departure.

I'm sorry. I'm getting gloomy again. Can you blame me? What do I have to be happy about?

The clock is ticking. As much as I don't want to face more disappointment, I need to get myself out there. I need a man, and I need him quick. The chances of me getting pregnant are already in decline. I've not got a husband yet. Not even a boyfriend.

Wendy would be up for a girls' night. But where would we go? Only the worst sleaze balls seem to approach me in nightclubs. I'm sure I have a sign on me 'weirdos, please approach'. You know, the ones that think they can dance too close as soon as they set eyes on you. They follow when you move to another area of the dance floor. Then they just happen to be in the next club you try to escape to. It's all very unnerving. Besides, at thirty-four, I'm too old for nightclubs.

Ever practical, I open up my laptop. Before I can talk myself out of it, I set up an online dating profile. Well, it makes sense. And a friend of a friend met her husband this way. Where else am I going to meet eligible bachelors? And this way I get to check them out first.

It's alarmingly quick and easy to do. I search for some recent photos in my files, add a few details, try to think of something witty to say, and hey presto, Molly is online and asking for love. All I have to do now is wait to see what comes in.

Buoyed by my positive action, I return to my wedding flower plans. One of my brides is going for a beautiful, soft, wildflower look, complete with cornflowers. It's extremely elegant with a rural feel.

The other Friday bride is opting for bright bold sunflowers, and very little else. I love them both. Two very different brides, brave enough to do things their own way.

Confident I know what I'm doing, the duster and vacuum cleaner get whisked around, so the room's all spic and span for the bride's consultation tomorrow. I place my portfolio on the table. There's a fab photographer who's taken some wonderful shots of my wedding bouquets, and some brides have passed on some of their photos too.

There's some work emails waiting for my attention on my laptop when I turn it back on, which I respond to. Then I upload the photos from my camera and start editing them. A small gasp escapes my lips as a photo of Paul appears on my screen, but I quickly click to the next one. I'm looking for flower shots to use.

Editing photos takes a surprisingly large amount of time, but there's finally some new additions on my social media pages. Marketing people speak of the importance of keeping up an 'online presence' and I do try my best to follow that advice, but it's a mighty effort to do so.

My tummy rumbles, and I realise it's beyond dinner time. Time has vanished. How did it get so late? Spinach and ricotta cannelloni get popped into the oven to warm up, along with some garlic bread. Spinach is good for you, isn't it?

Once it's cooked, I take my meal into the lounge on a tray, and plonk down in front of the TV. I've earned a rest. And after my mother's visit, this large glass of wine has been well and truly earned too.

I feel relaxed at last, but the wine glass is empty. I go to get some more from the fridge, and also pick up the bag of peanuts I bought earlier. Nibbles are a natural accompaniment to TV watching, and I've heard nuts are a good source of energy. I'll need plenty of that over the next few days. It's going to get busy.

A few hours later I wake up in front of the TV. I must have dozed off. Oops! I drag my aching body upstairs and flump into bed. But wouldn't you know it? I'm awake now. It's too hot, and I can't get back to sleep. The window's open, but only hot air seems to be coming in. I've even got my fan going, but the noise is annoying.

I toss and turn for hours. Sleep eludes me, and the voices of nagging doubt have snuck in.

"You'll be alone forever," they tell me, "Look at you. You're fat and ugly, and nobody wants you. How do you think you'll get a husband looking like that? Nobody wants you. If they did, you'd be married by now, wouldn't you?"

These vicious voices sound quite similar to my mother, funnily enough. I try to shut them out, but their nagging is persistent, and I feel their blows strike deep within me.

The alarm clock kicks in, and my heavy arm bashes it until it shuts up. Bleary eyed, I head to the bathroom. That was maybe three hours sleep in total. I feel wretched.

A shower at least washes off the sweat of the night, and I put on a light summery dress. It's still smart enough for the visitor today. I can't face putting on anything else. The mirror shows me a hippo in a sack as I walk past.

I shlump downstairs and put on the kettle, needing an extra strong coffee this morning; black with two sugars. A bowl of cereal gets crunched, but I'm still hungry. Needing more energy, I have a couple of slices of toast too, washed down with some orange juice.

I'm so tired I feel sick. It's been hot and humid all week, making sleeping incredibly challenging. I've been silently praying to a God I don't believe in for a break in the weather.

Heading straight down to the 'creation station', I gather flowers for today's weddings. The bouquets are being made this morning, as they need to be as fresh as possible so they can last all day. It's a frantic rush, and my adrenaline's pumping as I go.

Within a couple of hours they're both done and I rush upstairs for a very quick shower, a splash of makeup and some smart clothes. One has to look professional.

After driving my van around to the back of my house, I carefully load all of today's flowers in. It takes a while as I need to be really gentle and place them carefully. One bride's flowers are on one side, separated from the other. The bouquets and buttonholes are loaded last, as I'll be dropping those off first. I've got notes by each one, and their addresses are on the clipboard which is with me in the driver's cabin.

At seven a.m. I start making my way to the first bride's house. My smile is genuine as I pass her the beautiful bouquet. She's in her dressing gown, and her hair's in curlers. The bridesmaids receive their bouquets, and the buttonholes go to the mother who's come to the door. They've arranged for someone to take the boys' flowers to them as they're nearby.

I then make my way across town, a twenty minute drive to the next bride. There's squeals of joy as the door opens and a whole host of girls come to collect their flowers. I get swept up in the excitement, but don't linger long.

My next stop is the reception venue of bride one. I have eight table arrangements to place here. It's not a massive wedding, but it will be beautiful nonetheless.

And then it's off to the final venue of today. I have time, but still hurry as much as possible, whilst still displaying the flowers to show them off at their best. It'd be horrible if the florist was still onsite as the wedding party arrived.

Phew, and I'm done. It really is another roasting hot day. I'm glad the deliveries managed to get done early, but it's already lunchtime. I stop off at a drive-thru, and order a chicken wrap meal. It's too hot to eat much, and I had a chocolate bar to keep me going earlier. My trusty flask of coffee also helped.

Having read somewhere that you're supposed to have hot drinks in the heat, I stick to coffee. It's a welcome boost of caffeine as I drive around like a thing possessed.

The wrap is easier to eat than a burger as I drive. I know you're not supposed to, but I'm a busy woman with places to go.

The shower is a refreshing relief when I get home. It's a hurried one, but I was so hot and sticky after my errands I needed it. My makeup gets slapped on just in time for the doorbell to chime. I found to my cost, that putting makeup on first thing can result in a panda-eyed mess answering the door, so have learned to put it on last minute.

Business face on, I go to the door.

"Hello, I'm Molly," I greet the two women at my door, along with a handshake.

"Hello," a nervous looking bride-to-be says back, trying to smile.

Her mother appears to be far more confident, and is the first to follow me through the house.

"Tea or coffee?" I ask brightly.

"Coffee please," answers the young lady.

The disapproving frown from her mother doesn't escape me, but she doesn't contradict her daughter.

I have everything all laid out in the kitchen, and disappear momentarily, having seated the ladies down at the table, so they can peruse the portfolio.

A large cafetière with cups and a plate of biscuits is carried through on a tray by yours truly. I have to be a good hostess. I won't be the only florist these people see, so first impressions are everything.

"Have you booked your venue?" I ask the important question.

It's surprising how many haven't at this stage, but it gives me a good idea of the style they may be looking for.

This bride-to-be has in fact booked a very nice location already.

"Lovely. Have you got a theme in mind?"

"Vintage," says Natalie, the one getting married.

"Traditional," her mother interjects.

Now, vintage can mean different things to different people.

"And do you know what colour the bridesmaids will be wearing?"

This is important too, as it gives a colour theme, sometimes without the bride realising. It's sensible to pick out the accent colours in the flowers, so everything is complimented nicely.

"Pastel pink," the mother tells me at the same time as Natalie says lavender.

"Oh darling, pastel pink is far nicer for the traditional look we're going for, don't you think?"

Oh dear. Round one is starting. I offer the plate of biscuits forward, hoping to sweeten the situation.

"Either would work well with the vintage feel," I suggest.

Natalie picks up a biscuit and nibbles gingerly. I take one too, just to be polite, you understand.

"Are there any flowers you had in mind?"

"Roses," says the mother.

"Well, I really want to have some lavender in the bouquet," Natalie ventures.

"Ooh, that would be lovely. The scent is really calming too, so that's an added bonus," I tell her, but hope to win the mother over with this information.

I get an unconvinced raised eyebrow.

"We could have some lovely white peonies, pale pink roses, interspersed with lavender," I add, flicking to something similar in the portfolio.

I'm relieved to see two smiles pointing towards me. But then we have to start discussing the awkward topic of budget. I don't know why it's a huge surprise. Wedding magazines are excellent at listing the amounts you should expect to pay for all things wedding. And my prices aren't that far away from those.

We start to agree initial ideas, but I sense a dissatisfaction from the mother still. I personally love the idea of lavender buttonholes, but the mother thinks it's too feminine and wants something more traditional. I'll supply a quote for each, and leave the decision to them. There's a time and place to challenge, and I've softly made suggestions for compromises.

As soon as they're gone I go out to the garden and have a cigarette. It's always stressful trying to walk the diplomatic line in these meetings. As I'm having a puff, a little bee flies around a few times before heading off in search for pollen.

I pour myself another coffee, sit back down at the table and start sifting through my notes. I want to compile a quote whilst the information's still fresh in my mind. There's a few options to list out, including a 'what you've asked for' vs 'what you said you want to pay for' spin, not that I'll phrase it that way, you understand. There's biscuits left out on the plate, and without really thinking, I munch my way through them as I do my sums.

As my email gets fired off to Natalie I realise it's way past dinner time. Fortunately, I bought two packets of sandwiches yesterday, and I managed not to devour them both. Today it's a yummy egg mayo which gets gobbled down with some crisps. In an attempt to make up for the biscuits, I have an orange juice and not cola with them.

I tidy up, load up the dishwasher and head down to the 'creation station' to make a start on tomorrow's flower arrangements.

A wave of dizziness washes over me. Glancing at my watch I see it's later than I thought. I grab a coffee and some biscuits to help fuel my work.

The thrill of seeing my art come together in front of me is addictive. The way they go from loose flowers to stunning displays is mesmerising. It's why I do this. It feels like I'm actually creating something good, and bringing joy to many.

The night passes as my hands deftly position flowers. My eyelids are heavy and are trying to close, but I don't stop until my work is complete. I can finally stagger to my bed at one a.m. Yet, despite my exhaustion sleep doesn't come easily.

The heat is stifling. I can barely breathe in this humidity. The window's open and the fan's on again. Hey, I'm naked, don't look.

I must have drifted off at some point as my alarm clock is trilling, waking me up. I hate that clock. I hate early mornings. But it's worth it, so my hefty arse gets dragged into the bathroom and I get ready for another full day. Right now, I'm questioning my career move. My whole body aches, I'm exhausted and it really is an effort this morning.

Chapter 9 - Deliveries

There's no time to dwell or dawdle. I grab a piece of toast with marmalade, and a cup of coffee. It's too early to face a proper breakfast. This mini sugar rush will help spur me on though, and that's what I need.

Adrenaline is still buzzing, and more coffee is fuelling me as I work meticulously on the displays. My plans are by my side, which are followed fastidiously. They're there for a reason. Everything has to be perfect. I don't want any crying bridezillas on the phone.

Hunger starts to gnaw at my stomach, growling its displeasure, but I push on through. These flowers must get done, and there's three orders to fulfil. Brides wait for no-one. If I stop, I'll start to feel overwhelmed.

Today is especially difficult as the last venue of the day is the same hotel I went to last week. You know, the one where I let myself become a hussy with Paul. My soul retreats into a cave as I think about facing the humiliation of returning there.

But brides come first. I have to push my feelings aside. My hand drags down my face as I try to focus on the task before me. I am a professional. I can do this. Beautiful bouquets will be delivered.

As if yesterday is on repeat, I load my van and make my deliveries. There's three today though, so my hurry is all the greater. I zoom from place to place, being as careful as I can with my precious cargo.

I go from bride to bride like a busy bee. A bouquet here, a bouquet there, buttonholes here, some table arrangements there. Smile, congratulate, deliver, away. Rush rush rush, busy busy busy. There's no time to pause for breath.

All done, only the last venue to go. The one which knows my shame.

Fabulous, the heaven's open as I drive to the hotel. It's appropriate somehow, like some sort of foreboding omen. But oh no, the brides. Does it have to rain now? There's weddings going on. Those poor girls. It's been bastard hot all week, and now look at it. Their day will be washed out.

My feet falter as I climb the stone steps to the entrance. Get a grip, Molly, you can do this. It's just another wedding. It's not the one you attended last week. Those people aren't here. A bright flash rips through the clouds, closely followed by a loud rumble of thunder as I reach the door.

My tummy flips and my heart sinks as I see the same lovely young male receptionist who checked me out. He won't remember that though. How many people does he see in a week? I'm being silly. Come on now, pull up your big girl pants, take a deep breath.

"Oh hello. Back again?" he smiles at me.

Oh great, he has to have a good memory.

"Purely business this time," I say, brandishing the flowers in his direction.

He smiles as he waves me through, confirming the room to be set up. I know already, but it's sweet of him to say.

I walk as fast as I can with flowers in my hand, and start laying the tables.

"Can I help?" the charming receptionist asks me on one of my trips past.

"No, no, I can manage, thank you," I dismiss, secretly hoping he'll insist.

He doesn't. The rain is still bucketing down as I rush outside again. Just a couple more tables to go, then I can leave here, eat and rest. My head is a little swimmy, reminding me to eat very soon.

Reaching the top step, my foot flies from underneath me, and the world goes black.

Piled in a heap at the bottom of the stone steps, and feeling completely embarrassed, I try to sit up. But a hand stops me.

"It's OK, take your time. Don't try to move."

I recognise the receptionist's silky tone. What? How did he get here? Is that his hand on my head? The bloody cheek of him. Is he taking advantage of my sorry state?

"You had a fall," he starts to explain.

"I know that," I say, sounding huffy even to my own ears.

My head is pounding.

"An ambulance is on its way."

"What? Oh no. You didn't need to do that." My face is scarlet, I'm sure.

"You've hurt your head. It's bleeding."

"Oh."

So that's why his hand's on my head. He gently helps me sit up, ever so slowly. As my hand is guided to my head, I realise there's ice wrapped in a towel there, and I'm being encouraged to keep the pressure on.

This is apparently so he can pour me a glass of water from the jug which seems to have been brought out here. I must've passed out, but how long for?

He passes me the glass, and takes over towel duty whilst I sip.

"There, how are you feeling now?" he asks with obvious concern.

"Embarrassed."

"Are you hurt anywhere else? I could not see anything bad."

"No, I think I'm OK apart from my head. I feel a bit bruised, but I think I'll be fine."

"Well, you fell with style."

Did I mention before I thought his accent was Italian? His charm levels seem to confirm I was right. And now he's talking to me a bit more, his accent is more audible.

"I'm so sorry."

"For what? Falling? I do not think you did it on purpose."

"Well no, but I'm still sorry. I'm being such a nuisance."

"Not at all."

"Oh, but the rest of the flowers."

"Are being taken care of. In fact, here's Karen now."

The young lady, whom I assume is Karen comes to sit on the step next to me.

"Oh good, you're alive," she says, thinking she's funny, I'm sure.

"I'm so sorry. I didn't mean to be such a nuisance."

"Not at all. It was quite fun. The flower bit, not the collapsed florist part."

"I'm glad to hear that," I say with a laugh which makes me grimace.

My body hurts all over. I don't think anything's broken. It just hurts a lot.

"Phhw, take it easy," she says, wincing with me.

"It's OK, Antonio. I think we have it from here," she says to the man in question.

Yep, definitely Italian.

"If you are sure. OK. Well, take care, Molly," he says sweetly.

Oh, he knows my name. My heart beats a little more rapidly.

"I'll try. Thank you."

I try to turn to watch his cute butt walk away, but it hurts too much, so I face forwards again, elbows on my knees, my hand still clutching the towel to my head.

Karen peels it away a little to have a look. "I think the bleeding's stopped, but keep it there anyway."

I realise the rain's finally stopped, but I'm drenched through. I must look like a drowned rat. Embarrassment floods me as much as the water.

"I really am very sorry."

"Please stop apologising. It's not your fault. And you're not to worry. Your flowers all look beautiful, I'll move your van around to the rear car park later, and you can arrange to have it collected at your convenience. It's no bother."

"Thank you."

She really is very sweet, and I feel humbled in my sorry state. She kindly chats away about nothing of consequence as we wait for the ambulance to arrive.

Once they get here, the ambulance crew check me over, but as I'm sitting up they are apparently less concerned than they would've been.

"We're going to take you to hospital, so the doctors can take care of you, Molly," the lady paramedic explains slowly but politely.

"Please, you don't need to do that. I'll be fine."

"You need stitches in your head, for a start."

"Oh, right. Is it that bad?"

"It's not the worst I've seen, but it does need stitches. You're not scared of needles are you?"

"Um, a little."

"You'll be fine. We'll take care of you. There's nothing to be scared of. You won't feel a thing."

She and her male counterpart help me up onto a trolley and fasten me to a board. It's slow progress. I've been sitting on the wet step for a while. Mix that with my bumps and bruises, and I'm really stiff.

"It's OK, take your time," the male ambulance technician tells me, at my side.

I manage to thank Karen who's still here to wave me off.

The rain is spitting again, and the ambulance people are very careful as they load me into their vehicle. I can almost hear them think, "Careful, this one has previous."

Oh, the shame. As if I hadn't dishonoured myself enough in this hotel last week, I just had to put the icing on the cake, didn't I?

I find myself lying down on the trolley thing in the back of the ambulance, unable to move with my neck in a collar and my head being strapped down. This is a precaution apparently, as I was sitting up when they arrived, but they don't want to risk any further injury as I'm transported. Whatever. Just get me there quickly. I hurt all over.

The lady goes round to the front of the ambulance, and clambers into the driver's seat. I can't make out what she's saying into the radio receiver.

The male paramedic stays with me in the back whilst we are slowly driven to A&E. He's quite chatty. I suppose he's checking me for any signs of damage as they deliver me to hospital.

Chapter 10 – Admission

"Is there someone we can call?" the paramedic asks me as the ambulance ambles on.

The pressure pad on my head feels weird, and my stomach churns as the vehicle bumps down the road. My legs and arms feel bruised, stiff and sore.

My thoughts fly through my brain fog and on to Wendy in response to the paramedic's question, but I'm stopped from forming the words on my lips.

"You should have someone to wait with you, and give you a lift home. You'll probably want a change of clothes too."

Well, bollocks. If someone needs to go to my house first, it's my mum who has a spare key. She's not allowed to use it unless there's an emergency, and it dawns on me this might be just such a case.

"My mother," I admit in defeat, "but oh, my bag, I left it —"

"This one?" he asks with a smile, picking it up from the floor.

That's right, Karen had retrieved it, and handed it to me as I was getting into the ambulance. It's all a bit of a blur, quite frankly.

"Yes, that one," I admit, feeling stupid.

My phone is passed to me, and I hit the dial button, but the paramedic takes it back from me.

"It's probably best if I explain," he says gently.

Not wanting to face my mother's voice with a sore head I let him. It'd probably be a bit difficult to talk on the phone like this anyway.

"Hello, it's Steve from the South West ambulance service here. There's nothing to worry about. Molly took a tumble and is on her way to hospital for a few stitches. Please can you meet her there with a change of clothes? It's a bit wet outside and your daughter's a little soggy."

He says all this calmly and good-naturedly. He makes it sound like I'm just going for a walk in the park and want to meet my mother for lunch. Normal behaviour, nothing sensational. Her daughter hasn't made a complete tit of herself, and is not currently lying, battered and bruised, in an ambulance. Lalala.

Nonetheless I hear her cries from where I'm sitting. The phone is pulled rapidly away from poor Steve's ear as he recoils.

"You volunteered," I whisper with a grin.

"No, she's fine. Just some bruising and a little cut which needs some attention. Are you alright to drive, madam?" he answers her, still with a cool calmness.

She's obviously causing a scene, and he's now worried about her ability to drive. But they wrap up the call, and he confirms she's on her way. I'm both pleased and mortified by this. Does he know what he's just done? The ear bashing I will soon receive?

We arrive at the hospital, and I find myself being wheeled into the Emergency Department.

A doctor is checking me for any visible signs of head trauma.

"OK, Molly. I have to go now, but it was lovely meeting you. You take care now," Steve says.

"Thank you," I tell the paramedic meekly, and watch him walk out the door.

The doctor continues his checks. A light is shone in my eyes, making me wince. And then I have to follow his finger with my eyes as he waves it side to side then up and down.

I'm left in a bay and am told someone will be with me as soon as they can. It's foolish, but I feel abandoned. Steve the paramedic was so nice to me, and his presence was comforting. Now I'm all alone in a busy place, and realisation hits me. Unwanted tears start to fall down my cheeks with shame and indignity.

"Oh dear, are you alright?" an elderly lady asks me from the next bay along.

"I'm fine," I reply, unable to swipe my tears away; my movement still restricted.

My tears tickle my ears as they trickle down.

"I don't think that's quite true now, is it?" she says as she approaches nearer.

"No, not really. But you have your own problems."

"I'm waiting for my husband. He had an argument with the pavement, but he'll be fine. It happens when you get to our age."

"I had my own argument, but with a set of stone steps," I admit.

There's something about this woman that makes me want to tell her about the events of the day. Maybe it's because she reminds me of my grandmother. I give her the highlights and she makes soothing noises in all the right places.

"It must have been quite a shock. Dear me, you poor thing. But you're here now. They'll take good care of you."

"Yes, but now my mother is on her way."

"Well that's good."

"No, not really. I don't mean to sound ungrateful, but—"

I'm cut off by the woman herself. My mother has entered with a bag of clothes, and is shrieking at me.

"Molly, there you are. What have you done now? Do you know the trouble you've caused? And to get an ambulance called out? Really, what a fuss."

I'm in no mood for this. I feel bad enough already.

"Hello, Mother. Thank you for coming."

A heavy silence descends as we wait.

A nurse arrives, and makes lots of notes after asking many questions and taking some blood. This makes me feel queasy; I hate needles. And there's more of them as anaesthetic gets jabbed into me, right near my wound. Ow! Ow, ow, and more ow. Then I'm sewn and bandaged up.

A machine then gets hooked up to me, apparently for an ECG. All this activity is making my head whir.

The nurse declares my blood sugar is low, so she gives me some glucose gel to swallow. There's no quibbles here. I'm really hungry. Breakfast was many many hours ago. I tell her it's probably why I passed out in the first place.

"It's all my own stupid fault," I apologise many times.

A lovely doctor sees me next. A smile decorates her elfin face, which is framed by her short brown hair.

"I'm sending you for a CT scan," she tells me.

I have a head injury, and the unconsciousness seems to be cause for concern. I don't understand why. It was just one of those stupid things.

My mother looks worried as she re-joins me. She had disappeared during my assessment. I expected her to moan about me putting these people out and causing a fuss. But no, she actually looks concerned. There's creases in her brow, and everything.

"Well, they know best, darling. Best do what they say," Mother affirms with a pat on my hand when I update her.

I suspect the kind older lady has had a word. Maybe she's an angel? She certainly seems to have performed a miraculous transformation.

"Are you feeling any better?" My mother actually sounds meek.

I'm stunned for a moment. "Yes, a little, thank you."

A hospital porter arrives and delivers me to the CT scanning people. Mother trails behind.

"I'm scared," I tell her as we wait.

"There's nothing to be scared of. They're only going to scan you. Come along now, where's my brave girl?" It's half admonishing and half comforting, and I suddenly feel like I'm five years old again.

As they take me into the room I catch the concerned look on my mother's face. I wonder where my brave mum is. Hypocrite.

I'm manoeuvred onto a table thing which slides into a big machine. They tell me to lie very still, which is not a problem. But the sudden urge to pee is. They put some dye into my tube thing which the nurse had inserted, and my mouth and…down there now feel like they're on fire. Oh my God, am I actually going to wet myself? Please, no. I clench as tightly as I can to try to avoid another catastrophe today.

I'm very relieved when it's over and get taken back out to my mother to await the CT results. With my underwear still dry, I'm happy to say. My pee has to go into a cup instead though. Eurgh!

The elfin faced doctor from before is the one who delivers the news. "There's nothing overly obvious, but we're admitting you for observation overnight as a precautionary measure."

"Oh no. There's really no need for that. Please. I'm so sorry to have put you to so much trouble already. I should've eaten more. And I don't have any overnight things."

"We have this season's must have, a lovely hospital gown for you. All the other patients are wearing them. And I'd rather be safe than sorry. Also, I'm referring you to your GP for a fasting blood test. Your blood sugars aren't quite what they should be."

"Yes, because I hadn't eaten enough."

"Please humour me and let me do my job. Your health is important. Don't ignore it."

I try to protest a little more, but after a lecture I concede. This is ridiculous. It was a stupid accident. Apparently, the length of time I was unconscious is enough to earn me a bed for the night.

Finally free of the trolley, I carefully change into the gown, and transfer to a wheelchair. A porter pushes me along to a ward. My poor mother accompanies us, not even muttering one sound of annoyance.

She plonks the bag of clothes on the chair, and sees me settled in before she's ushered away.

"I'll be here with Dad in the morning to pick you up, darling. At least you'll get some low-fat food here. Get some rest," she tells me with a rueful smile.

I can see through the façade. She's as worried as I am. I've never had to spend time in hospital before. It's all clinical and depressing, and it smells funny. Yes, it's a good thing to be clinical in a hospital, but you know what I mean.

There's other people in the observation ward, but they're not exactly up to conversation. What am I doing here? I don't belong with these sick people. I have things to do.

Having sent Wendy a surreptitious text, she's promised to pop in when her shift's over. She conveniently works at the same hospital I'm in, but in the Intensive Care Unit, not this area. I don't know how she does it. She has a heart of gold.

These beds are really uncomfortable. Having a bruised arse probably doesn't increase the comfort factor. And it's a bit hot. I'm sorry, but I have a right to moan, don't I? Today has been terrible. Well, the whole week really. What a catastrophe.

Here I was, telling you about a nice average week of a florist, and I land myself in here. And the food's terrible. They brought me some dinner, and even I struggled to eat it, despite not having had a proper meal all day.

So, you find me hot, hungry, hurt and feeling more than a little sorry for myself. Which is exactly what Wendy finds too as she pops in.

"How's the patient?" she asks cheerily.

Honestly, it's like there's nothing wrong and she's just visiting me for coffee.

"Hot and hungry," I moan.

"Have they not fed you?"

"Yes, but it was awful. Can you be a friend and get me something from that fast food place on site, please? Pretty please?"

"No. You're supposed to have well balanced meals which help you heal, not clog your arteries with fat. Besides, they'd fire me if they saw me sneaking fast food into here."

"But Wendy," I moan.

"But Molly," she mimics, making me realise how childish I sounded.

"Fine. I'm sorry."

"But I did bring you these," she says, hoisting a bunch of grapes from her big bag and putting them on the table next to me.

"Oh very funny," I say sarcastically, but a laugh comes out anyway.

And actually, I'm hungry enough to pick a few and eat them.

"You're in very good hands. Do what the nurses tell you. I'm sure they'll let you out tomorrow. You already seem your usual grumpy self," she teases.

"Thanks for stopping by."

I can tell she's about to leave. Her feet are edging away. She must be exhausted after her shift. It was good of her to pop by at all. And I was just sullen. Nice one, Molly.

"Honestly, thank you. I didn't mean to be so grumpy."

"Show me a patient who isn't," she whispers with a wink.

"Go on. You go home and rest."

"OK, but I'll come over to yours when you're back home to make sure you're alright."

"You may have to get past my mother."

"Molly, she's not that much of a dragon. And she came here earlier, didn't she? She does care."

"I know. She was surprisingly subdued actually."

"She must've been very worried about you. I'm sure it came as quite a shock."

"Oh she got over it. She still managed to refer to my weight before she left."

"All's well then," she says with a smirk.

"Yeah, I suppose it is. Now go. Go on. You're supposed to be on your way home."

"I'm going, I'm going."

She squeezes my hand gently before she disappears, and I find myself alone once more.

I'm not sure how, but I manage to doze off. A nurse comes to check my 'vitals', which disturbs me. This happens throughout the entire night. Foolishly, I hadn't realised the observations would be quite so…observant.

Other patients get their checks and someone chucks up. The sound of sloppy vomit smacking the floor is enough to make me heave. Sleep is not forthcoming, so tired can now be added to my list of complaints. Hot, tired, sore, hungry, cranky; that just about covers it. And if I'd just eaten some bloody lunch all of this could have been avoided. Oh, add annoyed at myself. Just a regular bundle of joy, aren't I? Sorry. Please hug me.

A doctor comes to see me in the morning. He makes me promise to make an appointment with my GP for follow up blood tests, and does some final checks before confirming I can go home.

With the paperwork sorted it's time to leave. My body argues as it gets squeezed into my clothes. All I want to do is go home and have a hot bath. Fortunately my stitches won't stop me doing this. I'm not allowed to get them wet, but my head won't be in the water as I bathe.

As promised, both my mother and father arrive to collect their wounded daughter.

"How are you, poppet?" my father asks with a gentle hug and a kiss on my cheek.

"I've been better," I sigh.

"Let's get you home then."

There's no wheelchair escort this time, so my father supports me as I waddle out on bruised limbs to his car. I'm given the rare privilege of sitting in the front seat. Is there a royal wedding, or a similarly grand event happening today?

My father is always a cautious driver, but he's especially slow as we make our way to my house.

Chapter 11 – Visitors

"Mother, I've only been away for a day," I tell her as she brings a couple of carrier bags of food into my house with her.

"I didn't know what you already had in your cupboards. I didn't want you to starve."

I feel slightly guilty. She was only trying to look after me. But it's easy for her, she's naturally slim.

"Sorry. Thank you."

She directs me to sit down at my dining table, whilst she whips up some baked beans on toast for me and a pot of tea for us all. My father keeps me company, wittering on in his own special way.

Mother goes up to run me a bath, not too hot as instructed, whilst I eat.

"The bath's ready when you are," she chimes as she re-enters the room, and helps herself to tea.

"Thank you."

I'm relieved and grateful she's helping me, and not using every spare minute to lecture me. Yet it's uncomfortable too. I'm not used to it, and it feels weird to be looked after.

I get up and start walking towards the stairs.

"And where are you going?" I ask, as I realise my mother's following me.

"The doctor said you weren't to be left alone whilst bathing."

"Oh no. You've not seen me naked since I was a toddler."

"Don't make a fuss. I have a chair outside the bathroom. I'll talk to you through the door."

"Oh. Good. Thank you."

Phew, crisis averted. Yesterday was embarrassing enough. I don't think I can take any more.

Looking at my reflection, I look like Mr Bump from the Mr Men books. A big bandage is wound around my head. My eyes are puffy, and my arms and legs are all sorts of colours as the bruises come out on full display. The overall effect is rather dramatic.

When my mother told me she was going to talk to me through the door, I thought she'd just shout the odd, 'How are you doing in there?' every now and again. But no, she's rabbiting on about all her friends and neighbours. Did I know Barbara has done such and such, Sylvia isn't speaking to so and so, and blah blah blah? I don't think she's paused once to check if I've actually responded.

Her noise is disturbing my peace, and is the opposite of helpful. But it's my mother. This is her caring for me.

I really want to wash my hair. It feels grimy and icky, but I'm not allowed to. I have to wait forty-eight hours. Eww!

Well, my muscles feel better for a quick soak, but my bruises are still smarting. I struggle to haul myself up and out of the bath, but manage. Even if it had killed me, I would've managed without 'mother assistance'.

I gently towel myself dry and ease the tangles out of my hair. Apparently, you can't even see the bit they had to snip away to suture my wound together, according to my mother. I don't know, it's at the back so I can't see. The area's too tender for me to touch. I'll just have to take Mother's word for it.

At last, I feel almost human again. Clean body and clothes, and some food in my belly works wonders.

As my parents are still here I feel obligated to be sociable. My bed is calling to me. The lack of sleep seems to have caught up with me. But duty first. Mother goes down the stairs in front of me.

"I'll break your fall should you have another episode," she says.

"Mother, I'll break your neck if I land on you."

"No arguing, darling."

Fortunately, the journey down is event free. There's no collapsing daughters, safety mat mothers and not even any broken bones. Amazing. Wonders will never cease.

Father has made himself comfortable in front of my television. He has the remote control firmly in his grasp as he sits in my armchair. Some sort of nest of blankets and cushions has been fashioned on the sofa. I could point out it's mid-summer, but I refrain. I've probably been ungrateful enough for one day.

"I'll make us some more tea," my mother sings as she goes to the kitchen.

It doesn't feel like my home anymore. My visitors have turned into invaders. They've taken over. I'm not even allowed to answer my own front door.

"I'll get it," my mother decrees, rising to her feet.

"Hello, Mrs Wilkinson. Is Molly up to visitors?" I hear Wendy ask.

Am I at my home? Or have I been trapped in some time warp and transported back to my school days?

I hear my mother start to demure, as if she'd turn my own friend away from my own house.

"Of course she is," I yell from my sofa prison.

"Oh good."

Bless her, she must've pushed passed the mother barrier, as she's now smiling down at me. "I told you you'd be out today, didn't I? How are you?"

"Sore, but better than I was, thank you."

"Any headache or nausea?"

Always the nurse.

"No. Well, no more than is to be expected. My head's throbbing, but nothing to be concerned about."

"I brought you this," she says, holding out a bean bag bolster cushion thing.

"You can place it on the good side of your head, and it'll help support you without hurting your sore bit," she explains.

"Ooh, lovely, thank you," I comment, immediately trying it out.

My head sinks into the soft squishiness and it's blissful.

"Oh, isn't that thoughtful?" my mother says, but in a tone suggesting otherwise.

I don't know why she has to do that. It was actually very thoughtful of Wendy, and I appreciate it very much. I'm quite happy snuggling into my new-found comfort.

She bravely ignores the comment and tries to continue, "Have you got everything you need? Do you want me to pop to the shops?"

"I have it all covered, thank you," mother says in an even more clipped tone.

Wendy is only trying to be a good friend. My mother does not have a monopoly on me. There's no need for her rudeness. It's really grating on my nerves. I'd say something, but I really don't feel up to arguing at the moment.

"You look tired. Are you resting enough? Would you like a hand getting upstairs?" Wendy asks.

"I have to admit I am very tired. Maybe a nap would be a good idea, but I think I'll manage on my own thanks."

This was more for my mother's benefit than Wendy's. I'm being treated like an invalid. But apart from my stiff limbs, I really am fine.

"OK, make sure you do. You need your rest. Whether you want to face it or not, you've been through trauma. Please don't push yourself. I know what you're like."

"Alright, I promise."

"Good. Then I'll leave you in peace."

"I'll walk you to the door."

"Oh no you won't," mother tells me.

"Mother, I can walk. And I can go straight up to bed after."

There's some grumbling from her corner, but she doesn't stop me.

"I'll pop back tomorrow. Text me if there's anything you need," Wendy whispers as we get to the door.

"Thank you. I'll let you know when the coast's clear," I whisper back, giving her a grateful hug.

"Now go and get some rest."

"Yes, sir," I say with a smile and a salute.

The door closes behind my friend, and I turn to face the stairs. They loom large, as imposing as a mountain. But the climb must be faced. I won't get any sleep down here. Deep breaths, I can do this.

My hand reaches out to the rail, which is used to help pull my poor big body up the stairs, one at a time. My back and bum are particularly ouchy. I'm out of breath by the time the summit is reached, but I'm there.

My bed beckons and my feet carry me towards it, welcoming its soft marshmallowy goodness. I flump down on top of the mattress. Now I'm back out in the real world, I've noticed that the rain didn't help with the humidity. If anything, it seems to have added to it. But sleep claims me, regardless.

As I wake up, feeling groggy, I look at the clock. It's been hours since I came up here. A visit to the bathroom is required before the trudge downstairs.

I've woken up hungry and thirsty, so my next quest will be for food and drink.

Oh, my parents are still here. I was expecting them to have left by now.

"Ooh, she's up. How are you feeling, darling? We took it in turns to check on you whilst you slept," Mother announces.

"Thanks, but I'm alright. Otherwise the doctors wouldn't have released me from hospital. You really don't have to worry and go to all this trouble."

Hint hint, you can go now.

"It's no trouble. Now, what would you like for dinner?"

"I don't know. I'll have a look in the freezer."

"You go and sit down. I'll make something nice. Now, I bought some salmon."

I can't help my involuntary wince. Salmon is so boring.

"Don't look like that. It's good for you, and you need the nutrition."

I'm not quite sure if she's referring to my need to heal or to lose weight, but it's probably best not to enquire. There's also no point in arguing. There is no real choice of food being offered. My mother wishes to cook salmon, so that's what we shall have.

I silently join Father in the lounge and stare at something on TV until dinner is ready. Some sort of nature documentary was on, I think. I wasn't really concentrating. My mind was wandering onto other things, like how to eject my parents from my house, how the hospice probably won't get any flowers this week, and how much I have to do.

We're called to the table, where steaming pale pink fish is waiting. My stomach churns at the sight and smell. Overdone, soggy vegetables are loaded onto my fork along with overcooked salmon. I try to scoop on some parsley sauce, but there's not much of it, and it doesn't help anyway. It's all totally bland.

Bless him, my father seems to be struggling too. Only my mother seems to be eating with any form of enjoyment.

Wine is denied to me. Apparently, as I'm taking paracetamol I shouldn't consume alcohol. But it would really help wash down this slop. Mother thinks squash is a suitable dinner drink. Squash? Really? She really needs to leave before I start acting like the child she seems to think I am.

"Mmm, that was delicious," I lie as I finish a final mouthful of food, and push my plate away.

"There's fruit salad for dessert."

"Oh, I couldn't possibly manage anything else."

I can, and fully intend on heating up a microwave meal as soon as she's out the door, or at least have some crisps.

"It's made already. It's good for you."

The salmon was supposed to be good for me, and yet my stomach seems to think otherwise. Facing lots of acidic fruit seems like a bad idea.

Despite my protestations, she brings in bowls of fruit. I put a spoonful in my mouth, and rapidly realise its odd texture. It's bloody tinned fruit. No wonder it was "already made". Just not by her. Oh, it's horrible. There's no cream or anything to help liven it up. At least it slips down my throat easily.

My yawn is exaggerated once we're all finished. My arms get stretched up too, just so it doesn't escape my mother's attention. She doesn't move.

"Oh, I'm tired," I try.

"You get to bed then. I'll do the washing up before we retire, so don't you worry."

Pardon? What?

"Err, I have a dishwasher. And hadn't you better be getting off home before dark?"

"Don't be silly. How can we leave you in your moment of need? We'll stay the night to make sure you're alright."

"Mother, I'm —"

But my father comes to my rescue. He clearly wasn't consulted either.

"Now, Joan. Molly is all grown up. The hospital doesn't think she's in any danger."

"But what if she goes into a coma overnight?"

"If there was any chance of that she wouldn't be at home. Come along now, let's leave Mols to recover in peace. We've done our good deed for the day."

Mother hates it when he calls me Mols. She says it makes me sound like some sort of tunnel rat. But she ignores it on this occasion, as he's causing greater offense by suggesting she leave my presence.

"I can't possibly."

"Joan, she's a big girl. She can take care of herself."

He slowly nudges her towards the hall. She's ruffling her feathers and protesting all the way.

"I'll be fine, Mother. Thank you for everything. You've been wonderful."

Cough, cough. The words almost stick in my throat, but I have to commend her effort. It really was good of her to come to my rescue.

"Very well, if you're sure. You know where I am. Just telephone if you need me."

"I will do."

She's ushered out, and I give my father a quick hug. "Thank you."

"Needs must," he confides, before hurrying out to open the car door for my mother.

After nipping outside for a quick cigarette, I scurry into the kitchen and load the dishwasher. I can't be bothered to heat anything up, so grab a large packet of crisps and a cola, which disappear as I channel hop. I swear television programmes have gone downhill. But I need mindless drivel right now anyway, my mind is too busy.

Chapter 12 – There's More

Would you look at that? I went to bed and woke up again in the morning. Well done me for not suddenly dying in the night.

I'm still grateful that my father managed to convince my mother to go home. It was really lovely of her to care, but she just doesn't do it in the right way. And this is my own space. It doesn't feel right sharing my home. I'm an independent woman. Alright, I'm a pig-headed woman.

It's later than I'd like by the time my hippo self lollops out of bed. The doctors' surgery will already be open. I promised I'd phone this morning to make an appointment for a blood test.

Breakfast is more important though. Toast and marmalade for now. The butter dribbles down my chin as I bite into the thick white slice. After a large coffee I'm finally ready to make the call.

The line's jammed. I don't even get into the queue. I re-dial and re-dial, until finally it rings. The recorded, droning voice of a bored receptionist tells me the surgery hours, lots of useless information and finally announces my place in the queue.

It takes ages. The repeated announcements are really annoying. Yes, I know, I heard the first fifty times.

"Hello, _ surgery." The voice sounds cheery yet carries a warning to not waste her time also.

How do they do that? I'm sure there's a doctor's receptionist school where they have to go for training. Oh right, I should say something.

"Hello, please can I get a blood test app…"

"Hang on, please."

She didn't even let me finish. Rude! I'm left hanging in silence as she taps keys in the background.

"I have one two weeks Thursday."

"Oh, um."

"That's the earliest we have."

"But the hospital seemed to think it was more urgent."

"You want an emergency appointment?"

Yes, those blood test emergencies are so common, aren't they? Quick, rush me to…the blood nurse.

"I suppose so, yes please."

There's a tsk before more key tapping.

"It's a fasting one, if that helps," I offer, hoping she's still listening.

"I can fit you in Wednesday morning at nine-thirty. Don't eat or drink anything except water for twelve hours before."

"OK, thank you."

I hang up, shock rippling through me. Twelve hours? No proper drinks either? Oh, this is going to be horrendous. Is it really necessary? And what sort of emergency takes forty-eight hours to attend?

Feeling grumpy, I'm heading to the kitchen to make a cup of tea so I can console myself with biscuits.

Whilst waiting for the kettle to boil I phone the hospice to apologise and explain my absence this week. They're very sweet and ooze sympathy. Daft, they look after far sicker people every day. This is nothing, a little cut really.

I wander around, trying to get myself organised. I'm still in my pyjamas as I go into my workshop to tidy up. It's still too hot to breathe, but I take things slowly. The door's still open, in an attempt to get some fresh air.

The little bumble bee comes buzzing in and keeps me company. I swear it's checking I'm OK. That knock to my head must've been harder than I thought.

The sky's clouding over as I make my way back indoors. I really hope this means a storm is about to break. It's been well over a week now. This heat is unbearable; simply stifling.

The icky sticky mess that is me wanders into the kitchen. It doesn't help that my hair is yet to be washed, thanks to doctor's orders. Ham, pickle and cheese gets piled onto a plate, along with some of the crusty bread my mother bought. A large glass of orange juice is poured too. And perhaps a few crisps. This is what makes up my lunch.

My morning's exertions have tired me, so I snooze on the sofa, with the aid of my beany cushion. The vital things have all been done. I can claim a few minutes to rest.

But hours have gone by when I'm woken by the sound of my doorbell. It must be Wendy. Bless her, she's so good.

"Oh, what are you doing here?" I exclaim as I find Paul on my doorstep.

Good God, he has a bunch of flowers. Crazy stalker.

"I didn't have your phone number. Sorry. I heard what happened and wanted to see you were alright."

Of course, Paul. It wasn't just an excuse. I believe you. Not.

"I'm listed as Holly Molly in the directory."

"Oh, right. I guess I wasn't thinking. Here, I got you these."

The flowers are shoved in my face. They're cheap, nasty supermarket ones.

"Um, but maybe flowers for a florist wasn't the best idea?"

Oh crumbs, did my disdain show?

I hastily tell him, "It was a lovely thought. Thanks. But I'm not really up to visitors."

He had to see me at my worst, right? Not that I care. I'd rather not see him again after what happened.

"Right, sorry. As long as you're OK?"

"As well as can be expected."

"I guess I'll go then. You know where I am if you need me."

Does he have to look like a hurt puppy as he says that? He came over here, unannounced, uninvited and is somehow surprised I'm not welcoming him with open, bruised arms? Give me a break.

"Sorry. I just woke up. I'm still a bit groggy. Thanks for stopping by."

How do I politely tell him not to repeat this, though?

"Right. OK. Bye then."

"Bye," I chime as I close the door firmly.

The flowers drop to the floor as my hands cover my face and I huff out a sigh. What on Earth? Did that just happen? I feel embarrassed for him. What an idiot. What was he thinking? How did he get my address? I suppose it's listed in relation to my business, but then he would've seen my phone number too. So why didn't he just phone?

The doorbell rings again. Oh please don't be him. My stomach tightens as I open the door again.

"Oh, Wendy, I've never been so glad to see you. Come in, come in," I greet her, tugging her arm.

"I'm pleased to see you too, but why are you quite so glad?" a rather bemused friend enquires as she gets pulled into my hall.

"Paul was here."

"Paul? As in Paul, Paul?"

"Yes, the one from the wedding disaster, ex colleague, Paul."

"Oh my God."

"Quite. I didn't even know he had my address."

"And he clearly didn't think either," she says, stepping around the discarded flowers.

"I know, can you believe it? Flowers. Not very nice flowers."

"Oh dear. Negative brownie points for him."

"What possessed him? We had a one night thing. That was clearly all he was after."

"What did he say?"

"He said he'd heard what had happened. I suppose the mother grapevine was busy spreading the word again. Honestly, is nothing secret around here?"

A flash of light makes me jump.

"Was that lightning?"

"I think it may have been."

A distant rumble of thunder confirms it.

"We're safe and warm anyway. And I brought Chinese. I thought you may need it after your visitors yesterday," she says, holding up the white carrier bag.

"Oh, you're a star. Thanks. She fed me salmon. I thought I was going to puke."

We go into the kitchen and dish up the array of sticky food. We take the piled up plates, along with glasses of wine into the lounge. Takeaways are informal food, and it just feels wrong eating it at the table. We're quite happy sitting on the chairs in my lounge, tucking into the sweet, crunchy goodness.

"You wouldn't believe the effort it took to get my mother to leave," I tell Wendy between mouthfuls, "My father had to intervene. She was only thinking of staying the night."

"No!"

"Oh yes. It was like I was a toddler again. She ran a bath for me, and for one horrid moment I thought she was going to sit in the bathroom and watch."

Wendy giggles.

"It wasn't funny. She ended up sitting on a chair the other side of the door."

Wendy is roaring with laughter now. I can't help but join in. My mother, the drama queen. Guaranteed to make the most of any situation. What do you mean I clearly had a good teacher?

"You've had quite an exciting weekend, haven't you?" Wendy says as she manages to catch her breath.

"That's one way of putting it."

Thunder crashes and lightning floods the sky outside.

Chapter 13 – Appointments

Jan arrives at his usual appointed time the next day, and I'm semi-decent. My hair's clean, hoorah. It feels so good to be able to wash properly. I was still careful not to get my head too wet though. The bruises on my arms and legs have started turning all sorts of pretty colours as they begin to heal.

Last night's storm has cleared the air. It's drizzling on and off, but at least it's cooler. I'm wearing a lightweight long-sleeved top with jeans for my delivery. No, I'm not going to any special effort. But one can't wear pyjamas when dealing with a fellow professional. This is business.

We offload the flowers into my workshop.

"It looks like you have a new friend," he comments, pointing at the bee who's flown in with us.

Have I mentioned I really like his Dutch accent? Well, I do. His 's's make a 'sh' sound.

"It's taken a shining to my floral nest here, I think."

"Or it could just be a loved one in spirit telling you they are near."

"Oh, you don't believe in that nonsense, do you?"

"Who is to say what is nonsense and what is not?"

My shoulders shrug noncommittally in response. I thought the Dutch were more practical, sensible types. Oh well, it takes all sorts.

I close the large door behind him as he goes off. These flowers must be prepared and put into fresh water.

"Hello," I say softly and cheerily.

Yes, I'm talking to a bee. Yes, I know this makes me look crazy. But I swear it buzzes back. OK, I'll go and lie down as soon as I'm finished here. I may have concussion.

But as I go back into the house my tummy reminds me it's food time. Using some leftover ham and crusty bread, I make a quick sandwich. This is accompanied by crisps and orange juice.

Oh crap, I've not picked up my van yet. No rest for the wicked. I telephone a taxi company. I don't want to put anyone else to any further bother. My parents have driven far enough, and even if Wendy's not at work she should probably be resting. She works so hard.

So here I am, sitting in a taxi, making my way to the hotel of doom. To be fair, it's not the hotel's fault. It's all my own. But going back is not an exciting prospect. The splendour of the place is now obscured by my own veil of embarrassment.

The driver gets paid handsomely as I thank and dismiss him. My feet take small steps towards the building. I need to face the receptionist.

"Ciao, Molly."

Oh good, Antonio is here. Does he ever leave? It just had to be him.

"Hello. Listen, thanks for helping me the other day."

"It was nothing. I am glad to see you well again."

"Well, thank you. I'm here to remove my van, which has been cluttering up your car park."

"Not at all. It is in the rear car park for you."

He disappears into the back office, and returns with my van key.

"Thanks again."

"You're very welcome, bella."

Oh, he has a cute smile as he says that. Ahem, off I go to reunite with my little workhorse. I've no time for distractions.

Happily, the van starts. I confess that I was a little worried. It's only been a few days, and it was a silly thing to worry about. But the relief is there anyway.

My energy is waning, but I manage to drag myself round a supermarket to top up my food supplies. A chocolate bar sneaks into my mouth before I drive home. What? I'm tired, and need the energy.

It's late afternoon by the time I get back home. The food gets packed away, and I flop down onto my sofa with a cup of tea and some biscuits. It doesn't look like I'm going to get a nap in. And no food will pass my lips from nine o'clock tonight.

Butterflies flutter in my tummy as I think of my blood test. The needle itself is scary, but what the test may find is even scarier. The doctor hinted I may have diabetes. But I can't have. Can I?

Honestly, I'm terrified. What if I do? What happens next? Visions of me having to inject myself appear in my head. It doesn't bear thinking about. It's too horrible. I know some people have to, but I've no idea how they cope with it.

The rest of the evening gets worried away, and a microwave meal gets eaten. I treated myself to a roast dinner one as it's my last food for a while.

Sleep doesn't come easily. Fear has me in its grasp, and it doesn't want to let go. I feel sick.

"You're too fat. You did this to yourself. If only you'd not stuffed your fat face so much you wouldn't be in this situation. Well, you'll pay for it now, you hippo," that familiar internal voice lectures me throughout the night.

A very worried, sleepy and hungry me arrives at the doctor's surgery Wednesday morning. I report in and go to wait uncomfortably in the, well, the waiting room. There's other people in here, and some of them are coughing and sneezing. Sick people go to doctors. I'm not sick and don't belong here. They'd better not spread their germs to me.

Finally, my name gets called. I follow the nurse as if going to my doom. Sensing my reluctance, the nurse is very good and tries to put me at my ease. She directs my eyes in the opposite direction as she sticks the needle in.

"There we go, you're doing very well. So, you're a florist?"

"Argh, yes," I try to ignore the pricking sensation of the needle going in.

"That must be nice."

"Yeees, it is. Flowers make people happy, which makes me happy."

"Do you do weddings?"

"Yes, mainly weddings actually."

"I'm getting married next year."

I don't know why, but I'm surprised by this. "Oh lovely, congratulations."

"Have you got any business cards?"

"Really? You want one?"

"If that's OK."

"Sure, when I can reach my bag."

"There we go. All done."

"Really? Already?"

She smiles at me as she sticks a little bandage roll thing to my arm. Once she's done I reach into my bag and give her one of my cards. You never know who you're going to meet, do you? Who would have thought today would result in a potential client?

I'm actually smiling as I leave the surgery, still pleasantly surprised by the chance encounter. There's emergency chocolate bars in my glovebox, and one is utilised. Ah, food! I go to a drive-thru on my way home too. My bravery needs to be rewarded, and I didn't have breakfast. The nurse didn't even give me a good girl lollipop.

Back at my house, there's time for a quick tidy up and a shower before this afternoon's client gets here. It feels good to be returning back to normal. Overall, the past couple of weeks have been traumatic. But I'm finally finding my feet again. And my body is aching less as the bumps and bruises heal.

This afternoon's bride is bringing a friend, and some Prosecco is chilling in my fridge for them. This will be mixed with some orange juice for some Bucks Fizz as we talk through options. And there's some peanuts and little cheese biscuits for nibbles.

The bride told me she'll be arriving after she finishes work, so I want her to feel pampered. Everything's all laid out when they arrive.

We chat through some very exciting, modern ideas as we sip our drinks and munch away. It's a lovely relaxed atmosphere, and we're all bubbling with excitement.

There's some nibbles left over after they've gone. It'd be rude to waste them, and it's a hassle trying to get them back into packets, so I polish them off myself as I wait for my dinner to heat up. Oh dear, some Prosecco is left too. What a sumptuous dinner.

Feeling a little tipsy, I make sure everything's tidied up, and allow myself some R&R in front of the television. Ahh, that's better.

***

In the morning I have a slightly groggy head. Oops, too many bubbles last night. Oh well, it was worth it. It was nice to chill out.

My phone rings mid-morning. It's my doctor's surgery. I'm invited to go in for an appointment to discuss my results, but I decline as I'm too busy. The receptionist kindly arranges for the doctor to phone me instead.

"There's no nice way of telling you this, Miss Wilkinson. You have prediabetes," he tells me when he calls.

"Um, is that diabetes or not?" I ask, a little confused.

"No, but it means you could very well end up with type 2 diabetes unless you make some changes. You are borderline diabetic. There's lots of people who manage to avoid the condition. Your BMI is above thirty-three, which indicates you're severely obese."

Oh great, even my doctor is calling me fat.

He continues, "There's a dietician at the surgery you can make an appointment with. I'd recommend seeing her to talk through your options."

I end the call and let reality sink in. I'm fat. Fat enough to put my health at risk. My health is already in bad shape. A part of me knew this, but it's not nice hearing a health professional tell you. Tears are dripping down my face. What have I done?

Chapter 14 – Put My Money Where My Mouth Is

I telephone my mother, who of course gives me a full verse of 'I told you so'. Feeling even worse, I end the call. It hurts as I know she's right. This is all my fault. I'm fat, ugly and stupid.

So, I call Wendy, who of course comes round as soon as she hears my sobs on the phone. She's greeted by a big blubbering mess.

"Deep breaths. Tell me, what the matter is," she says calmly, grasping my upper arms.

Even Wendy couldn't decipher my words on the phone.

"He…he…said I'm fat."

"Who did?"

"My doctor."

"Were those his exact words?"

"No. He said…severely obese."

"Oh sweetie," she consoles, giving me a hug.

"And…and…I have…prediabetes."

"I'm so sorry."

More hugging ensues as I cry my little eyes out.

"But at least it's not actually diabetes. You can do something about it," Wendy tells me.

"Yeeees…I have to go on a diet." My sobs get louder at this prospect.

The next several minutes are not pretty. I'm in pieces. Wendy goes and makes a pot of tea as I try to calm myself. The hot, sweet liquid helps a little.

"So, what's the plan?"

She's very practical. There's a problem, deal with it. I'm very good at this too, just when giving advice to others, and not myself.

"He said I can talk to the dietician at the surgery."

"That sounds like a good idea. My friend Gail has done really well. She joined a slimming group. You could try that?"

"And have all those people judge how fat I am?"

"I don't think it works like that. You're all in the same boat, surely?"

"Maybe. But I'm not sure I can face it."

"What if I go with you?"

Wendy isn't exactly skinny herself. I'd never call my friend fat. But maybe we could both benefit from losing a bit of weight.

"Would you really do that?"

"Well, I've sort of been thinking about it anyway."

"I'll think about it."

"I'll find out when the group meets, and we can go together. We can just go to one meeting to see if we like it. What's the harm of trying?"

I can't think of a reason not to. At least not one that Wendy would accept. She's in one of those 'don't mess with me' moods.

OK, I can do this. I need to do this.

***

It is with great reluctance that I now stand before you, outside the hall, awaiting Wendy. I'm here. I made it this far. My first ever slimming group meeting. Some other people have gone in already. They look reassuringly fat. But there was one woman, who quite frankly doesn't look like she belongs. Why would someone that slim need to lose weight?

I'd like to say I've carried on business as usual. Well, I have, on the surface at least. Brides have requested flowers, and they've been delivered with a smile. But I'd be lying if I said this moment hasn't been constantly on my mind. I'm not good in large groups, especially ones which will be looking at the fat hippo I am.

I'm a nervous wreck, and grab Wendy into a reassuring hug when she arrives.

"You ready?" she asks me.

I can feel my lips scrunching to one side. "Not really."

"Come on. We'll be fine."

My hand is in hers as she practically pulls me inside. Is it too late to start kicking and screaming? Why am I doing this? I feel sick. Fortunately, before I can create a scene or even run away, a lovely smiling lady approaches us.

"Hello, ladies. I'm Hazel. Are you here to join us today?"

"Yes," Wendy replies emphatically before I even open my mouth.

"Lovely. Welcome. Come this way, and you can take a seat for a bit. I'm just going to see if there's any other new starters today. I won't be long."

We're guided to a corner of the room. There's a line of people queueing at a till on the far side. And another queue waiting at what I presume are scales. And a large semicircle of chairs, where some people are sitting already. Oh crumbs, there's even a bloke here. I thought it would be women only.

They're not expecting me to weigh myself in front of people, are they? It seems a bit open. Oh, please don't tell everyone the number. I know they can see what a whale I am with their own eyes, but to have that number confirmed? I don't even want to hear it.

Oh cripes, Hazel is approaching.

"Sorry about that. OK, have either of you attended one of our groups before?"

We both shake our heads, no.

Hazel holds up a little folder, and hands us each our own booklet.

"No problem. In a moment I'll get you to sit with the group, and I'll weigh you at the end of the session."

She proceeds to tell us about the basics of the diet programme. Apparently it's a lifestyle change not a diet though. I fail to see the difference.

Oh, I can still eat pasta and potatoes? Hey, what are you trying to pull here? Carbs on a diet? This is never going to work. But bread is restricted. Hm, well we'll see.

There's a list of vegetables which are super good, and to be encouraged. And fruit. There's another list of food which I can eat lots of. A list of what looks like dairy, and another listing fibre rich foods, which I need a little bit of each day. And pages of the naughty food, which I'm allowed a very little bit of each day.

"Nothing is banned. You're not denying yourself," Hazel explains.

There's an awful lot to take in. I'm trying to listen, but my brain's whirring. I'm glad Wendy's here. I'm sure she's taking more in than me. She was always the better listener out of the two of us, which I relied on in school.

We're led to sit down in amongst the big group. There's people either side of us, and they smile their greetings as we take our seats.

Hazel addresses the group, and tells us all about important updates, and highlighting articles in the magazine. Each person has their chance to say what their week has been like. Some have lost, some have gained, and some have maintained.

The people with gains are not pointed at and made to feel ashamed. No, they're met with sympathy and we discuss ideas how to make this week go better for them, including some great sounding meal ideas.

The lady who I thought was too slim to need to come here? It turns out she's a target member, and has lost four stone. She looks great. I hope I can be like her. How inspirational.

It's a huge relief to hear no actual weights read out; just how much the loss has been. Some have lost a couple of pounds, and one person has lost a massive eight pounds. Each and every person receives a round of applause, even if they've gained. It's surprisingly supportive and positive.

Honestly, I thought there would be a lot of fat shaming. But no, there's only gentle words of encouragement.

Before I know it, the end of the session is called, so Wendy and me go up to the counter to pay and stand on the dreaded scales.

"It's just a starting point," Hazel kindly points out.

I clamber onto the scales. I'm not surprised. The doctors told me my weight. It's not miraculously changed. Well, it's gone up a little. My heart sinks as the large number gets written into my very own book. I'm encouraged to set a target weight.

I don't know what to say. I just don't want to be at risk of getting diabetes, and not be fat. We agree a target of a five stone weight loss, as that gets me into my healthy BMI range. That sounds like an awful lot to lose. Can I do this?

I go home alone and start reading through all the information. It's a daunting prospect. But the slim lady has given me some hope. She's done it. It's worked for her. Maybe it can work for me too.

It turns out that orange juice is on the naughty list. I thought I was being healthy. But it's high in sugar. So, that can be reduced, for a start.

The recommended sugar intake for the day? Oops, that's been and gone on my coffees alone. So, I need to at least reduce the amount of sugar in that.

Toast is alright. I need to change to wholemeal bread, and then that can be counted as my fibre for the day. That's good news.

The people in the group seem to recommend making your own meals. But there's microwave ones which the group brand has created, so I can still buy those for when I need to have something in a hurry.

But what do I cook? It's only me. One of the ladies tonight said about cooking in batches and freezing them. So I can eat some straight away, and have the rest another evening. That would be quick to heat up too. I suppose that's doable.

There's so much information here. My head hurts, and I want to dive into a packet of biscuits and escape from it all. I won't. But I want to. Actually, there's not many bad things left in the cupboards. I ate my way through most of it, knowing I'd need to say goodbye to my treats. This *may* be why my weight was even higher than the one the doctor told me.

Whichever way I look at it, I need to face up to facts. I have to lose weight. My health depends upon it. This isn't going to be easy, but I have to do it.

So, what should go on my shopping list for tomorrow? Wholemeal bread, eggs, low fat yoghurt. That doesn't seem too bad. Grapes for snacking. Fine. Someone suggested jacket potatoes as you can bung them in the oven and leave them, so they're easy. Baked beans are on the OK list, so they can go on too, to go with the potatoes.

Sandwiches are out the window. Do you know how much sugar there is in bread? It's a lot. Plus the fillings in the sandwiches you buy pre made. That's going to be hard. I eat a lot of those. What do I do instead? Salad? Bleurgh.

I log onto the website, and discover some nice noodle salad recipes. Quick, easy, and look achievable. OK, I'll try. It's too hot for soup. There's something called crustless quiche, which could be made on my quiet days, and then can be portioned out to last a few lunches.

Dinners could be trickier. Let's have a look. Oh, that's not so difficult. There's plenty of quick pasta recipes. And curry; result!

OK, there's enough on my list to get a start. One of the ladies told me to buy lots of fruit and vegetables and have a play. She made sense, but it's a bit scary. Maybe after a few weeks I'll have a go. Meat and two veg was what people used to say as a rule of thumb, and it does seem to ring true.

List done. Plans made.

Chapter 15 – Food for Thought

There was no brown bread in the house, but I don't think one little slice of white toast is going to ruin the whole week.

My weekly flower delivery arrives courtesy of Jan. Prepping the flowers can wait. My tummy's rumbling.

Hunger, we're told, can often be confused with thirst. Therefore, instead of reaching for the snacks, I'm drinking a glass of water. It's bland and boring, and making me long for coffee. Not terribly satisfied, it's time to head to the shops.

The supermarket has some of those trendy drinks bottles on sale; you know, the ones where you put fruit in a little compartment. Hopefully, that will make water more interesting.

All sorts of healthy items get loaded into my basket, and subsequently passed along the conveyor.

Sweat's trickling down my forehead by the time I get back home. It's supposed to be less humid now, according to the weatherman. Another glass of water gets consumed as I pack my shopping away. Bored.

Cooking isn't appealing at the moment, so I'm going to have one of the recommended pasta snacks for lunch. As it's soaking, I wash up my new water bottle and stuff in some ice, water, strawberries, watermelon and mint.

The pasta doesn't taste too bad, and the fruity water is a vast improvement. I top up the bottle and take it around with me as I disappear into my 'creation station' to feed the flowers and make sure they're happy.

My life is already getting disturbed by this diet. Today feels all topsy turvy. I hope the poor flowers don't mind this delay. And that's just one part of it. If I'm to start preparing meals I need to plan my day differently.

It's all feeling a little too much. Everything's changing, and it doesn't feel right. I send Wendy a quick text to see how she's doing, and to report on my own progress. Her response pings back almost immediately.

"Not as bad as I feared so far. We'll be fine."

I'm glad she's coping better than I am. This afternoon's snack is a banana. It fills a hole, but it's not biscuits, is it?

I bung the potatoes in the oven, and decide to take a nap as they cook. I thought all this healthy stuff was supposed to give me energy, but I'm feeling really drained, and a little bit shaky.

Dinner this evening is accompanied by a coffee. I've been missing it all day, and I'm allowed some. It only has one sugar in, but it's not too bad. I could get used to it.

Day one is completed on target. Ta da!

***

You're not supposed to, but I stood on my bathroom scales just now. No difference, damn it. Impatient? Me? OK, you got me, but I wanted something to change. Surely there should be a little sign of hope for my efforts? Just a teeny weeny one?

Nope, off I shlump. There's a funeral to do flowers for. It's so sad. This chap was a husband and father, only in his fifties. It's no age, is it? Life is so cruel sometimes. Another victim of cancer. Such an evil disease.

Unable to help it, tears fall as I put the arrangement together. It makes me think of my own father. He has the patience of a saint, and is always quietly there in the background. He came to my rescue last week, didn't he? I'm a grown adult, but still need my daddy. Especially if I do ever manage to get married. He should be there to give me away.

Just imagine it. My father leading me up the aisle, like Amelia's did. Beaming with pride. Making a silly speech. Dancing with me in the evening. Nothing should be able to take away those precious moments.

My little bee friend is back as I busy myself with the sad task. Hopefully these flowers will help lift the mourners' spirits a little.

Trying hard not to get too forlorn, I take the displays to the funeral home to be laid on the coffin, and make my way home as fast as I can. Please note, there is no stop off at a drive-thru on my way back. I'm determined to make the Asian noodle salad today.

That road to hell is still paved with good intentions, isn't it? I'm staring at the recipe for the salad, and it involves putting things in a food processor. It's all a bit fussy. Nope, I'm not doing it. Maybe I can make it when I have a bit more time? Hunger is calling.

Instead, I opt for the chicken Caesar salad. Can you believe I'm allowed bacon? Next week I think I'll buy a roast chicken and use leftovers for this recipe. But for now, there's a little packet of cooked chicken with my name on it. It's cheating, but give me a break, I'm trying.

The dressing is quite easy. Fromage frais and a few bits in a bowl; mix mix mix as the bacon sizzles. Chuck some lettuce leaves on a plate. Bish, bash, bosh, job done. Mmm, and quite yummy. I even get to have a little bit of cheese. This meal is definitely being filed under 'to be done again'.

Tidying up awaits. Don't feel you have to follow me down the garden. There's only so much flower trimming stuff you can see, I'm sure.

***

I'm being a good girl, and filling in my food diary with each morsel which passes my lips. I'm staying within my limits, and trying to eat more veg.

Oh, it's coffee break time, so this is an opportune moment to update a bit more of my food diary now. It's alarming to see the difference in my diet already. It turns out I was being bad even when I thought I was being good. For example, the cereal I was eating was high in sugar, and the portion size was far too big.

Muesli gets weighed out for breakfast, and is actually enjoyable once some low fat yoghurt and fresh berries are mixed in, and left overnight. No more toast. And I'm not even hungry. I may actually be eating more food than normal. Can this be right? Weigh day will tell, I suppose.

Fruit is being consumed like there's no tomorrow. And my poor loo is being flushed more often. Hopefully the increased peeing is down to me drinking more water, and not because diabetes has caught up with me. I have an appointment to check that in a couple of weeks' time.

The only thing I've not done so far is increased my exercise. But work keeps me busy, and I bustle around quite a lot. One step at a time, eh? I can't do everything all in one go.

There's a new spice rack in my kitchen, and it's starting to get filled up. I'm making a curry tonight, and not with a jar of sauce. This is crazy. I never thought I'd do this. But those sauces are full of sugar, and apparently making your own tastes nicer. There's a good takeaway locally who will deliver should this go horribly wrong.

Let's see…fry off some spices and onions, mushrooms and peppers. I've chopped and sliced everything already. It took a while, but hopefully it'll be worth it. Chuck in some garlic. Then some chicken. It smells lovely. Then some stock and a tin of tomatoes. Sizzle sizzle, bubble bubble. Cover and simmer. Well, that was easy. Now I have forty-five minutes to do a bit of housework.

The vacuum cleaner gets whisked round, only pausing long enough for me to put some rice on. A packet of microwave rice was tempting, but I'm doing things properly. And there's more portion control this way.

My kitchen smells amazing. Augh, my mouth is literally watering as I dish up my masterpiece. And I'm allowing a very small glass of wine to go with it. It's so awesome I can do this. And my hard work should be rewarded, don't you think?

Oh my God, this curry is gorgeous. Did I really just make this? And why didn't I do it before? It was so easy. And yes, so much better than the stuff from a jar. And there's lots of vegetables in it, so it's good for me too. Wowwee! The best bit? There's loads left over, so I can put some in the freezer and have some more another day.

I send a text to Wendy, "I just made curry. Call me Delia Smith."

"Well done. I'll be calling you Nigella by the time we're through losing weight. Where's mine?"

"Haha. Not quite a domestic goddess yet. The rest is going in the freezer. But you can have a bit if you want."

"I'll pop by for a doggy bag tomorrow."

A thought pops into my head; poor Wendy works so much. Her shifts are long and many. If we club together, I can buy and cook and she can benefit from the yummy food. I could make up fridge packs, or she can pop by after her shift, time permitting. Why didn't I think of it before? Mental note; chat this through with her tomorrow.

Chapter 16 – Ups and Downs

It's been a busy week, but I've been mainly good, making some healthy choices. I've not really missed the biscuits yet, as I've been trying to replace them with other things. And a few crisps have been consumed within my allowance.

Wendy's working, so I'm here in the group on my own. To say my nerves are getting the better of me is an understatement. There's a dance party in my stomach, and there's even sweat on my brow. I know I've tried really hard, but other diets have let me down in the past, so who knows if this one will work?

The queue's out the door. There's lots of people here, and the wait is doing nothing for my nerves. Everyone else is chatting, asking how each other did this week, and catching up. But I don't know anyone else here. My arms are wrapped around my middle as I shuffle along, one step further towards the truth.

"Hello, it's Molly, isn't it?" the lady behind me asks.

She's been talking to someone else who had already weighed in, but that lady's now gone to make a coffee. I'm almost the same height as her, which is comforting. Her brown bob bounces as she turns to face me properly.

"Hello. Um, yes."

"I'm Tracy. How was your first week?"

"OK, I think. I suppose the scales will tell me."

"Don't be nervous. Some people lose in their first week, some take longer for it to show. The main thing is you're here and you're trying."

"Thanks. I really want to lose weight."

"We all do," she replies, smiling with understanding.

"I suppose so."

"You'll be alright. Did you find anything you liked?"

"Oh yes, a lovely curry. I'd never made one before, not properly," I say, looking away.

"Well done. That's fabulous."

My head snaps back in her direction at the praise. "And there was a really nice chicken Caesar salad, but I got hungry quite quickly."

"Try putting some new potatoes in it too," Tracy says with a knowing look.

"Ooh, that sounds good."

"It will help fill you up for longer."

"Thanks."

We natter until I reach the desk and pay my money. The lady there explains I can buy several weeks at once, which works out at a discount, and I'll be entitled to a free recipe booklet. Maybe. I need to be convinced this works before I commit.

Round to the queue for the scales. Oh, this is moving agonisingly slowly. I just want to know if I've lost anything, or if I'm still a hippo. Bless her, Tracy is talking away at me again. She's lovely; helping to distract me from my impending doom. But now I've arrived at the scales.

"OK, you can get on," the person manning the scales tells me.

My shoes have been discarded already. Taking a deep breath, I mount the weighing device. I'm sure I hear it moan in pain underneath me.

"Well done, you've lost six pounds."

"What? Are you sure?" I yelp.

"Yep, it's right there," she says, tapping my book with her pen.

"Oh my God."

I virtually bounce off the scales.

"See. I told you you'd be OK," Tracy tells me.

In shock, I go and take a seat in the big semicircle and send Wendy a text to tell her about the miracle.

Tracy joins me a few minutes later, taking the vacant chair next to me. She's full of congratulations, and informs me she lost one pound this week, which she's happy about.

I'm still amazed at my own loss. Six pounds? Wow. Just wow. I hope I can lose lots next week too.

As we go around the room I hear, "One or two pounds a week is a good steady weight loss."

Hazel, the consultant announces, "And everyone give a big round of applause to our new member, Molly, who lost six pounds in her first week."

I squirm in my chair, blushing madly as people clap and cheer.

"Well done, Molly. How did you find your first week? Was there anything you liked?"

"I loved the curry I made. I actually made it from scratch," I tell the group quietly.

Some appreciative 'ooh's go around the semicircle.

"I had jacket potatoes and beans one day, but it's a bit hot for that really."

"You could try swapping to sweet potatoes. They microwave in about five minutes, and they go really nicely with tuna in a bit of light mayonnaise, and some peppers. Maybe a bit of salad on the side too," another member suggests.

"That's a lovely suggestion. Thank you, Tim. Does that sound like something you'd like, Molly?" Hazel asks.

"It does actually. Thank you."

Hazel moves on to the next person, and I try to remember some of the tips others are suggesting as we go round. Hang on. Is that excitement I'm feeling? I do believe it is. I'm actually excited about some of the things to try this week.

***

I really need to change my shopping day. I've had to wait for Jan and his delivery, and have made an omelette for lunch. One tip I learned last night was to not shop on an empty stomach. Maybe more naughty snacks do go into my trolley that way. Good advice.

But it's already mid-afternoon, and I don't feel like going. Don't get me wrong, I'm forcing myself out, but it's a struggle. And now the group are teaching me all these good tips, my head is starting to get to grips with the whole plan. Organisation is key.

My laptop was whirring last night as I had a look for more recipes and compiled a shopping list, spurred on by my magical weight loss and the lovely people in the group. There's enough for me to cook a few meals for Wendy, and to generate some leftovers too, so I'm not cooking every night.

It's quite challenging going up and down the aisles of the supermarket. At the end of most of them are the special offers, and none of them are healthy. I am having to force my feet to walk past all the tempting multi buy crisps, chocolate, biscuits, and even wine. My neck cranes round, gazing at the naughties as I pass. Talk about testing my willpower. This is torture. Sweat is forming on my upper lip and brow with the effort. My breathing is becoming shallower. Please, I just need to get through this.

I'm so relieved to get out of there. Maybe I should order my food online for a while? But I don't like other people choosing for me. I don't know. Perhaps it's worth it, just whilst I get used to my new diet. Does that make me sound like a foodaholic? Gosh, maybe I am? If there's an open packet of biscuits, or anything for that matter, I do feel compelled to finish it. Is that normal? Or is it in fact a form of addiction? Eek.

As the shopping gets unpacked I want to cry. A multipack of crisps and a big packet of biscuits had found their way into my trolley. I don't have to eat them. They can sit at the back of the cupboard. Calling my name. Pleading to get munched. Stop it! No. I can do this. I am in control.

I'll work out the naughty value of them, and incorporate them into my allowance for the day. It's fine. No panic.

Tsk, I was in such a good mood earlier. I was proud of myself for losing six pounds. That's almost half a stone already. It's amazing. But already I'm beating myself up for failing at shopping.

I log onto the slimming group's social media page, and tell them what's happened. Maybe sharing it will help me? I instantly get lots of supportive messages, which is nice. And as I scroll down I can see lots of food pictures. Someone has a snack tray, so their daily allowance is contained, and she doesn't go over the limit. That seems sensible.

Time to check my work emails. There's not too many, but I take my time, making sure to respond fully, and without spelling mistakes. I need to look professional.

It occurs to me I've not checked my personal email. My boyfriend quest has been completely sidetracked by food issues. Well, maybe it's all for the same cause. Once I'm thinner maybe I'll have more of a chance?

There's quite a few emails from the dating site. This looks positive. Perhaps I'm not a hideous hippo after all?

I open the first message and gasp in horror. How can someone send such a horrible message?

"Try looking in a local field for your match, you fat heffer."

Despite the fact he can't even spell heifer, this message still stings. Well, stings like a knife going through my heart. That's more of a stab, isn't it? And hurts a whole lot more than a sting.

Message after message of hatred flashes up on the screen. What have I ever done to these people? Why do I deserve such awful messages? I really am a fat, ugly hippo.

"See, nobody wants you," my cruel voice chides me.

There's a few 'like' type notifications. Most of the guys I click on are real losers, though. Not that I'd ever be mean enough to say that in a message to them. I simply ignore them. There's one guy that looks nice, but then again familiar. I bet he's used a stolen picture of a minor celebrity from the internet. Jerk! I ignore him too.

Tears are flowing freely by the time I finish reading all the vitriol. I text Wendy who promises to come over after her shift in a few hours.

I'm so stupid. I knew nobody in their right mind would want someone like me. Stupid, fat and ugly. Whatever possessed me to try online dating anyway? It's not like actual in-person dating has worked for me. Stupid, stupid, stupid.

Before I know it, I'm staring at an empty packet of biscuits and pot of tea. What have I done? Oh God, I'm so stupid.

The doorbell rings, and I plod towards the door. Wendy wraps me in a hug and comes to sit down. She immediately spots the empty packet.

"Oh dear," she comments.

"Oh, what am I going to do? I'm alone and fat and stupid."

"Now stop that. You are beautiful. I know you have to lose a bit of weight, but we're doing something about that. You lost six pounds already. And you're really intelligent. Look at what you've achieved. You run your own business. Not many can do that. Come here."

I find myself getting hugged again. It's very nice of her to say those things, but I don't really believe her. It's nice to be hugged, but I wish it was a man holding me.

Chapter 17 – Gains and Losses

I've deleted my dating profile. It's only going to make me feel worse about myself, and as Wendy says, I really don't need that kind of negativity in my life right now.

I promised to be honest here, so I'll admit this hasn't been a great week. I ate my way through all the crisps, and went up the road to buy some large bars of chocolate too. My mood refuses to budge. I'm stuck in the deep blue pit of depression. There's just no clawing myself out of this one.

Thank goodness for Wendy. I don't know what I'd do without her. Well, I do, but maybe that's too much honesty. It's not a good thought. I'm so glad she can come round and prop me up as much as she does. It's not fair though. She shouldn't have to. I feel selfish. Cue more self-loathing, pushing me further into my pit. See? Hopeless.

So, another week, another weigh in. When I get on the scales I discover I've miraculously lost the other four and a half stone, I've got engaged, and live happily ever after. Hm, not even in my wildest dreams do I get that lucky.

Fine, I've put on three pounds. There. I've admitted it. I only have myself to blame. Me, and those horrid men who thought because I'm a hippo I have no feelings. Maybe I have too many feelings? I've been told I'm too sensitive. Is that a thing? How do I change it?

Wendy's working again, and has promised to go to a different group this week. I'm here, suffering the humiliation on my own.

"And let's give a big round of applause for Molly. She's come in facing a gain, but it's still a three pound loss overall. Well done, Molly."

Everyone claps, but it feels a bit forced and I don't feel worthy. They're clapping even though I've gained? That is not to be rewarded. I start to well up under their scrutiny. This of course is immediately pounced upon by the consultant.

"Is there anything we can do to help?"

"Not unless you can make me look like a supermodel, so men don't say horrible things to me online."

"Pardon?"

"Oh nothing really. I hit the biscuits and chocolate because of a nasty experience," I tell her, wincing.

"There's no food confessions here. We don't need to know what happened in the past. It's gone."

Lots of heads nod in agreement, as well as murmurs to back this up.

"Is there anything which can get in your way this week?"

"Well, err, no."

There's really not, is there? Except me. And I choose to get out of my own way.

As I'm making my way out the door one of the young women stops me.

"I'm so sorry about what happened. Which dating site was it?"

I tell her. No, I'm not telling you. That would be indiscrete, and I could get into all sorts of trouble.

She suggests a different one, and sings its praises so much I'm actually considering it. I really hope it's not another den of lions ready to maul me to shreds.

As soon as I get home I look up the site. This one has a fee involved, but maybe that will keep the trolls away. I hope so. It looks good. To hell with it, I'm going to create my profile before I can talk myself out of it. It can't hurt any more than the existing pain.

Holly Molly has a really busy week. There's little time for anything else except work. But I'm being good, aiming for a loss on the scales this week. Another gain would be awful. I refuse to go back to square one.

Sunday arrives before I'm able to check my personal emails. There's some suggestions of prospective people via the new website. It feels a little sordid, flicking through men this way, like they're menu options. Today, I'll have the horny cocktail, please, waiter.

Drastic times call for drastic measures though. So, I swallow my pride and force myself to hunt for a boyfriend. There's nothing to say they'll like me in return. Oh well, in for a penny, in for a pound.

At least these profiles seem to have genuine photographs. And a couple like the same things as me. Not that there's many hobbies and interests on my list. I do actually like long walks on the beach, but that's a bit clichéd. Try as I might, I'm just not very interesting.

This is a dilemma. If I'm putting out boring hobbies aren't I getting boring men in return? The selection so far isn't anything to get overly excited about. But I give the OK to one of them, whilst forming the resolution to think of something more fun to put on my request list.

An email pings back almost immediately. Wow, he's keen. Too keen? Should I be worried? But his message is sweet.

"Hello there. I've been notified we're a good match, and I'm really happy about that. You seem really nice, and might I add pretty? I hope that's not offensive. I don't want to sound creepy. So yeah, hi."

He even signed off with "xx Andrew". Aww.

"Hi Andrew. You seem nice too. I can't remember the last time I was called pretty. You look handsome. Do you really like being out in nature?"

I'm being forward, I know, but he started it.

"I really do. There's something so freeing about being out in the forest. Something energising yet peaceful. Don't worry, it won't be a first date suggestion. I can't have you thinking I'm an axe murderer."

I chuckle to myself, yet have to admit the thought had crossed my mind.

"I believe I specifically said no axe murderers on my request list ;-)"

"That's how you know I'm not one. So, would you like to meet up? Maybe in a pub?"

He's funny. I like him. And suggesting a quick drink, somewhere public; that was very sweet and considerate.

"Sure. Sounds like a good idea."

We arrange a time and a place. It's only when I switch my laptop off that the panic starts to set in. Oh, what have I just done? I have no idea who this Andrew really is, yet have arranged to meet him for a date. This is crazy.

I send a text to Wendy, who phones me straight back for more details. And what do you think? Bless her, she's going to hide out in the pub so she can keep an eye on things. She's amazing.

Bless him, Andrew's been really patient. We've exchanged some more emails. Our date is set for a week's time. Sundays are better for me, even though I'll be tired from the days and nights before. Weekend evenings are a bit of a no-go for me, but he was really understanding about that. And as we wanted to meet in a pub, Sunday lunchtime seemed a good time.

I'm in a really good mood. I lost three pounds this week, so am back to my first week's success weight. Yay! As Hazel pointed out, the beginning number has changed on the scales, which is exciting. The little oops is forgotten, and I'm looking forward to another loss this week.

Business has been going really well too. It's such a relief to feel like things are really beginning to take shape after the last couple of years. It's been really hard work, and was a massive risk.

So, a slightly more confident me walks into the pub today. I scan the busy rooms, and spy Wendy in the corner. Who's that with her? It looks like she's managed to get a date too. But there's no time to dwell on that now.

Where's Andrew? My brain is busy comparing the face in the photo to those all around me. I can't see him. Feeling self-conscious, standing here looking like a complete prat, I opt for approaching the bar and ordering my own drink.

I get a gin and slimline tonic. Are you proud of me? I'm making a better choice, and saved some of my weekly allowance for this. I'm only having the one anyway, being a responsible driver. Andrew will know I'm here as my van's quite obvious. The 'Holly Molly' logo gives it away a bit.

Somehow, I find a small empty table, tucked away, but I can keep my eye on the door, for when Andrew arrives. I have no reason to doubt him. He seemed honest and lovely.

Time ticks on, and my optimism wobbles. He's over fifteen minutes late. Where is he? I'd put it down to busy traffic, but this is getting silly now. I take another sip of my drink, which has almost vanished.

My glass is empty, and forty-five minutes have gone by. This is clearly not going to happen. Maybe he arrived without me seeing, and he took one look and scarpered? Maybe I'm uglier in real life. He thought he could cope with slightly chubby, but seeing how heavy I really am, perhaps he thought better of it.

I catch Wendy's eye as I get up to leave. When I'm almost at the door a voice halts my progress.

"I'm sorry, are you Molly?"

I turn around, and squint at the short, brown haired man before me.

"Hi, I'm Andrew," he says, offering me a hand to shake, which I don't take.

"No you're not."

"I promise I am."

"Where have you been? I've been here for ages."

"I'm sorry, I didn't see you there."

"Well, it's no wonder I didn't see you. You lied to me. You're nothing like your photo. I don't date liars. So if you'll excuse me."

Not waiting for an answer, I turn on my heels and walk briskly out the door. The bloody nerve. I thought he was trustworthy. But he can't even be honest about his appearance. Fine, he wasn't exactly handsome, but I would maybe have given him a chance. But he had to pretend to be someone else entirely. And if he lied about that what else was he lying about? Bloody men!

I hear my phone sound the alert for text messages, but wait until I get safely home before reading them. I've been checking my rearview mirror the whole way, making sure Andrew hasn't followed me.

The first text is from him, trying to apologise. *Tap, tap, tap. settings, block number*. I'm not interested. You lost your chance, buddy. Naff off.

The second text is from Wendy, bless her. She saw what happened, and made sure he didn't leave the pub. Her work friend went over and had a word, apparently. Oh, so that's who he was. A guy from work. That was very nice of him.

I text back my many thanks for them both. I'm so lucky to have such a great friend. I may have mentioned that before. But Wendy really is fantastic, isn't she?

As annoying as his actions were, I'm weirdly not that upset. Sure, he lied about his appearance. He was much shorter and nowhere near as handsome, incidentally. But it's his loss, isn't it? It's reassuring in an odd way; he didn't do a runner. He was still interested, even if I wasn't. Is it weird to feel flattered?

Chapter 18 - Loser

This diet thing's going well. I'm really getting into the swing of it. Honestly, I'm eating more than ever, and still losing weight. Sounds too good to be true, right?

But my sugar intake has been reduced considerably. Gone are the takeaways and microwave meals, and fresh food has replaced them. I don't think I've ever eaten so many eggs before, and have even managed to get the hang of poaching them.

My clothes are starting to feel loose, new ones will need to be purchased soon. Can you believe another three pounds was lost this week? I got my half stone award in group. It feels marvellous. I got given a certificate and a shiny sticker for my book. Hazel passed me a big bag weighing half a stone, so I could feel how much I've lost. It's astonishing. I can't believe I was carrying that around just a month ago.

And get this, I got the slimmer of the week award too. Me! Over two weeks I've lost the most in the group. Wendy was there and I'm sure she clapped the loudest.

Is it completely egotistical to admit it felt really good? I actually felt proud of myself, like I'd achieved something. Everyone else cheered me on. I don't know, it felt supportive. More than that, I felt respected. Yeah, that's the feeling. Respect.

Maybe I'll treat myself to a little reward. It probably shouldn't be a food one. I don't want to ruin my hard work. I'll have a think about it.

In the meantime, another potential chap has popped up on my radar. He's quite good looking, but not enough to arouse suspicion. Hopefully this is a real profile photo. I ask him to send me some more snaps, just to be on the safe side. Jerry willingly obliges.

The photos I've received are hot. He must be at the gym, or something, judging by the background, and the fact he's in shorts. Oh, and he's topless. That's a pleasant surprise. He's more muscley than I would've given him credit for.

His emails aren't as sugary sweet as Andrew's were, but that can only be a good thing, right? I admire Jerry's forthrightness. It must be a good sign. He's got straight to the point, and we're meeting Sunday lunchtime, but not in the pub where I met Andrew. No, we're meeting for lunch. He specified the restaurant. This wasn't very gallant, but I've looked ahead, and there's some good healthier choices on their menu, so have agreed.

Whilst in the supermarket I pass the makeup aisle. Perfect. A little treat to reward my diet success, and that will help enhance my appearance for my date with Jerry.

I've not bought new makeup in ages, so it's quite a thrill. As soon as I get home I try it out to see if it makes me look respectable. There, expensive, but apparently worth it makeup. It's as good as I'm going to get anyway.

Lots of fresh ingredients for this week's taste sensations were also purchased. I'm getting quite adventurous. Singapore Noodles is on the menu tonight. No Wendy again, so I'm risking it. It's only me.

There's lots of ingredients for this one, but I'll use the rest in my other dishes this week. I think I'm developing a noodle obsession. But they're quick, easy and tasty.

The week disappears in a blur of nervous activity, but am really glad to be so busy. It's helping keep my mind off the date a bit. I'm rather anxious about it. The last one was such a disaster.

Wendy's swapped her shift, and has roped in her colleague again. He must be keen on her to undergo these excursions. But I've not even seen her to quiz her on the subject; she's been really busy.

So here I am. Entering the restaurant, dressed up to the nines, ready for love. The waiter greets me, and directs me to the table where Jerry is already sitting. Well, that's a good start. He's here, and does actually look like his photo.

I've spotted Wendy too. She's engrossed in conversation with her lovely co-worker, but she risks a discrete wave to indicate she's seen me too. I'm starting to suspect she's on guard duty just to have the excuse of spending time with the guy, you know.

"Hello, you must be Molly," Jerry greets, half standing and kissing the back of my hand.

Oh my, I could get used to this.

"Yes, and I'm hoping you're Jerry, otherwise this is very awkward," I say with a smile.

"Yeah, that's me. It's lovely to meet you in person. The camera didn't lie."

"No, it didn't, did it?" I can't help it, a smirk spreads across my face.

He really is quite charming. My luck seems to have decided to take my side at last.

We order our food and fall easily into small talk. He's easy to speak to, and is saying all the right things. Embarrassingly, I've begun giggling like a schoolgirl. I'm sorry, but I'm not used to this flattery.

As we wait for dessert, Jerry excuses himself to go to the loo. Wendy's friend does too. Oh gosh, I hope he's not going to approach Jerry and say anything we'll all regret. You can take protectiveness too far, you know.

Wendy gives me a little thumbs up from her table, and I answer her with a massive grin.

Her date returns first, and his face looks like thunder. Oh dear, I hope nothing awful transpired back there. He's talking to Wendy who tries to signal something to me, but Jerry walks back to our table before I can decipher her mime. And our desserts have arrived.

As we finish eating Jerry asks, "So, your place or mine?"

"I beg your pardon?"

"Oh baby, you heard me."

"Yes, but I don't think I quite believed you. Are you really suggesting..?"

"Well, yes. What did you think?"

"I thought we were on a first date is what I bloody well thought," I tell him, my voice rising.

"Dates lead to…"

"Oh my God, what do you think I am? Who do you think you are?" My mouth gapes open.

"Your date."

Oh, I want to swipe that smirk off his face with my fist.

"Of all the pig-headed, arrogant…" I'm so angry I can't even finish my sentence.

I get up, flinging my napkin down.

"Is everything alright?" a male voice asks.

Oh I could kiss him. Wendy's friend is coming to my aid.

"No, it's bloody well not. This arsehole thought he could buy me one meal and I'd jump in the sack with him."

"There's no need for a scene, love. Just because someone says they want to shag you."

"Come on, we're leaving," Wendy's blokey says.

Oh, I don't even know his name. But he's a far safer prospect right now. Wendy's by my side too now as we all walk out of the restaurant.

"Oh Molly, I'm so sorry. I tried to tell you. Gary overheard him in the gents. You tell her, Gary."

"He was on the phone to his mate. I hid in a cubicle. He was all full of how the fat ugly ones are the best as they're so desperate they'll sleep with the first man who shows them any attention. That everything was all in the bag. I'm so sorry."

"Oh my God. He was only on the date because he thought I'd put out? That I'm ugly?"

"Gary, you weren't supposed to say that bit. How could you?" Wendy reprimands.

Poor Gary looks askance, clearly unaware of his faux pas.

Tears spring forth. I'm standing in the restaurant car park and crying like a baby. Well, wouldn't you if the same happened to you? It's one thing calling yourself every name under the sun, and quite another for someone to actually use it to their own advantage.

"Look, the guy's clearly an arsehole. Ignore him. Who cares what he thinks?" Gary ventures.

But it's no good. The damage is done.

"But I bought new makeup and got all dressed up. I tried my best, and I'm still fat and ugly."

"Gary, I'm sorry, but I'm going to drive her home," Wendy apologises.

"That's OK. I understand." He pecks her on the cheek and quietly gets in his car, driving off into the distance.

"Keys," Wendy demands, holding out her hand.

I fish in my handbag, and hand them over. She's on my insurance, as she's helped me with deliveries occasionally. I never thought it would be used because I was incapacitated. But I'd never see the road through these tears.

I blub the whole way back to my house.

"What's wrong with me, Wendy? I keep attracting losers who want to take advantage of me. Why can't I find a nice guy? Am I really so hideous and pathetic?"

Many other woeful things come out of my mouth through sobs. There's not much Wendy can say. She of course offers placations as fast as she can think of them. But they do nothing to soothe my ravaged soul.

I'm never dating again. It's not worth it. I'll just have to die an old maid. All alone. Maybe I'll buy some cats.

Wendy mops up the Molly shaped puddle, and ushers me into my own home, and pours some wine into glasses. To hell with the calorie value. I don't care. The first glass gets downed. It quietens me down enough to attempt conversation.

"The right man will be out there, Molly. You'll see."

"Will he? What if I'm supposed to be on my own? What if this is my life?"

"Do you want to be on your own?"

I shake my head.

"Then you'll find him. I bet he's out there right now, looking for you."

"You really think so?"

"He'd be mad not to. Look what he's missing."

"What? An ugly, red eyed, teary hippo?" I ask, swiping at my eyes, my breath hitching.

"Will you please stop calling yourself that? No. He's missing the most beautiful person I know, inside and out. You're kind and caring, and I think you're pretty."

"Jerry didn't."

"Who cares what Jerry thinks? Do you want to listen to an arsehole?"

"No," I confirm on a half giggle.

"He's obviously not worthy of you. Clearly not the one. A Mr Wrong if ever I saw one. Shagging around like a tom cat. So don't waste another thought on him, and carry on the search for Mr Right."

I manage a weak smile as a second glass of wine gets gulped down.

Wendy spends the rest of the afternoon with me, and we finish off two bottles of wine between us. She has to phone for a taxi to take her home, which I give her the money for. It's my fault after all.

The room spins a little, so I lie down on the sofa. Staring at the slightly blurry ceiling, I contemplate my life and all Wendy discussed with me. Is Mr Right really out there? If you're out there, please come and find me. I'm right here. I'm a large target, you can't miss me. Hello!

Chapter 19 – If You Can't Say Something Nice

Time to face the music. Wendy's at work, thanks to me. She swapped shifts so she could be my minder, and is now stuck there. This does not make me feel happy. And now I'm here on my own again, about to face up to my failure.

As I finally get on the scales they tell me what I already know. There's a gain. Two pounds is pretty good considering the quantity of wine that I consumed yesterday. And there may have been crisps. And some chocolate.

"A gain this week for Molly, but only a little one. And she's still lost seven pounds in total. Let's give her a round of applause for staying to group, everyone," Hazel cheers brightly.

Actually, their applause feels quite nice today. Oh, how desperate for approval am I? But yes, I need this, to be reminded of the weight that's been lost. I have achieved something. And there's not one disapproving glance cast in my direction.

"I had an oops yesterday. My date thought that I'd be easy because I'm fat and ugly."

"Oh my God," someone gasps amongst other shocked sounds travelling around the semi-circle.

"But you're not," the lady next to me says firmly.

I shrug, my eyes cast towards the floor.

"The mirror and scales tell a different story. I'm a hippo."

"No no no. You're not allowed to call yourself names like that," screeches the target member.

"Pardon me?"

My gaze shoots over to her. I'm shocked into listening.

"If you wouldn't say it to a friend then don't say it to yourself."

"Yes, quite right. That's a very good reminder, thank you. We can sometimes be our own worst enemy, can't we?" Hazel takes up the conversation.

Receiving murmurs and nods of agreement, she continues, "I think we've all said things to ourselves that we'd never say to another person. We have little voices in our heads, like the angel and demon on the shoulders in cartoons. But when was the last time you listened to the angel? As we go around the rest of the room, I want you to tell me one thing you like about yourself. Starting with you, Molly."

"Um, err, I like, um, my eyes?" I reply, shrinking into my chair.

"There we go, that's a start."

We go round the rest of the room and listen to what everyone else has to say.

At the end, Hazel announces, "Now, when you go home I want you all to look in the mirror, and write down five things you like about you. It can be something about the way you look or the person you are inside. Keep that list somewhere that you'll see it to remind yourself."

***

At home, I plonk myself down on my bed and gaze into my mirror. Let's see. What good is there in me?

1) Eyes – they're brown and hint at mischief beneath

2) ~~My hair?~~ No scratch that. It's red, and has been a great source of teasing over the years

   Err, caring – I'm a kind, caring person. I donate flowers to the hospice, and care when others are struggling.

3) ~~It's no good, I'm staring at a hippo in the mirror.~~ My hands. They create lovely flower displays that others enjoy.

4) Oh look, there's my smile – I like that, it brightens up my whole face, making me look friendly

5) Last one, five…um…~~not my temper~~…my courage. I'm brave, tackle challenges head on. Usually.

There, I've done it. I found five good things. Yay me. I can go to bed happy tonight. Hey Mr Right, look what you're missing out on. Come get me. I have a good heart and hands. You lucky man, you.

Hm, this might need a bit of work. How do I find myself? I don't think a trip to India or Tibet, or anywhere like that, is within my budget. So, where do I go? What do I do? And what am I actually seeking?

To be honest, I'm still a bit of a mess. The past couple of days have been horrid. I want to eat my way through a chocolate mountain and pretend the world doesn't exist. But I've already seen a gain on the scales. That's my second one, and I've only just started. I must do better.

***

You know those nights when your head just won't shut up? Yeah, one of those. I didn't sleep much at all. As Hazel would say, my devil voice was speaking to me. I was trying not to listen, but couldn't help it. She was pretty insistent. And how can I deny it? I am fat and ugly. Didn't Jerry prove that point? What a nightmare.

I still can't believe that man. Who does that? If he didn't really find me attractive what was he going to do? Oh, that horrid phrase springs to mind, "You don't look at the mantelpiece when you're poking the fire." Eurgh. I can't help the image appearing in my mind; of Jerry doing me from behind. It's foul on so many levels. I feel unclean, and a little sick. Was he really so desperate for a hole to fuck? Pardon my language, but that's what I was to him. Horrid horrid man.

The point is, I must be putting out some sort of desperation signal to attract scum like that. What am I doing so wrong? There's a whole long line of users and abusers in my history. I'm a nice person with so much love to give. It's not fair. What do I need to do? I'm trying here. I'm trying so goddamned hard.

I'm sorry. I'll wipe these tears away. You don't want to see more weeping from me. This is getting absurd. It's pain after pain after pain. And I'm tired. Just so bloody tired. Exhausted. I'm not sure how much more I can take.

Is it even worth trying again? I seem to keep digging myself a deeper hole. I simply can't face it. I'm not even entertaining the idea right now. I need to form and regroup after this latest catastrophe.

Jan is due today. I don't know where the time goes. It only feels like yesterday since his last visit. I'm still not interested in him. I'm not. Stop it. I just like his cheerful face.

He always seems happy, and has a way of cheering me up. He spends such a short time in my presence, but it's enough. I wonder if he feels the same way. No. Seriously, not like that. I mean it. I do wish you'd behave.

Anyway, he's here now, so stop smirking. He disappears round to the 'creation station' and I go to open the door.

"You are still in need of a guardian, I see," he says, nodding towards the bee who has joined me again.

"Oh stop. You had me saying hello to it a few weeks ago. I felt so foolish."

"And what did it say back?"

"Buzz," I tell him, poking out my tongue before laughing.

He joins in the laughter before wishing me a good week and departing. See; cheers me up. Who would've thought I'd be able to laugh today?

Yesterday was a bit dismal. I had a hangover, but still managed to take some flowers to the hospice and even dragged my arse around the supermarket. I'm not terribly sure what went in the trolley. I was in a bit of a daze, and the lights made my headache worse.

Right, I've got to prepare these flowers for storage, before making lunch.

"You really are a funny little thing," I tell the bee who insists on watching me.

It was sweet at first, but after what Jan said, it's now a bit creepy. But it's not harming anyone. It's not stung me. Fortunately, I think the flowers are a more tempting prospect.

My mood has been shored up a little by Jan's youthful exuberance, but I'm still lethargic. I can't be arsed to make anything spectacular. There's no leftover chicken as I went out Sunday. Eurgh, don't remind me.

So, I grab some salad leaves from a bag, bung them on a plate with tomatoes, ham and pickled onions. It's not exactly a feast, but my stomach doesn't want much else. I'm sure it wouldn't say no to crisps and chocolate, but it's not getting those, so tough.

I chomp my way through unenthusiastically. Let's face it, it's pure subsistence. I added a tinsy bit of low fat dressing, but it's not enough to make it interesting. Ho hum.

There's a consultation due this afternoon. I really don't feel like it, but business is business. And to be fair, I don't think the people coming want to be here either. It's another funeral.

These things do put one's life into perspective, don't they? I mean, here's me moping, and this family have lost a loved one. My problems are nothing in comparison.

With that thought firmly in mind, I open the door with a very different attitude when my clients arrive. Oh, it's so difficult. My heart goes out to them. Their grief fills the room with its silence. Their down-turned looks and red eyes speak volumes of how hard this is.

I try to make the appointment as quick as possible, so as not to prolong their agony. I provide them with hot drinks and biscuits, but manage not to eat any myself. But then neither do they.

All my words of sympathy sound empty and hollow. There's really nothing to be said in these circumstances. Nothing will help heal these wounds except time.

Chapter 20 – Saint Nick

I've been a right old misery guts. It was really difficult to shake off what I can only call a bout of depression, really. Let's just say I was very low. I think even Wendy felt like giving up on me.

My birthday went by largely unnoticed. Mother made me get dressed up to have supper with her and Father. Jeans and a jumper really would've sufficed. We didn't go anywhere. But she insisted. She fed me cake, and it all made me feel worse if anything. Thirty-five and still on the shelf. Bong! Old Father Time is striking, the sands in his hourglass continue to flow.

Wendy tried her best, but all my energy would allow was a girl's night in. It was nice, but not exactly anything special. It's my own fault. I didn't feel like doing anything.

My weight has fluctuated too. I faced some gains as well as losses. Comfort food is still my go-to in times of crisis. It's a hard habit to break. I tried to make better choices, and think damage limitation was achieved. I certainly didn't go off the rails as once would've been the case.

But as we now head into October I'm the lightest I've been for a long time. Fourteen stone six is my current weight. It's not where I wanted to be at this point, but it's better than it was. Only another four pounds and I'll get my one stone award.

Hazel and others in the group keep reminding me of what I've achieved so far, and their support is helping me through.

I've not been on any more dates. I thought it best to give it a rest for a while. And Holly Molly was busy. But as the peak wedding season has now died down there's more time for reflection. I can't keep relying on Wendy, it's not fair. But nor can I turn to my mother. She insists on reminding me of the ticking clock.

The doctors are keeping a close eye on me. I've been for a couple of check-ups. My BMI has gone down a little, but they'd like to see further improvements in that area. That's doctor speak for 'eat less, you fat cow'. They're only doing their job, and have my best interests at heart, but I can't help feeling judged.

Some people get terribly sad at this time of year, but I have to say it's improving my spirits. The gorgeous golds, reds and browns of autumn have arrived along with that musty smell in the air. My evenings are spent under a blanket with candles lit, a good book and a little drop of red wine. It's within my allowance, it's OK.

Bigger news is that I've got a date lined up tomorrow afternoon. It's midweek, but it suits us both. He's a shift worker, and his name's Nick. If his photos are real, he has brown hair and grey eyes. He sent me extra photos, and only one of those is topless. Even then, that's because he's on a beach in that one. We've been taking things slowly. We've kept it to email contact only until now.

Nick is a good name, isn't it? There's a nice, solid sound to it. I was sad enough to look it up, and it means people's victory. Doesn't that sound noble? And of course, we have jolly old Saint Nick. Maybe he has gifts of joy in the sack?

I'm just walking into the coffee shop now. A youngish, tall, slim man with brown hair and grey eyes was sitting at a table, but is now approaching me. His hand is outstretched, and I take it.

"Hello, Molly?" he checks as he shakes my hand.

"Yes. Nick?"

Fine, that's a fairly safe assumption, but it never hurts to be careful.

"That's me. Look, I ordered you a small cappuccino with skimmed milk. I forgot to ask, but from what you've told me, I thought that's what you'd go for. I'll get something else if you want."

"No, that's fine. Thank you."

He leads me back to the table where my coffee is waiting. My head is telling me to be cautious. This man is a stranger, and he's already got a drink waiting for me. What if he spiked it? I'm sure there's unscrupulous men about who would put date rape drugs even in coffee. But it's the middle of the day in a busy coffee shop. He wouldn't, would he? Awkward.

He must've sensed my reticence. He picks up the cup and takes a sip.

"See, it's safe."

Oh my God. Did he just do that? I can't help but laugh at him.

"Oh good. So now I have your spit in my coffee. Thanks," I say with a chuckle.

"Oh right. Sorry. I don't have germs or anything. You were looking at that cup as if it were a red apple in a fairy story."

"Oh dear, was I? I'm sorry. I've just had such a run of bad luck with dates."

"You too? I thought it was only me who was cursed."

"Really?"

"Yes. But you're still here, actually look like your photo, not crying, and haven't started lecturing me yet, so it's going well. I'd go so far as to say you seem perfectly normal." His grey eyes glint with mirth.

"Haha, I don't think many would call me normal. But did you really get the false photo thing too?"

"Yeah. I take it you did too."

"Sadly, yes. How many people out there actually do that? It's outrageous."

"Tell me about it. It's crazy. What do they think's going to happen? As soon as you meet up it's obvious. Mind you, it took me a while to find her, given I was looking for someone who looked completely different."

"Snap," I say through my laughter, "Oh, I gave him a complete earful before beating a hasty retreat, I can tell you."

"Good for you. Well done. I wish I'd been there to see it. I had to creep away as soon as possible without seeming rude to mine."

"How very British of you."

"Well one can't cause offense, even in the face of such deceit."

"Oh quite," I say, still laughing.

We both try to calm our laughter. We've already attracted the attention of others in the coffee shop. I don't overly mind. It's nice to laugh.

"I have to admit it's why I wanted to meet here. It's not as big as a pub, and doesn't require the length of time of a whole meal if you turned out to be…" I start.

"Please, say no more. I quite understand. I was happy to meet you here too, for much the same reason. It's such a relief to find you're as lovely as I thought you'd be."

I blush wildly at the compliment. "You don't have to say that. I know it's not true."

"Not true? Molly. What on earth makes you say such a thing?"

In all fairness he looks genuinely shocked.

"Well, there was this guy…" I begin.

"Actually, no. I don't want to hear it. I don't think that sentence is going to end well. Please, let me prove to you that not all men are dreadful," he tells me, looking earnestly into my eyes.

"OK," I whisper.

I'm really touched. Oh dear, I think I may be a little bit in love already. He'd better not ruin it all now. Please don't ask me back to your place, Nick.

He doesn't. We have a very pleasant conversation, and he walks me to my vehicle afterwards.

"Molly, this has been fun. Would it be OK to do this again?"

"I think I'd like that."

"Good. Maybe we could risk a whole meal?"

"I think that would be an appropriate next step," I say with a grin.

"Fine. I'll be in touch once I know my schedule. Sorry. It's all a bit up in the air."

"That's alright. I'll try to fit in, but obviously I need to mind my own work."

"Of course, of course. We'll work something out."

He leans in and plants a little peck on my cheek. But it sends thrills right through me as if it had been a snog. My heart's beating so rapidly I fear it may take off and fly away.

I get into my van, and drive away, beaming like a cat who's got the cream.

I send Wendy a text to let her know it all went OK, and I've not been abducted or verbally abused, or anything. Regrettably, she wasn't available for the full minder duty today, but she was at the end of a phone. I was very brave and ventured out alone. And I'm very glad I did.

Nick's lovely. He's funny and interesting and nice looking and, oh, you get the idea. Lucky number three, eh? How very clichéd of me. Well, fate has its own way, I suppose.

Please disregard my nonsense of loving him. Of course it's far too soon to be talking such silliness. I was swept away with the moment. But I do have a strong liking for Nick. I can't wait to see him again. I hope we can arrange something soon.

Oh, listen to me. I'm getting carried away like some giddy schoolgirl. Ahem, I am calm. I am a grown woman. A sensible one.

Ooh he's sent me a text already, and I'm inwardly doing a happy dance.

"It was lovely to meet you today. I hope we can meet again soon. Thank you for not being a crazy person."

That makes me laugh again.

"I hope so too. And thank you too, for not being a git."

"Haha. I'm a git free zone."

He's so funny.

I busy myself about my household chores with a definite spring in my step. In fact, I've put my iPod onto the docking station, and am currently prancing around to the rousing music of the ELO. That's the Electric Light Orchestra. "Mr Blue Sky" is playing. It's one of the happiest songs I know, and suits my mood marvellously.

Tonight's dinner requires a few more bits. It's a crisp, sunny day and I've decided to walk to the local shops as soon as the housework's done.

I make it there and back in record time, and not one extra item snuck into my basket. I need to make doubly sure that my diet's on track now. I want to look nice for Nick. And of course, for health reasons.

***

We've been emailing and texting like two young fools in love. But we've not had the chance to meet again until now. It's Tuesday evening. This feels like a proper date. An actual evening meal. And I feel even more nervous this time. Now I have something to lose. Before I was merely hopeful. Please don't disappoint me now, Nick.

There's a slight concern over the timing. He said he's a shift worker. Please be telling me the truth. Please don't be secretly married.

Nick's not here yet, and I'm sitting alone in the semi-dark, busy restaurant. He will turn up, won't he? He's not had second thoughts. Did I come on too strong? Maybe a few less texts would've been more appropriate.

Does he think I'm trying to ensnare him? Must not speak of marriage. It's not even a thought. Slight fib, it is, but not in a serious way. More in the 'time's ticking' sort of train of thought. I'm babbling, aren't I? Am I babbling? Yes, probably.

A breadstick gets nibbled and a few sips of wine slip down my throat. My leg won't seem to keep still. My knee is bouncing up and down underneath the table.

There's a flurry of excitement at the door. It's him. Nick's taking off his coat and giving it to the waiter. Here he is. Be still my beating heart.

"Molly, I'm so sorry. I got caught up at work, and have only just come off shift. I came straight here," he says, leaning forward to peck my cheek.

"Well, you're here now, that's the main thing," I say with a patient smile as I take my seat.

"What is it you do?" The question's out of my mouth before I can stop it.

He's told me he's a shift worker, but he's been very cagey as to the particulars.

"I owe you an explanation, don't I? I do apologise, but you see, I find it changes people's perception of me. Honestly, some people have actually run away. I was afraid of frightening you off."

"Now you really have to tell me. I'm intrigued."

He clears his throat before responding, "Aher, you see, well, I'm a forensic pathologist."

Can you please pass me my jaw? It seems to have fallen onto the floor.

"A…a…forensic pathologist? Like CSI?"

"Yes, and no. I don't go running around solving crimes."

"No, of course not." Silly me.

"But yes, it involves autopsies. Sometimes I have to go to crime scenes. And I have to attend court regularly to explain medical issues. But there's a lot of admin involved too."

"I see."

"Do you?" he asks, maintaining eye contact.

"I have to admit it's a bit of a surprise. It's not exactly what I expected," I reply, looking away.

"I warned you. People always look at me differently."

"Well, you do deal with dead bodies for a living."

"Do you want to leave? It's OK if you do. I understand."

What a question. What to do? I take a sip of wine as a delaying tactic, and let's face it, to steady myself a little. A snap decision must be made. Is this too icky?

"No. I'll stay. It's fascinating. I'd love to hear more about it, but perhaps not over dinner."

"You're being very brave."

"Am I?"

"Yes, and you know it. Thank you."

"For what?"

"For not running out the door."

"Nick, you seem like a really nice man. It'd be incredibly stupid to run for the hills just because I don't understand your job."

Throughout dinner I concentrate on his hands. He cuts his steak with precision. All sorts of horrendous images of dead bodies spring to mind. I'm terribly glad I opted for the lobster linguine. It's not such a healthy choice for my diet, but it's certainly a better option for my appetite at this moment.

How can such a nice man cut up dead bodies for a living? It's just so...so grim. Oh dear, I hope this doesn't prove to be a sticking point. It's just a job, right? A very gory, sombre job.

Chapter 21 – The Not So Grim Reaper

Nick and I parted with another peck on the cheek last night. He's still funny and lovely, but there's this big cloud over him now. He cuts people up for a living. It's so morbid; gross.

It was difficult to concentrate on conversation as I struggled to come to terms with his revelation. Am I over-reacting? Is it really that bad? It's freaking me out. I'm not sure what sort of person would want to do something like that. Haven't you got to have a weird mindset? An obsession with death and gore?

Surgeons cut into people too, I know. But at least those are living people. To be surrounded by death all day must be damaging to one's mental health, surely?

OK, I'm making a big thing about this. I will just have to keep seeing him. The poor bloke, I don't know enough about him to dismiss him out of hand. I could be being completely unfair. He does seem very nice otherwise.

At least it explains the difficulty in meeting up. I imagine he must have odd working hours. And that also explains why he was on a dating site. It must be difficult, bless him.

There's a couple of wedding's coming up, so I still have my own job to worry about. Hopefully, I've done enough over the summer to keep me going over the quiet winter. People still get married, of course. It's just a lot quieter. And there's still funerals too. Oh great, I'm still thinking of dead people. Eurgh.

Come on Molly, head in the game. There's flowers to arrange. Pretty, lovely flowers, spreading joy with their scent. Lovely, lovely, lovely.

This isn't working, is it? Why is this such a problem? Grow up.

After almost an hour of being not terribly productive I give up. I grab my phone and send Nick a text.

"Sorry to bother you. But please can you tell me more about what you do at work, and why you do it?"

It's a while before I get a response. Eek, maybe he was sleeping? I don't know when he's working and when he's not.

"This IS a problem 4 u. I feared this. Prbly best 2 discuss in person. Can I come round 2mrw am?"

To my house? Ooh err, I'm not sure that's a good idea. What if he's a murderer? It'd be the perfect crime. He could cover his own tracks. Maybe that's why he works in the morgue?

"Meet for coffee same place as before?"

"Fine. 9am?"

"Fine."

Oh dear, that didn't go well. It felt awkward and terse. I think I've upset him. But I need to know, to understand. You wouldn't believe how much I wish I could feel differently. But it is what it is.

Flowers have been prepped, and businessy stuff has been dealt with; emails, phone calls, admin etc. Dinner for one is done. Oh, it's spaghetti bolognese tonight. There's lots of vegetables in it, and all made by me. It's not hard. Meat, veg, herbs and a tin of tomatoes. Doesn't take any longer than the jar really.

Of course, my old microwave version would be faster, but that's been banned. Well, I do have some low fat options, but that's only in case of emergency, or Saturday nights when I'm simply too tired to cook. But even then leftovers are utilised more. Like tonight's dinner. It's hard to get small packets of lean beef mince, so there'll be some ragu put in the freezer.

Is it weird to say my insides feel cleaner? I'm not sure how to describe it. I just feel better. My skin's cleared up a lot too. Fewer spots are erupting, and my hair's less greasy. Perhaps there really is something to this healthy eating malarkey.

After dinner I go out into the garden for a quick cigarette. Yes, I'm still smoking. You can't really expect me to give up junk food *and* nicotine all at once. Who do you think I am? If anything, my nicotine intake has increased as it replaces some snacking habits. Sorry. But we all need to have our vices. Wine has been reduced as well as the unhealthy food, so this is what I'm left with.

***

It's 08:50 and I'm here at the coffee shop already. I'm usually up early anyway, and I was pacing the floors at home; too anxious and restless. Today's meeting feels like our most important one yet. It could make or break us.

Of course, Nick's in the queue already, so I make my way over to him. There's no friendly peck on my cheek to greet me. There's an awkward distance between us.

"What do you want?" he asks.

"It's my turn to buy."

"Don't be daft. Tell me, or you'll just get a cappuccino."

"Well, that's actually what I want anyway, please."

"Fine. Why don't you go find a table whilst I wait?"

It's too awkward to remain by his side, so I go and sit down as bid. There's an anxious wait. There was only one person in front of Nick, but coffees take time to make. It feels like an eternity before he finally joins me.

"So what do you want to know?" he asks as soon as he sits.

"Wow, straight in with no hesitation?"

"Molly, you have questions and I'm happy to answer them. So get it off your chest."

"OK. Um, so err, how did you get into it?"

"My father was a surgeon, and I was moulded to follow in his wake. But whilst I was studying I discovered forensic pathology as a possible direction."

"But isn't it morbid? You're surrounded by dead bodies."

"But they're just bodies. Look at it from the other way around. Often I do autopsies which put the minds of families to rest. Maybe their loved one has died suddenly and they need answers before they can come to terms with what's happened and start to heal."

"OK, so that's a good thing."

"And there are cases where people have died in suspicious circumstances. Even in a small way, I help the police catch the bad guys. I may not be out patrolling the streets, but the information I give can certainly help."

"Well, yes, when you put it like that. But they're still dead."

Nick sniggers a little. "Well, I certainly hope so. I'd have the fright of my life if someone sat up on my table."

OK, that made me giggle a bit too. He has a fair point.

"Oh, you know what I mean."

He becomes serious again. "Yes, I do. But I repeat, they are just bodies. There's no essence of who they were. It's a shell. Their soul has already moved on."

"Their soul? You're a scientist. Do you really believe in that sort of thing?"

"For me it proves it. I look at you, full of vibrancy and vitality. You're beautiful and feisty. But the bodies which come to me? No, there's nothing. Cold and vacant. Soulless."

"Wow."

"So many people think they're helping by being doctors and surgeons. And they do help a lot, but death is no stranger to them either. At least I know my clients have no chance at survival. Do you know the stress of that fight, to keep someone alive?"

"No, I don't suppose I do."

"Nor should you. But it's horrible. I'd see my father sometimes, when he'd come home after someone died on his table. He'd try to hide it, but it all took its toll. Every time was a failure to him. But what I do, I can find meaning to the madness."

"So it's not because you like cutting people up?"

He really does laugh now. "Would you ask a surgeon that?"

"No, yeah, maybe. I don't know. Do they?"

"Haha, no. At least, I don't think that's why most of them do it. My father liked being able to save people. Healing was his profession."

"And it's not because you're a Goth?"

"No. I find bodies fascinating, not necessarily death itself."

"Oh, that makes sense, I think."

"Our bodies *are* fascinating, don't you think? They're highly sophisticated machines. They work 24/7. Ceaselessly replenishing cells. It's extraordinary."

"I don't think mine's extraordinary."

"But it is. Everyone is. Even you. Especially you."

My eyes are transfixed on a coffee stain on the table all of a sudden. It's nothing to do with the blood rushing to my cheeks at all.

"Does that help?"

"Yes. Thank you. I'm sorry."

He places his hand over mine, making me look up into his serious eyes. "Sorry for asking? I'm glad you did. It's better than disappearing. I'm always happy to answer anything you have to ask. Never apologise."
"Thank you."
"So, if we're OK, do you mind if I go now?"
"Um, no, that's fine."
He's leaving me now? What? Did he really mind being asked, and was just being nice?
"I've only just finished work for the night, and really want to go and get some sleep."
"Oh. Sorry. Oh, and you had coffee. Now I feel really bad."
He leans over and pecks my cheek. "You worry too much. I told you, I'm happy you had the courage to ask. And that was decaf."
Aww. He's so lovely.
"OK, you're excused."
"Why, thank you. You're most kind."

We finish the last dregs of our drinks and he walks me to my van.

"Until next time?" he asks hopefully.

"Until next time."

He goes to place a precious peck on my cheek, but I turn my head so it lands on my lips. Naughty, I know. But the man earned it. He must be exhausted, but came to meet me, to explain away my concerns. The peck lingers into a kiss. We both stop before it develops into a full-on snog. We're in a public car park, and he needs to go and sleep. Poor man doesn't need to get over excited.

We reluctantly part ways and I return home to housework and flowers.

Chapter 22 – Epic Fail

Well, Nick's convinced me he's not a psycho killer or a death-obsessed maniac. We've been emailing and texting, but between his work and mine we've not managed to meet up again yet. It's been two weeks since we had our coffee chat.

My weight is going down. Progress is slow, but at two pounds per week, it's good steady progress, apparently. I've got my one stone award, which is wonderful, but there's still another four to go. I can't help but feel a little frustrated. Still, if it continues like this, my two stone award will be achieved by Christmas. That's my target for now.

Two stone in three months? This is possibly considered a good goal, but I want more. My health is still at risk. And then there's Christmas itself. The time of feasting and gluttony. I'm sure to see an increase over the festive season.

My five stone target feels like it's miles away. I'm trying to remain positive, but it's an effort. One day at a time. It will happen. I need to keep focussed and stay strong.

Wendy's her usual wonderful self. She's losing weight well too. And she's been terrific. I've updated her on the Nick news, and she made me see sense. I was comforted after my chat with him, but she helped get rid of the last shred of doubt. She works in a hospital, of course, and told me how silly I was being.

She also suggested I treat myself to a spa day as my reward for losing one stone already. It's important to celebrate your progress, according to Wendy.

The colder months aren't helping. I want to eat stodgy food, but there's ways around that. Casseroles and my new slow cooker are proving useful. I've even made some soups. There's a really good tomato soup, which almost tastes like the famous one from a can, but contains far fewer calories. Who knew a humble little pickled onion could make soup taste good?

I've also found a really great way of making hot chocolate. Using my daily milk allowance, I heat some in a pan. Mix in two teaspoons of chocolate hazelnut spread, then the rest of the milk and heat. It's really quick, and tastes really naughty. It helps stave off some chocolate cravings too; like a hug in a mug.

November is very nearly here, and there's not been a tremendous amount of progress on 'Operation Bride'. So many pass through Holly Molly's doors, and I provide them with beautiful flowers. But they serve as a constant reminder that my own special day is a mere hope, a pipedream.

All of these things are running through my mind as I get ready for this evening's date. Yes, a grown-up evening date. Nick and I have finally managed to get some time together.

He let me choose the restaurant, so there's healthy options planned. I refuse to let this dating thing interfere with my weight loss. In fact, I need to try extra hard at the moment if I'm to have any hope of surviving Christmas.

Recently, I had to buy some new clothes; dress size has changed, yippee. But I'm still losing weight, so I didn't want to buy too much either. This dieting thing can be quite expensive, you know. But this evening I'm wearing a little black dress. OK, it's quite a big black dress, but smaller than it would've been. Don't worry, it's not a tight-fitting number. I have far too many wobbly bits and bumps for that.

My makeup has been carefully applied. No trowels involved. And my hair has been scooped up in a French twist.

I'm as confident as I can be as I make my way to the restaurant. Excitement is the overarching feeling actually, but I'm trying desperately not to let it show. We've already gone through a few nervous meetings, and I'm beginning to feel confident with Nick. He still wants to keep seeing me. Goodness knows why, but he does.

However, I am the first to arrive again. Trying not to outwardly cringe, I follow the waiter as he leads me to a table for two, and feel other eyes upon me.

"Can I just have a water, please?" I ask the waiter as he enquires as to my drink preference.

He gives me 'the look' but returns with my requested beverage. I refuse to order any nibbles. No breadsticks, no rolls, no antipasti. I have a plan, and I'm sticking to it.

My phone vibrates in the bag at my feet.

"So sorry. Stuck at work. Something's come up. Can't make it tonight. I'll make it up to you."

Why could he not have said sooner? Now I need to extricate myself from this awkward situation. How do I leave the restaurant alone with any dignity intact? There isn't a way, is there? I catch the waiter's eye and let him know.

I make my exit, head held in shame, avoiding all eye contact. Oh the shame! My cheeks are burning by the time I reach my van. I'm not sure I can forgive him for this humiliation.

Once home, I reach into the freezer for a diet ready meal. No leftovers have been thawed, I'm in no need to cook, and my tummy is rumbling. It too is complaining that it's not getting the delicious food it was promised.

I poke at the food on my plate, and force some of it down, but there's a bitter taste in my mouth. A large glass of red wine doesn't help rid me of the taste. And nor does the cigarette. The bitter taste of disappointment is a hard one to get rid of indeed.

The biscuits are calling my name, but I shut my ears. My special hot chocolate gets made instead, once pyjamas replace my dress. Curling up on the sofa, I flick on the TV find a chick flick to watch. Funny how they never get stood up in films.

Tears pool in my eyes as girl meets boy, boy treats girl and they live happily ever after. Well, that did the opposite of cheering me up. I find a nice dark series on Netflix to immerse myself in. Binge watching should be an Olympic sport, I'd win gold for sure.

It's late, but my doorbell's ringing. Bless, I did text Wendy earlier, so she's probably come to offer her shoulder to soak up my tears. But I don't really want to right now. I just want to forget tonight ever happened, and wind down for bed. Alone.

As I open the door a bunch of flowers greets me.

"Hello. I'm so sorry. Please forgive me," the flowers say.

Fine, it's the voice behind the large bouquet which is audible. I have to point out these are very good quality flowers. Where did Nick find them at this time of night?

Taking the bouquet, I reply, "Well, I suppose I'll have to now. How did you know where I live? Wait, Holly Molly, right?"

"Right. Err, and those were always for you. I bought them this morning, in preparation for our date. I was honestly looking forward to it. I'm gutted I was a no-show, please believe me."

"Oh. Um, do you want to come in?"

"I don't want to intrude."

Oh crap, I'm in my pyjamas. My hair's a mess, and my makeup's probably run.

"Well, you've seen me now, so you may as well come inside."

"You still look beautiful," he soothes, planting one of those lovely pecks on my cheek.

He allows me to lead the way into the lounge.

"Did you want a cup of tea?" I ask, scooping up empty cups and plates hurriedly.

"I really did ruin the evening, didn't I?" he asks, looking up through his eyelashes.

"Um, yes."

What? Was I supposed to lie? To pretend I hadn't had to do the walk of shame? Pour salve on his conscience? I was hurt, and I'm not going to lie about that. Sorry, not sorry. Well, maybe I am a bit.

Nick continues to apologise. "I really am sorry. I will make it up to you, promise. Work has a nasty habit of getting in the way. There's not much I can do about it."

"Hmmm."

"Oh, you're still unhappy. You have every right to be."

"I was already sitting in the restaurant."

His mouth forms an 'o' shape as his hand slaps his forehead and gets dragged down his face. "Oh no. Molly. I thought I'd catch you before you went in. I sent the text before we were due to meet."

"You did?"

"Yes."

"I didn't receive it until fifteen minutes after you should've been there."

"I must've had a weak signal, and it got delayed. Argh, now I feel like a complete arsehole. No wonder you're so upset. I can only apologise yet again." His fingers clutch through his hair as he speaks.

"It's fine. It's not your fault. You tried. Anyway, tea was it?"

I'm still standing there with arms full of detritus and flowers.

"If that's not too much trouble."

"I'll just be a jiffy. Make yourself at home."

As I wait for the kettle to boil I contemplate going to get changed. But it's too late. It would be too weird if I changed into my original outfit for the evening, wouldn't it? No, my pyjamas and dressing gown will have to remain in situ. I can brave it out. At least I don't have bunny slippers. They're actually quite pretty ballerina style ones.

Finding a vase, I put the flowers in water. There's no time to cut them and arrange them properly. They're in their packaging in the vase for now.

Refastening my dressing gown belt, making sure it covers as much as possible, I carry two mugs of tea in to the sheepish looking male on my couch.

"I made you resort to watching dreary rubbish. I don't think I've ever hated my job before."

"No, don't hate it. Not for me. I'm not worth it."

I take a seat next to him on the sofa, and place the mugs on the coffee table, on coasters, of course.

"Why do you keep doing that?"

"What?"

"Putting yourself down."

"I get it in before anyone else can, I suppose," I tell him with a shrug.

"And do they? If you stopped, would anyone tell you the nasty things you do?"

This gives me pause for thought.

"Maybe not now. Well, my mother always will. But maybe not anyone else."

"But they used to?"

I nod slowly.

"Aw, Molly, come here."

Without hesitation he pulls me into his arms and kisses my forehead.

"You deserve so much more."

I try to absorb his words, but can't. But I do snuggle into him. It feels wonderful to have a proper cuddle. He strokes my hair with long soothing movements. Bliss!

There's a slight disturbance as he reaches forward for his tea, but then jostles around until I'm lying across his lap and he can continue stroking my hair. It feels oddly intimate, yet surprisingly natural.

Maybe this evening wasn't an epic failure?

Chapter 23 – Awakening

Oh my God. I've woken up, it's morning, and Nick's still here. We're still on the sofa in a couple's tangle. I'm sure this wasn't his intention when he came round. I must've fallen asleep on him. How embarrassing. What do I do?

I try to wriggle myself free, but the movement wakes him up.

"Good morning, beautiful," he mutters huskily.

"Morning. I'm sorry."

"Whatever for?"

"For falling asleep."

"Molly, it's the greatest compliment anyone's ever paid me."

My whole face scrunches up in confusion.

"That you trusted me enough to let yourself relax like that. It's really flattering."

"Hm, if you say so. Err, would you like some breakfast?"

"Yes please. I'm starving. I didn't have dinner last night."

Oh, he came straight here after he finished work without even stopping for food. How sweet is that? Oh cripes, I should've fed him.

The kettle goes on and I whirl around my kitchen in a frenzy. What do I give him? What does he like? A man spent the night in my house and I don't even know his food preferences. What kind of harlot am I? A bad one, I suppose. It's not like we had sex.

Oh, we didn't even have sex. A golden opportunity wasted. Was he expecting it? Have I disappointed him?

A pair of strong arms wrap themselves around my middle, making me jump.

"Just what you normally have is fine. Don't go to any effort. I'm not supposed to be here," Nick whispers in my ear.

We didn't have sex, did we? I'm sure I'd remember. This intimate contact feels like perhaps we did. Not that I'm complaining, mind you. It's most welcome. A giggle escapes me as I revel in the feeling of being a couple.

"Something funny?"

"Only me," I demure, "Right, muesli and yoghurt OK?"

"Sounds great."

I'm sure he's lying but dollop some into bowls anyway. Coffee gets poured from my cafetière. What? Of course that's how I make my coffee every morning. I'm not trying to make an impression (cough cough).

"Mm, this is really nice," he remarks as we sit at the dining table, eating.

"I'm glad you like it. What do you normally have?"

"I tend to grab some toast, or whatever's to hand. Sometimes one of those breakfast biscuits if I'm in a hurry."

"Ha, that's the sort of thing I used to do. This diet's completely changed the way I eat though."

"Well I think you're beautiful as you are."

"Will you please stop saying that?"

"No. Will you please start believing it?"

"I'll try," I reply into my bowl.

"In my line of work you really learn to appreciate it's what's on the inside that counts."

"Eww, is that autopsy humour? I'm eating," I moan, but laugh anyway.

"Maybe, but it also happens to be true. You're beautiful inside and out."

Once we've finished our little breakfast I start to collect the bowls.

"Um, I don't want to sound like I'm trying to get rid of you, but do you need to get to work?"

"I worked late, so I'll start late, phone calls permitting. I'll need to go home for a shower and change though."

"Great. I have some tidying up to do down in my creation station, but you're welcome to come down and have a look if you like."

"I'd love to see you at work."

"Fab. Give me a moment to freshen up and I'll show you. Why don't you go into the lounge? Oh, and just for the record, don't feel you need to reciprocate with the work thing."

He shakes his head and laughs as he goes into the other room and I load the dishwasher. I practically sprint up the stairs to shower and make myself look semi decent.

I don't want to keep him waiting too long, but I do put on a smattering of makeup. Yes, I know he saw me looking much worse last night, which is why it's even more important to look a lot better now. Do I want him leaving here with an image of pyjama'd me?

"Right. Ready when you are," I announce, re-entering the room.

"Lead the way."

He stands up from the sofa and trails behind me like a puppy. Honestly, he seems quite excited. He does know it's flowers, right?

There's cut stems and ribbons all over the place.

"This is the not so pretty end, I'm afraid," I apologise.

"Not a problem. It's still a lot prettier than what I see on my work table."

He picks up a broom and starts helping me sweep the floor.

"You don't have to do that."

"No, but I want to."

We soon have the place looking spic and span, and I give him a mini tour. He seems genuinely interested.

"Well, I ought to be heading off," Nick says, glancing at his watch.

My heart sinks a little. It's soppy, I know, but I can't help it. It's been lovely having him here.

"OK," I say anyway.

"Are you busy on Saturday?"

"I have a wedding to do."

"Oh, of course. If I remain free, would it be OK if I tag along?"

"Sure, why not? You're used to weird times."

Well, this could be fun.

***

Perhaps I should've thought this through. This wedding's at *the* hotel. You know, the one with the random act of manipulation, and the one where I took the great arse-over-tit fall. Apart from picking up my van, I've not been back since. It's just my luck that it appears again now. Please break the curse. Please don't keep appearing in my life to torture me.

Is it fortunate or unfortunate that Nick doesn't cancel on me today? Well, whichever, he's turned up right on time, and with takeaway coffee, bless his heart. I prepared as much as possible last night, and worked on my own this morning. I didn't want to do too much with Nick here; he's distracting.

We go back down to the 'creation station' and I show him what I've been up to.

"Ooh, impressive. You did all this yourself?"

"Of course. This is only one wedding. I sometimes have three or four in one day."

"All this for one wedding?"

I can't help laughing.

"Yes. There's this bouquet for the bride, then the smaller ones for the bridesmaids, buttonholes for the groom and ushers. Then there's all these table arrangements for the wedding breakfast," I explain, pointing to each as I go.

"Wow."

"And I'm just finishing this last one. There's two bouquets for the mums as thank you presents too."

He watches me as I tie the stems into a cellophane wrap. It makes more of an impact somehow. And the mums usually appreciate the drama of it.

"Wait here, and I'll bring the van around," I tell Nick as I'm done.

We load up the van and get in. I pass him my folder with the details for the drop-offs.

He stays in the van as I take the first batch up to the bridal party, and then to the boy zone. Then it's off to the reception venue. The hotel looms at the end of the driveway like a big doomy thing.

Nick comes in with me as we start taking arrangements inside.

227

"Hello, Molly. Ah, you have help, I see. You are not to be trusted out on your own, eh?"

Great, it's Antonio, and he's still humorous.

"Hi, Antonio. Yes, we don't want any accidents, do we?"

Externally, my tone and gestures suggest I'm joking along with him. Internally I'm stabbing him with his own pen.

He again needlessly informs me of the room which is to be used. It's right here in the folder which Nick is still clutching. Probably should have told him he could leave that in the car. Oh well. We head on through.

"What was all that about?"

"I'll tell you later. It's a long story."

I've not told him about the falling event yet, having managed to successfully bypass that embarrassing tale. Why add clumsy to the list of faults he knows about?

"OK. Mysterious, but OK. Nothing I should worry about?"

"With Antonio? No. He's fine," I tell him, giggling. Really? Antonio? Give me some credit. He's charming. Too charming. If he was at all interested in me, it'd be a flash-in-the-pan sort of relationship.

We soon finish our task. This is so much easier with two pairs of hands. Nick brings in the arrangements as I fuss with them on the tables, ensuring they're shown to their best. With a quick final spritz of the flowers it's time to make our exit.

As we're about to descend, my feet hesitate on the top step. It's silly, but it feels like tempting fate. I thought I was covering my emotions well, but Nick's looking at me inquisitively.

"Are you OK?"

"Yeah, fine," I lie, gratefully accepting his arm which he's offering.

I keep forgetting how analytical he is for a living, so keep getting surprised at his observations and care as a result.

"Well, I think we've earned a lunch out," he says, clapping his hands.

"Oh, you do, do you?"

"Yeah, what do you say? Your choice."

I drive us to a countryside pub. There's a roaring blaze in the fireplace, and it feels really cosy. We escaped the worst of the rain today, but it's quite cold out. I scan the menu.

"Would you hate me if I have the sausage and mash?" Nick asks.

"No, not as long as you give me a little taste."

"Done. What would you like?

"Ham, egg and chips please. And a diet lemonade."

"OK, I'll be right back."

I think I can account for the chips. They'll be naughty. And the eggs are probably fried. But it was the best option. Otherwise it was pie or scampi, and they are far worse. Oh well, it's only one meal. I can cope. Can't I?

Nick comes back to the table with our drinks. He's got a pint, of course. What a bloke.

"So, what was the story back at the hotel?"

Damn, I hoped he'd forget about that. I tell him the whole sorry saga of falling down, and how that led me to going on this diet. I'd only told him it was doctor's advice and not what led up to the diagnosis before. Can you blame me? It's incredibly embarrassing, and I wasn't going to volunteer the information. Now he knows what a lummox I am. But he's not mocking me, or even laughing.

"That sounds painful. It must've been scary too."

"It was both of those things. But I survived. I'm fine. And it helped me get the medical intervention I clearly needed. It's all good."

"So, something good came out of the bad?"

"Exactly. It was like an epiphany, or something."

"That's a very good way of looking at it. See, you *can* be positive."

Chapter 24 - Shortcut

Feeling full of delicious food, we've made our way back to my place. As soon the van stopped Nick came to open the door on my side.

"Where are you taking me?" I ask him, as he leads me away from my front door.

"I need a stroll after that lunch."

"A stroll? But it's freezing."

"We'll have to walk faster to keep warm then. The rain's stopped, and look, the sun's trying to come out."

I'm getting out of puff as he leads me down unknown roads and paths. He walks faster than me; his legs are longer. Our arms are linked, so I'm forced to keep up. Unable to take any more, I tug on his arm, slowing our pace a little. My chest heaves, trying to take in more air.

"Sorry. I'm just excited," Nick says.

"Excited? About a walk?" I ask between gasps. Where are we going? Maybe he's an axe murderer after all? He's taking me somewhere quiet to do the deed. I'm too young to die. I'm not even married yet. You can't kill me before I've got married. That's not fair.

To my great relief, we've arrived at a park, surrounded by trees. There's a few brave families and dog walkers about. Oh good, they can bear witness should he try to murder me.

"I love this park," he tells me.

All the better to kill you here, I think.

But what I actually say is, "Wait. I know where we are. How did we get here so quickly? It's taken, what, ten minutes?"

"Ha, I knew you wouldn't know the shortcuts. You're such a driver. Yes, the roads take you the long way around. It's one of those weird times when it's quicker to walk."

"Oh, how wonderful."

Murder within convenient reach; spiffing.

"You're not too worn out, are you?"

"Of course not," I lie.

Anyone got an oxygen tank on them?

"I love being out in nature, and here it is on your doorstep."

"I suppose it is."

What will his murder weapon be? Maybe he's trying to induce a heart attack? Very clever. Nothing to incriminate him. Merely an unfortunate incident. There's a kiosk, which sparks a coffee craving, but as we get closer I can see it's closed. Oh well, I'm sure it's lovely in the summer.

Oh good, there's a bench and we seem to be heading towards it. Eww, obviously it's still wet from the rain earlier. Aww, but Nick's taking off his coat and laying it down for me to sit on.

"Aren't you going to get cold?"

"I'll be OK. I think you need to rest more than I need the warmth."

Despite the cold, sweat's trickling down my forehead and back. I'm longing for a little sit-down, so accept the kind offer.

"I'm so sorry. I didn't mean to walk so fast. I only wanted to show you the way. Now you're losing weight I thought it might be a nice route for you to take. It's not far, and a lovely walk. I just got a bit carried away."

"Well, I should increase my exercise."

"So you've said."

"Have I? Oh, have I been a diet bore? Sorry."

"Not at all. But you always have this little worry crease here, every time you say it," he tells me, pointing to my brows.

Oops, I must've said something about it without realising. I know I told him about trying to lose weight, but it was more so he knew I wasn't going to be large forever. That something was being done about it.

He lets me sit here in silence for a few minutes. It really is lovely here. The winter sun is shining through the trees, there's a few hardy birds singing, and a feeling of calm envelopes me.

We walk down by the river before heading for home. He's much slower now. And no murders have taken place, I'm happy to report. Mind you, I wouldn't have been able to report it if I had been killed, would I?

"Would you like to come in for coffee?" I ask innocently, as we approach my door.

"I thought you'd never ask."

Oh, there's his cute cheeky grin.

"Not like that, I mean coffee coffee."

"Sure, that would be good too," he says, with a shrug, his eyes sparkling like diamonds.

He's so naughty.

I get the mugs ready, and pop spoonfuls of coffee and sugar in as I wait for the kettle to boil. Those arms wrap around my waist again, but this time there's a kiss on my cheek and tingles run through me.

Nick's lips travel down to my neck and nip ever so gently, turning my insides to molten lava. Oh, we're going there, are we? OK then.

My bum leans against the kitchen counter as I turn around in his arms. His grey eyes are dark and intense as he looks down into mine. My neck cranes up so my lips can find his. All boilers have been lit, and my lust is firing on all cylinders. So is his, by the feel of things.

I quietly take his hand, and start to lead him upstairs to my bedroom.

"Are you sure?" he checks.

"Oh yes."

No more words are required. We know what's about to happen. Butterflies are flying around my stomach, and some acrobats seem to have joined them, and are busy doing somersaults. Nick is about to see me naked, and it's still daylight. Oh God, what am I doing?

My bedroom only overlooks the garden, but I pull the curtains anyway. That might help hide me a bit; diffused light.

My clothes get ripped off by my own hands, and I jump straight under the duvet on the bed.

"Hey, slow down," Nick complains.

He starts to pull the duvet away.

"Please don't. It's cold," I plead.

"Ah ahh, come on, I'm dying to see."

"You won't want me anymore."

"Molly, I couldn't want you more. Please share with me. Trust me."

"But I'm ugly."

"If I thought you were ugly I wouldn't be here, would I?"

"You've not seen the worst of me."

"Do you know how many bodies I've seen? I'm sure you haven't got anything I've not seen before."

Damn, he has a point.

"Maybe I'm covered in purple fur."

"Well then, I definitely have to see."

That makes me laugh. He tugs the duvet down far enough to reveal my boobs.

"Well, I like what I see so far. Disappointingly, no purple fur though." He waggles his eyebrows playfully.

The man's brazen in his own nakedness as he sits on top of the duvet, at my feet. There's the hint of muscle definition in his torso. His physique is slender. He's not rippling or bulging with muscles, but fit all the same. Talking of bulges, that's a decent size, and standing proud.

Oh my, his mouth has found one of my nipples. That does all kinds of things to me, and I can hear myself moan in pleasure.

A chill whispers along my tummy as the covers get pulled down further. Nick's hands massage down from my boobs and across my stomach. I cringe as I feel him grab a fistful of flesh.

"You're gorgeous, Molly. Relax."

"How can you say that?"

"Because I have eyes. And because you feel great."

"Please stop grabbing my flab."

"I'm not. I'm finding something to hold onto for when things get rough later."

Oh my, he makes that sound sexy.

But I still shudder as the duvet is completely pulled aside, and it's only partially because of the cold.

"Part your legs for me, Molly," he commands.

"I can't."

"Yes, you can."

"Nope. Can't."

Oh, this is normally all under cover stuff. It's not even dark. He'll see everything.

"Yes. You can," he whispers more firmly and slowly. His fingers travel lightly across the soles of my feet, and my legs retract of their own accord as I burst into laughter at his touch.

"Told you so," he says with a wicked grin.

He wastes no time, and seizes the opportunity. Oh my God, his mouth is *there*. Oh, his tongue...is…is…

"Oooooaaaaah," I cry as my world explodes.

"My beautiful woman," he whispers as he travels up my body.

He looks very pleased with himself.

"Do you, err, have umm, protection handy?"

"Actually, I have some in this drawer, which is lucky for you."

"Oh I have some in my pocket, but my trousers are all the way over there, on the floor. I suddenly don't want to leave this bed. No idea why."

He nips my neck as he says this. Mmm, good excuse. I don't want him to leave either. The packet gets chucked at him as I nestle into the bed.

This time there's no argument, my legs are open for him. I'm so ready. Part of me is relieved he's not flipped me on my front. But I don't have time to dwell on past conversations with others.

"Oooooah," I gasp as he enters me.

"Oh God, Molly."

He thrusts in and out, sending me into ecstasy. I grab his bum, urging him on.

"Argh, you feel so good," he says through gritted teeth.

Our bodies slip and slide and I lose myself in him, surrendering every bit of me. All that I am is his.

"Oh, Nick!"

My hips buck under him, begging for more. My nails dig into his flesh as we rage on; our sweaty bodies deliciously moving together.

His hand travels up the side of my body, gripping on, as he dives ever deeper inside.

My neck arches backwards as he squeezes one of my nipples, forcing a cry of ecstasy from my lips.

As he sucks on my neck I am lost.

A kaleidoscope of colours bursts behind my eyes as I climax. That's a first. Normally it's a dark floaty place. But this is something entirely different.

I'm vaguely aware of his groans, as if they're coming from a far off place.

"Sorry. You're too sexy," he apologises, "I was planning on taking much longer."

His voice brings me back down to Earth. Admittedly, it was no marathon session, but still the most wonderful sexual experience of my life.

"It was perfect," I manage to murmur.

He pulls me to his side and holds me. Maybe he is a murderer after all? I feel like I'm in heaven right now.

Chapter 25 – Sorry

The rest of the day disappears in hugs and kisses;
utter bliss. No work phone calls for him. I wish I
could freeze this moment forever, but sadly time
ticks on.

We had a big lunch, so I rustle up a quick pasta dish
for dinner. The heating's been turned up, and Nick's
wearing my dressing gown over his boxer shorts as I
lounge around in my pyjamas. He insisted.

Apparently, I look "cute" in them. After what
happened earlier, I'm going along with his wishes.

We're cosied up on the sofa, and a film's playing on
the television, but we're not paying much attention
to it. We're lost in our own little world.

"Is it OK if I stay the night?"

"More than OK," I find myself preening my
response.

Ahh, does life get any better than this? I'm as snug as
a bug in a rug.

We comfortably chatter until we can't keep our eyes
open any longer. We make our way back upstairs.

"Don't want to add to your energy bills," Nick quips
as he turns the thermostat back down as we pass it.

It really is unnerving sometimes; how observant he
is. He notices everything.

"Besides, I'll keep you warm," he adds, instantly
making my insides melt again.

We snuggle down in bed together. Ha ha, get me. I'm
getting spooned. Who'd have thought it? He does
that hair stroking thing, and I am lulled into sleep.

There's strange music playing. It rudely wakes me up. What is that? Where's it coming from. There's a scuffling next to me. Oh yeah, my boyfriend's here. What's he up to?

"Hello?" I hear him say from a distance.

The music's stopped and he's not by my side. Sodding phones! He's actually taking a phone call. Glancing at the clock, it confirms it is the small hours of the morning. Who phones at two o'clock am? Is it some sort of advanced feathered friend? An owl, perhaps?

"Molly, I'm so sorry. I have to go. It's work."

"What? At this time?"

"Afraid so. I really am sorry. I'll make it up to you."

Nick's out the door before I can say much. He had warned me about his work hours. But surely the person's dead. They'll be dead for a good long time to come. Can't they wait? I'm very much alive and I have needs.

It takes me ages to get back to sleep. I'm all upset. Today had been so lovely, and his work had to go and ruin it. Aren't I allowed one good day?

***

I obviously did get back to sleep, as I'm opening my eyes in daylight. There's a cold empty patch next to me in the bed. It would be unreasonable and childish to cry just because I didn't get my own way, because Nick has other priorities, more important than me. So I don't. No, these aren't tears. I have something in my eye. Fine, I'm crying. Happy now? I'm being a complete baby.

How many mornings have I woken up alone? How often have I sort of liked my independence? There's nobody telling me what to do or where to go…or taking me for romantic walks, or treating me to a yummy lunch. Ahem, I seem to have lost track. My point is, I'm more than capable of being alone. I'm a grown-up. I'm used to this. But my yoghurt and muesli tastes sour as my mind lingers on the memory of the morning when Nick was here. My heart aches, knowing he should be here this morning, with me now.

Maybe he would have woken me up with morning sex. And we could've gone for another walk somewhere on our way back from taking my donation to the hospice. It's all empty hopes though. He's not here, and that's that. No amount of wishing will bring him here.

I shower, get dressed and ready the display for the hospice and make my, if not merry way, at least my lonesome path to fulfil my duty.

"Are you alright, Molly?" the wonderful lady there asks as I hand over the flowers.

"Yes, of course. Can't complain," I reply, trying to smile.

Oh, I'm the worst kind of human. Here's me feeling sorry for myself because my boyfriend had to go to work. There's children here who won't reach adulthood. Whose parents will mourn the passing of their little darlings. How selfish am I? What right do I have to carry on like this?

The supermarket will have to miss me. I'm in no mood for shopping. Yes, I'm still moping. Not as much. How can I with the painful reminder of those poor children? But I'm still missing Nick. Fine, I'll go, but I won't be happy about it. I point my van in the direction of the shops. Eurgh!

Look, the thing is, those parents have also reminded me I'm not one of them. I want children. I may have said that once or twice. It's natural, isn't it? Aren't women supposed to have this inbuilt thing? I certainly do.

My feet take me up the aisle to the lady care shelf. It'll soon be here again, that painful reminder which arrives each month, telling me what a failure I am. My womb is wasting away. My eggs aren't hatching. Chocolate also finds its way into the trolley. Leave me alone, it's near that time of month, and I have boyfriend issues. And I'll build it into my daily allowance. I won't eat an entire family bar in one sitting. Ahem, she says, taking the family bar out of her trolley, and replacing it with a bag of fun size ones. And poke my tongue out at you as I do so. Ppph!

Why are they called fun size anyway? There's nothing fun about them. Here, have a fraction of a normal sized bar of chocolate. Oh, thank you very much, what fun. No. It's a miser's bar. A stingy size. Don't suppose they'd sell many if they called them Scrooge size, though.

Oh shit. It's Halloween this week. I actually need to buy a big tub of sweets for trick or treaters. Honestly, it *is* for them. I do get tiny tots knocking on my door.

I'm sorry I was grotty, by the way. I'm all hormonal and upset, and didn't mean it. I know as well as you do, that the giant bar of chocolate would've disappeared, and I'd have used it as another reason to hate myself.

There's some snack bars in my car, the healthy kind. I stupidly didn't eat lunch before coming out. I wasn't thinking clearly, and now my tummy's rumbling. One of the bars gets munched as I set off for home. Alone.

Honestly, I'll snap out of this. Please bear with me. Some healthy soup gets heated up for lunch as soon as I'm home. There's nothing like a big bowl of comforting soup on a cold day, is there? The wind's got up out there. Birds would be forgiven for trying to make a home in my hair, it's such a messy nest. But there's nobody to impress, so who cares?

The bowl's not even half finished when my phone rings. Oh good, it's my mother to add joy to my day.

"Molly darling, it's been too long since we had a chat."

Has it? I thought she'd rung a few days ago. What's she after?

"Hello, Mother."

"How's that nice young man of yours?"

I really wish I hadn't told her about Nick, but she has a way of weedling these things out. Besides, if I hadn't told her, the mother grapevine would've, and then she'd have used that against me forever.

"Oh, my own daughter, too ashamed of her mother to tell her when she had a suitor," she'd have said.

Oops, I need to respond to what she actually said.

"He's at work, Mother. I'm fine, by the way. How are you?"

"Oh, mustn't grumble. Are you still losing weight?"

"Yes, Mother."

Is it possible to hear eyes roll, over the phone? Will she notice?

And what if I wasn't still losing weight? Why should I have to report these things to her? For heaven's sake. I'm a grown-up. I live on my own, and have done for some time. I haven't managed to do myself any serious harm, with the exception of that one brief hospital stay. Can't I be trusted with my own life?

"Oh, good. I hear you're doing ever so well."

Well, of course she's heard. I bloody well tell her, don't I? But what she's actually referring to is that someone else has mentioned it, one of her network of spies. Friends, I mean friends, of course. I can hear it now, "*Hasn't your Molly really slimmed down?*"

"Can I help you with anything, Mother?"

Do I sound as bored and grumpy as I feel?

"I was just calling to invite you both round to supper."

Oh God, I'm not sure we're ready for that. He'll run a mile.

"Well, it's rather difficult with his work."

"You let me know when he's available, and we'll slot in. It's no trouble."

No trouble, my arse. She'll go all out, thinking some grandiose banquet will impress the potential son-in-law. She's chomping at the bit to meet him, I can hear it in her voice. She must give her approval. I'm clearly unable to make a life changing decision on my own.

"I'll check with him and let you know."

The call gets ended as fast as I can manage. My soup's getting cold, and I can't bear any more confidence bashing today. My quota has been fulfilled, thank you very much.

I slurp down the rest of my soup, then layer up so I can have a cigarette out in my garden. Ahh, I needed that. What a day.

You know when some people say something's an emotional rollercoaster? That's what I feel like today. So many ups and downs, my head's spinning. My fingers swipe up, over my nose and eyebrows as I try to clear my head.

Nick keeps telling me to focus on the positive. So, what do we have here? Oh yeah, Nick himself. OK, his work called him away, but he's still mine. I have a boyfriend. That's a pretty good thing. And he's lovely when he's here.

But still some of the 'trick or treat' sweets and chocolate find their way into my mouth. I'm conscious of having enough for the kids though, so there's not too much harm done.

Chapter 26 – Treats and Trouble

My breakfast has changed now it's got colder. An egg gets added to the overnight oats along with some frozen fruit. Yes, cooked fruit is on the naughty list, but it's also good for me, so I'm sensible with the portions. It only takes twenty minutes in the oven. Healthy, warming and delicious with sustained energy. I'm raring to go.

Not that I have anywhere to go to. The 'creation station' gets a quick tidy, and I have a quick black coffee. It tastes quite nice now I've got used to the flavour.

It's too quiet. Sod it, I'm going to go out for a walk as the rain's let up. Nick, look what you've started. My feet tread the same route he took me along, and I soon find myself in the park. I'm not gasping for breath this time as I was able to amble along at my own unrushed pace.

Maybe I should get one of those step counter thingies? Some people in the weight loss group were talking about them last week. It'd probably encourage me to get out a bit more.

It's really nice, getting out in the fresh air. I'm sure it's clearing my head a bit. But I'm really ready for my soup when I get home.

Nick texts me as he's on his way home after his shift. He's full of apologies, and wants to see me this evening, but I brush him off. I have my slimming group and it's really important to me.

"Can I invite you round mine tomorrow evening then? I'll cook," he types.

"I hope you have something healthy in your cookbook."

"I might do."

"Not just beans on toast then?"

"Haha, very funny."

Our playful banter lightens my mood another notch. Having not seen his flat yet, and being curious to see where he lives, I agree. Plus, there's the promise of food.

I grab the chance to catch up on a bit of housework, which is also a mini workout, apparently. All activity is good according to 'group'. Then it's time to see how I've done this week.

Despite my slightly naughty lunch yesterday, I've still lost two pounds this week. The number at the front has almost changed again. Slow and steady wins the race. I'm still battling myself on this point of view, and am impatient. I want to reach my target more quickly, but my head knows that patience is required.

My laptop comes out when I get home. Realising I've not booked my spa treat yet, and being in the mood for some pampering, now's the time to look. My dress size has changed, so I'm not quite so scared of wandering about in a swimsuit and robe.

Oh dear, that deal includes afternoon tea; best not go for that one. Scones and cream? Bit of a no-no, isn't it? Pity. Um, what else is there?

That one looks good; it's a small venue, so shouldn't be too busy. I can get lunch, which offers healthy options, and includes a facial. I check the availability and book in for next Tuesday. It's a bit extravagant, but to hell with the cost, I've earned it.

The rest of the day is disappearing in a blur of anticipation. I'm struggling to focus on anything as I wait for evening to arrive, bringing hope with it. Is it weird to feel this excited? I'm itching to see Nick again, and his place for the first time.

But the time finally arrives. No awful text or telephone call has been received to cancel. I've booked a taxi to take me, so I can have a tipple should I wish to. I feel like Cinderella as my carriage takes me to my destination. Well, I'm not quite that glammed up, but you get what I mean.

He buzzes me in, and I climb the stairs to heaven. Err, his flat. I climb the stairs to his flat. His smiling face greets me at his door.

"Hello, gorgeous," he says before giving me a long, lingering kiss.

"Hello," I reply when I can catch my breath.

Phew, that was a welcome and a half. Wonderful smells waft up my nostrils as I follow him inside.

"Ooh, something smells good. I hope you've not gone to too much trouble."

"Nothing's too much trouble for my beautiful woman."

Aww, doesn't he say the nicest things?

"So, what is on the menu?"

"Molly Supreme."

"To eat?"

"That's what I said."

"No, actual food," I push playfully.

He's such a tease.

"Chicken balti, spoil sport. I looked it up, and it's diet compliant."

"Aww, thank you. But didn't you have to buy lots of ingredients?"

"I actually make a lot of curries anyway. I had most of the spices already."

"Really? You have time to cook?"

"Well, when I have the time I make them. Most don't take too long anyway."

"Mm, it really does smell good."

"And it's ready when you are. Right this way, madam."

He pulls out a chair for me at his dining table. That makes it sound huge. It's not. His flat is quite bijou. The lounge is bordered by the kitchen/diner. There's only enough room for a small table, which he's laid out beautifully by the way.

There's a simple black tablecloth, and white plates. Elegant wine glasses and stainless steel cutlery is glimmering in the candle light. It's very tasteful. I'm impressed.

Nick's standing at the kitchen counter, and I gaze on longingly as he dishes up. Honestly, the smells are amazing; all warm and spicy. My tummy gurgles in anticipation.

"I have some viognier wine in the fridge, or diet cola. Or would you prefer gin and tonic?" he asks as he brings in plates of steaming curry.

"Oh, you really have gone to a lot of effort. I'll have a wine, please."

It's torture. I'm sitting here with plates of delicious food as he pours our drinks.

"Don't wait, tuck in," he coaxes.

But my manners are too ingrained to let me follow his instruction. Not until the host sits and starts to eat will I join in. Is that weird? It's how I've been brought up.

His bum is barely in his seat when I pick up my fork
and start tucking into the curry.

"Ahhh, mmm, delicious," I admire honestly, once
I've finished my mouthful, of course.

I think I detect a slight blush on my man's cheeks as
he thanks me. My man. That sounds delectable too.
We don't talk much as we eat, but his eyes stare at
me longingly throughout. The candlelight dances in
his eyes, adding to the intensity. It may not be just
the heat of the curry coursing through my body as I
dine.

I shovel the food into my gob, anxious to get to the
next bit, yet also hungry. I know, so romantic, aren't
I? But a girl can have more than one need at once.
Demonstrating my best sultry pouty look, I sip the
last of my wine.

"So, what's for dessert?" I try to ask in a husky
whisper, but it sounds more 'strangled cat'.

He silently gets up and reaches for my hand. Oh my,
this seems to be going exactly where I want it to.
Oh look, we're in his dark blue bedroom. There's a
few candles lit in here too. He really has put some
effort into this seduction. It'd be rude not to reward
his hard work, wouldn't it?

I kiss him longingly. Every fibre of my being wants
this man. And when he looks at me that way my
insides melt.

He's taken control and is undressing me. His fingers
tease my skin as they brush against me in the
process.

I practically throw myself on the bed and allow him
to quickly undress and prepare.

I'm taken to a whole new world as our bodies unite.

Ahem, well that didn't quite go as expected. As soon as the writhing part began my tummy started making noises, and it felt like it was struggling with the combination of food and movement. Sex on a full stomach is *not* a good idea. Not my finest hour. Lying in his arms, he moves to kiss me on my forehead, seemingly satisfied anyway.

"Molly, I hate to say this, but I have work in the morning."

"Oh, you want me to leave?"

"Well…"

"Why didn't you bloody well say to start with? Why go to all this trouble?"

I storm off the bed and into his bathroom. It's not hard to find in a small flat. I go to the loo and get dressed whilst seething.

How bloody dare he? He lures me into his man cave to have his wicked way and then kicks me out once he's got what he wanted? I feel used and cheap.

He's trying to call to me as I grab my bag on my way out.

"Don't bother," I bite out as I march out of his door. I call a taxi from my mobile, and wait around the corner, so he can't see me. It's freezing cold, but the heat of my anger shields me a little. What an arsehole! I was all ready for a whole night of the wining and dining sort of romance. And what do I get? Curry and a hurry.

He hasn't even come out to search for me. Mind you, my phone has rung a couple of times, and I've ignored his calls. I can't speak to him right now, my words will get stuck in my throat.

The taxi doesn't take very long to arrive, fortunately, and I've had time to calm down a little. But the poor cabby still gets my address in a rather terse tone. I give him a bigger tip than I would've given normally, hoping that makes up for my behaviour. It's not like it's his fault. And he was wise enough not to pry. He silently drove me home in the dark. Cinderella never had this trouble. The dainty footed bitch. She was the one to run out. The prince didn't kick her out, did he?

Chapter 27 – Make Up

OK, so I've been licking my wounds for a couple of days. Some may call it sulking. But Nick really hurt me the other night. He built up my hopes and expectations then shat on my parade.

He's sent me texts and emails, trying to explain he didn't mean for me to leave immediately. Fine, I might've overreacted a little bit. I missed out on a couple of extra hours with him due to my temper, and I'm sorry for that. I just want to spend more time with him, but have been left frustrated.

We talked some things over, and we both still really like each other. And Christmas isn't far away. It's the worst time of year to be on your own. So, we're still a couple. He's going to try to spend more time with me.

Nick's actually due here soon. I'm cooking this time. Then I get to kick him out, ha ha, only joking. There's just enough time to update you on my slimming progress. I'm really happy as another three pounds were shed this week. I've got a new number at the start of my weight; hoorah. It must be the extra exercise, and I don't only mean the bedroom variety. I've started walking out most days, not always as far as the park, but I at least try to stroll around the block. Wendy's doing well too, and had a great loss on the scales this week.

Oh, and you'll never guess. Wendy's dating that Gary bloke. You know the one, the guy she recruited as my bodyguard. That's why she's not been round so much. Bless her, she didn't want to tell me when I was single, in case I felt abandoned. But seeing as I'm dating someone she confessed all. Of course, then I told her about my fight with Nick. Water under the bridge though.

Whilst I'm really happy for her, I'm also a little hurt Wendy felt she couldn't tell me her good news.

We're best friends, and we tell each other everything. I don't want to be a pity case. People shouldn't feel like they're walking on eggshells around me. Am I that stroppy? Maybe don't answer that.

My doorbell's ringing. Nick must be here. The butterflies are back in my tummy. I verily skip to the door.

"I'm so glad to see you," Nick says, his voice muffled by my shoulder as he wraps himself around me.

My arms wrap around him too. It feels so nice to be back in his arms.

"I don't like fighting," I tell him as I move so I can peck him on the lips.

"Neither do I," he says between kisses.

I made the right decision. He really is sweet, and I feel safe right here.

"But can I come in out of the cold?"

Oops, we're still in the doorway.

"Um, yes, sorry. Come in," I say on a laugh.

Now I feel bad for not having gone to more effort. I was still harbouring resentment and didn't go all out with the food. Besides, it's a lean time of year for Holly Molly, so I'm being a bit watchful of my pennies.

Of course it's diet compliant. Steak and homemade chips, made simply by cutting up potatoes into long chunks and cooking them in the oven. A grilled tomato and some veg served on the side. Not too shabby.

"Smells fantastic," Nick kindly comments as I lead him through so I can dish up.

Having learned my lesson, we don't head straight for the bedroom after we've eaten. Partly because I want to be sure he's here for a while, and partly to let the food go down a bit.

His fingers intertwine with mine and he takes a deep breath in. "You're a pain in the arse, you know that?"

""Hey."

"Let me finish, woman. See, you're just proving my point. Like I was saying, you're a pain in the arse. You fly off the handle at the slightest thing. But it's also what I love about you. That fiery passion. Your spontaneity, your exuberance, it's exciting. So much of my life is dull and predictable. But you? You bring this flame, and I can't resist. Even if it does mean I get burned sometimes."

Hold the phone. Did he just use the love word? It was about me, not that he loves me directly though. Does that count? Oh. This would be where I say something.

"I'm sorry. I don't mean to hurt you," I tell him, shaking his hand gently from side to side.

"I know you don't. Please know I don't want to hurt you either. Ever."

Aww, he's the moth to my flame. He won't harm me.

Music is playing quietly in the background, serenading us as we dissolve into a make-out session. He's really sexy and I've missed him. My body is keen to make up with him too.

Once we finally reach the bedroom gymnastics stage I'm trembling with desire. It's taken all my self-control to wait even this long. Our clothes get thrown off and we jump into bed. Making sure he's got protection, we go at it like rabbits. Sorry if that's a bit graphic.

We can't keep our hands off each other. My palms search his whole body, gripping on as our tongues entwine. My legs open, desperate to invite him in. I need to feel him, and his reassuring presence. He fulfils my desire.

It's hot, dirty, desperate sex. I feel he needs this as much as I do. His body pumps over mine with a ferocious pace. My body reacts to his, and it doesn't take me too long to find my release, shortly before he finds his.

I drape myself across his chest when we finish, and surrender to the satisfied feelings washing over me. I really needed that.

Refusing to fall asleep, I throw on some clothes so I can have a cigarette outside. It's post coital, OK? Don't roll your eyes, please. I know smoking's bad, but I need this too.

Nick joins me. Yeah, he smokes too. And I'm glad. It's really icky if one of you smells of smoke and the other one doesn't.

I make us coffee to warm up as we head back inside. There's a layer of frost outside already, and the chill's gone through to my bones. The hot drink helps thaw me out.

Nick's not run away yet. Actually, he ends up staying the night.

As I wake up in the morning there's a warm body lying next to me. Just kill me now, so I can die happy. I roll over and snuggle up to him, waking him up in the process. Oh well, it's not too early. The alarm clock hasn't gone off, but it's not too far away.

Mm, morning sex is luxurious. I probably should've brushed my teeth first, but I was caught up in the moment. I'm a very happy bunny right now.

I feel like a fairytale princess as I waltz downstairs to make breakfast for me and my man, humming all the while.

"Someone sounds happy," Nick announces as he joins me.

"That's because I am," I reply, grinning widely and planting a kiss on his lips.

His front is pressed against my back, and his arms are wrapped around my waist as I rustle up some bacon, mushrooms and eggs. I'm so glad I'm allowed bacon on my eating plan; I just don't eat the fat. But which is yummier; bacon or Nick? In this precise moment I can't quite decide.

He heads off to work with a full stomach and a few more kisses. The dream swirls around my head, as I imagine this is what married life would be like with him.

I dance my way through the rest of the day, singing as I do the housework and Holly Molly things. Life's pretty good.

Nick sends me a thrilling text in the evening, thanking me for an amazing time. Honestly, thrills run right through me as I read it, and a giggle might've escaped, like a love-struck schoolgirl.

Ah, happiness, there you are. I've been looking for you.

"I've been here all the time, waiting for you," happiness tells me.

Have I lost the plot? Maybe. I don't care. I'm happy, weeee. I want to yell it from the rooftops. Sorry, I'll stop whirling around with my arms out wide. In a minute. Just once more.

OK, I'm done now. Sorry. Look, I'm sitting down on the sofa like a grown-up. A grown-up with a mug of hot chocolate. It's OK, it's the healthy option one. I'm going to sit here and read. Not dream about my lovely night. Nope. Reading.

My phone beeps as my eyes read the same sentence in my book for the umpteenth time, my head's refusing to take it in.

"Missing you," Nick's text says.

Aww.

"Missing you too."

Things might get a bit slushy. It's OK, I'll catch up with you later.

Chapter 28 – Rejuvenation

I'm just about ready when Wendy rings the doorbell, bright and early. When I told her I'd booked a spa day she insisted on coming along too. Apparently it's not the sort of thing one should do alone. Who knew?

It's been ages since we had quality time together. I suppose we're both guilty of being side-tracked by our men folk. I'm really looking forward to having a good catch-up with her. Although, I'm less excited about doing so in a tankini. I had to go out and buy the little garment as I had nothing suitable which would fit.

Do you know how difficult it is to buy these things in winter? Especially when you don't want to reveal too much flesh, yet need a two-piece so you don't have to be fully naked when getting a massage. It's a tricky thing to get right. I may have lost weight, but I'm still no super model.

Is the spa therapist going to judge me? Is she going to be silently holding down vomit as her hands plunge through my folds of fat? There's so many rolls I could open a bakery.

"Morning, are you ready?" Wendy asks me cheerily.

"Yep, all set," I lie, grabbing my bag and leading the way to my van.

Wendy jabbers away on the journey to the spa. I'm concentrating on driving, so I let her ramble on about how wonderful Gary is. He does sound rather wonderful, and it's great they get to see each other so much. But I can't help the pang of jealousy which strikes me.

Nick and I are still struggling to find time together. But Wendy's a busy nurse, and Gary works at the hospital too. If they can manage their time effectively why can't I?

We pull into the car park and make our way to the spa's reception. I'm fidgeting. My nerves haven't been calmed by the sight of skinny people entering the building. I really am going to look like a whale. The receptionist makes us fill in forms and sign in before handing us a towel, robe and slippers. She directs us to the changing room, where we shrug off our outer clothes, and stuff them into a locker.

"Ooh, nice tankini," Wendy kindly mentions.

"Thanks. Yours is nice too," I reply, feeling awkward.

The robe is mercifully covering me as we patter into the spa proper in our foamy slippers. I'm grateful for Wendy's presence too; there's lots of pairs of women here. Although I think there some are here alone, and they don't seem fazed at all. Oh heck, there's a few men too, who I think must've been dragged here by their other halves.

It's quite quiet, and we feel compelled to speak in a library-like whisper as we acquaint ourselves with the facilities. Our treatments aren't until later, so there's time to relax first. We opt for a gentle steam room, easing our way into the spa world gradually. In my experience, women are often very chatty when they're grouped together like this. But there seems to be some unspoken sacred serenity at play here. It's sort of eerie, but kind of nice.

The steam room had one other person in it, who happily vacated soon after we arrived, so now we can talk a little.

"So, how's things with Nick?" Wendy quizzes.

I roll my eyes, which I don't think she can see through the steam.

"Hm, they're OK."

"Don't sound too enthusiastic, will you?"

"No, they're good. It's just, I don't know, a bit frustrating I suppose."

"Frustrating? Is he not good in between the sheets?" she teases.

I give her a wry look, again, which I still doubt she can see.

"He's fine there, thank you. It's more a matter of getting him there."

"Oh."

"He seems to get called away to work a lot," I explain.

"And you think it may not always be work?"

"What? No. Well, now I do."

"Sorry."

I can hear the guilt in her voice.

"I think it really is work. At least, I hope it is. But between his job and mine, time's a bit sparse."

"There's ways. If it's meant to be, and if you want to, you will make things work."

"I guess."

I change the subject. We're supposed to be relaxing, treating ourselves to some TLC, not dwelling on the bad stuff.

It's really hot, and I suggest moving to the next room before I feel ill.

"You're supposed to go and have a cold shower in between, I think. It's good for the circulation," Wendy says.

"You can if you like," I reply with a smirk as we get to the cooler air outside the room.

"Maybe a drink of cold water instead?"

We find a fountain, and sip some lovely fresh cold water.

"Sauna next?" Wendy suggests.

I pull a face, but agree. I'm the one who wanted to come here, so should be open to new experiences. Actually, the heat in the sauna is nicer. It's more intense but drier, and I don't have the same feeling of my breath being restricted.

Wendy and I start swapping funny work stories. It's familiar territory and we have a good laugh.

As we find chairs in the quiet area two therapists approach, quietly calling our names. I take a deep breath, and follow the poor girl who's been assigned to me. Wendy smiles encouragingly at me as we go our separate ways.

The therapist leads me to a small dark room, and instructs me on what to do before leaving to let me undress. I reluctantly take off my robe and tankini top, depositing them on a chair in the corner, and clamber up onto the massage table. I'm glad the therapist left the room as it's not an elegant process. The bed creaks and groans beneath me as I settle myself into position, my face pointing through the hole at the top.

"Ready?" the therapist asks breezily with a knock on the door.

"Mm hm," is all I can really reply from this position.

She mutters something about starting with the back massage and the oils she's going to be using. I don't really care, to be honest. I'm starting to doubt the wisdom of this trip. It's supposed to be a treat, but trepidation is taking hold. This lovely svelte girl is going to have to actually touch my back fat.

To her credit she doesn't say a word, or even mutter a sound of disgust as her hands start slipping up and down my back.

"Is that pressure OK?"

"Mm hm."

"Just let me know if you need a bit more or a bit less at any point."

"Mm hm."

Her hands make all sorts of shapes and movements along my back, and she digs in around my shoulders. It almost hurts, but in a good way. I think she's literally releasing my tension, as I begin to relax. This feels really nice, actually.

Is that tissue she's putting across my back?

"This will absorb the excess oil for you," she says soothingly, as if she read my mind.

Then she draws the towel back up to cover me. I'm as snug as a bug in a rug, and almost asleep. Not that I'm allowed to enjoy that feeling for long. She's stepped round to one side and is picking up one side of the towel and telling me to roll over.

I grunt and groan as I heave myself over to lie on my back. I hope she's not looking beyond that towel. She doesn't seem to be. I feel more like a whale than ever, but eventually manage to lie back down. How do people ever do this elegantly?

Undeterred, the therapist tucks me up in a towel cocoon, and makes sure my hair is all out of the way. She explains the facial procedure to me in an almost hypnotic voice.

"Oh, that's cold," I exclaim as the cleanser is apparently applied.

"Sorry. That's the worst bit. It'll be fine from here." Her fingers sweep across my face with different lotions in a gliding motion. OK, that's quite nice.

"What made you choose this job?" I find myself asking.

"I like helping people. And I've never been one of those who wanted to work in an office."

"Good choice. I did, and it's horrible. I'm a florist now."

"Oh, that must be lovely."

I end up telling her about my work. Not quite sure where this chatty mode came from. I don't know her. Why am I telling her all this? I go from work stuff to very personal details.

"How can you not like yourself? You seem like a really lovely person."

"That's very nice of you to say," I reply, thinking she has to say nice things to clients.

"I mean it. Look, I have a friend who may be able to help. Please don't tell my boss, I'd probably get fired for this. She's a holistic therapist, but doesn't work in a spa. She does things like Reiki and Emotional Freedom Technique."

"Um, I've not heard of those."

She's started putting some sort of gunk on my face which is drying already, making it difficult to move my lips. She lays something across my eyes.

"I'm going to leave the room for a minute to let you relax here with this face mask on. But when I come back I'll have her details for you. You can look her up online, then the choice is yours."

"OK, thank you," I say between barely moving lips and clenched teeth.

The whole world seems to disappear as I lie there alone in the darkness. The stuff on my face smells nice, and my thoughts drift off along with the soothing music.

Sleep has almost taken me when there's a little knock on the door, and the sweet girl comes back in and asks how I'm doing.

"Mm OK," I manage to murmur through semi-closed lips.

She removes the face mask, and wipes more stuff over a few times then gives my whole face a massage.

"There, how's that?" she asks once she's done.

"It feels wonderful," I say, feeling my face with my fingers, but speaking about the inner and outer feeling at once.

"Good. Here's the details of my friend," she says, handing me a piece of paper.

"Relax here for a few minutes, I've brought a glass of water for you. Take your time to get ready."

"Thank you so much," I tell her, feeling a little teary. She fortunately exits the room before any droplets fall. Why am I so emotional? It was only a massage and a facial. But I feel like a weight's been lifted from me.

I get dressed and head out of the room in a happy little haze. My therapist is waiting to guide me to the chillout area to wait for Wendy, who's already there when I walk in.

Saying goodbye and another thank you to the therapist, I sink down into the lounger next to Wendy.

"How was it?" she asks.

"Wonderful. So much better than I expected. I'm so relaxed. How was yours?"

"Lovely too. They're really good here. She really helped get some knots out of my shoulders."

The rest of our time disappears into a happy sort of dream. We have a lovely lunch, drift between experience rooms, and then regrettably head home, back to the real world. I don't want this time to end. It's the happiest I've been in ages.

I drop Wendy back at her house and thank her for a lovely day. Then it's back to my empty house I go. As I walk in, it dawns on me I don't mind the time alone. It gives me a chance to reflect on the wonderful day. As I chuck the wet things into the washing machine, my hand finds the note with the holistic therapist's details on. I miraculously remembered to take it out of the robe's pocket. Strike whilst the iron's hot, let's go and have a look.

My laptop churns into gear, and the website is loaded. Reiki, apparently pronounced *ray-key*, seems very interesting. I've vaguely heard about chakras, but this is apparently a way of balancing these energy wheels so the body works at its optimum level, thus reducing stress. The feedback seems encouraging. Maybe it's something I could go for. At least I don't have to get undressed.

Nick comes round the next evening, and the subject comes up when he asks me about my spa day.

"I think you should go," he says.

"Really?"

"Sure. If you think it'll help."

"You don't think Reiki is mumbo jumbo?"

"There's many things we don't understand in the universe, so maybe this stuff works."

"You never cease to amaze me. You're a man of science, and you're saying to try this?"

"Science doesn't explain everything."

Well, there's a shock. I was sort of hoping he'd talk some sense into me.

"If you boil it down, we're all energy, aren't we?" he continues.

"Well yes, I suppose."

"So maybe we can draw more energy? I'm not saying I believe it. Just that it may be worth a go. If it helps you realise how beautiful and wonderful you are it's worth it."

Aww shucks, my heart just melted a little bit. I give him a big smoochy kiss in gratitude. He's so supportive. When he's here.

He always says such lovely things, and in a way I want to believe him. Perhaps some of his words are starting to take hold. And he's so thoughtful. I feel rather spoiled by his attentions. Again, when he's here.

I drag him to the bedroom to show him just how grateful I am.

We have had an uninterrupted evening, and my joy is complete. It's been a wonderful couple of days. Can I freeze time here, please? I'm happy and want to stay here.

Chapter 29 – Realisation

For the first time in forever, my florist work feels as if it's getting in the way. I have urgent and important things which need to be done before I allow myself the luxury of looking into this Reiki thing a bit more. But I manage to get through it with my usual professionalism.

Finally, I have been able to grab a moment to have a nose around the internet. I want to read up on the therapy generally before going to see someone. It's a really odd concept, and I'm surprised Nick was so in favour.

He had a point it seems. Reading more, I learn about the universal energy which is just floating about, but gets channelled by the therapist into their client. I suppose you can liken this to electrical charge. And do we not all use and generate our own energy? Is it that farfetched when you think about it? A bit weird, yes, but suppose I can see how it might work.

There's lots and lots of people on the internet who say how it's helped them with things like stress and anxiety, depression, insomnia and a vague "emotional healing". Ah, and weight loss, that's what I was looking for.

Hm, by reducing stress and therefore cortisol levels, blah blah blah. It all sounds very indirect. There goes my magical cure. Oh well. This sense of balance and wellbeing sounds nice. I do feel 'off'. It's not something I can really put my finger on, just a sense of something not being quite right.

My trembling fingers pick up the phone and dial the local therapist's number. I'm slightly taken aback as she answers. I was expecting to leave a message. But no, she's talking to me calmly, and answering my questions and making an appointment for Monday. Eek, this is actually happening. It feels like a big, important decision, and the start of something. Oh, that sounds daft. Forget I said that.

The week goes by in the usual flurry of flowers. I've not seen Nick since our lovely evening together, but I've spoken with him on the phone. Wendy has also been preoccupied, but we've caught up via texts. I've told them both about my Reiki plans. Nick's still making encouraging noises, whilst Wendy gently teases me. I'm still sceptical, but am trying to go with an open mind.

Irene welcomes me with a lovely smile as I enter her therapy room. She sits me down to fill in a form and talk first.

"This is your first Reiki treatment, I think you told me, Molly?"

"Yes."

"OK, so in a moment I'll get you to lie down, fully clothed on the therapy couch. I'll start with some chimes which I'll hover over your body. When I'm ready to start I will be standing at your head, and will lay my hands on your shoulders briefly, but that will be the only time you feel my hands until the end. I'll hover my hands above each of your chakras."

Honestly, without even touching anything? At least massages give you contact, and you can feel them doing something. My scepticism is still lingering, and perhaps increasing.

"Do I need to do anything?"

"No. Just lie down with your eyes closed and relax. Let yourself open up to the energy."

"How do I do that?"

"Just lie there without actively thinking about it. It's alright, you'll understand," she says with a smile.

I take off my shoes and lie down, face up, as directed. A fluffy blanket gets pulled over me, and some plinky plunky music starts to play.

"Close your eyes, and take some deep breaths," Irene instructs in her soothing tone.

The clinging chimes sound above me, which makes me jump at first. I'm not quite sure about this. It's loud and odd, but I force myself to stay lying down on the couch.

Irene walks round to my head, and puts her hands lightly on my shoulders and tells me to take three deep breaths. My breath shudders at first as I inhale deeply and let it out slowly. By the end of the third exhalation I'm starting to feel more relaxed already.

The music floats around the room, and my ears tune into that as Irene presumably hovers her hands above my head. I'm only vaguely aware of some light air movement, and I'm trying not to think about what she's doing.

My thoughts wander without settling, drifting around like a bee hovering from flower to flower. But they slowly still.

Mmmm, peace, harmony, acceptance; the words are like flashcards in my mind and wrap me up in warm fuzzies.

A comforting drowsiness seeps through me, flowing like a warm stream.

Irene's hands are on my shoulders again, and she's saying something.

"Is that it?" I question on a squeak, slightly surprised.

"Yes."

"Oh no, did I fall asleep?" I ask, starting to sit up. Irene's hand gently rests on my shoulder.

"There's no hurry. Let yourself come to slowly. Wriggle your fingers and toes."

I do so whilst apologising.

"It's fine. It happens all the time."

I don't feel like I've been asleep. I don't know, but think this must be what a trance feels like.

"Did you hypnotise me?"

She giggles a little. "No, you just fell asleep. Part of you must've felt you'd be more receptive that way." Lifting the back of the therapy couch to support me, Irene helps me sit up and hands me a glass of water.

"How does that feel?" she asks.

"Um, weird. Different." My free hand goes up to cover my mouth, realising what I just said; it must sound so insulting.

"That's the usual response for people who come for their first session," she replies, smiling.

Phew, thankfully she doesn't seem to have taken offense.

"I'm sort of tingly," I tell her as the sensation buzzes through my veins.

"That's quite usual too. It's nothing to be alarmed about."

"I feel lighter too."

I do. Not like I've literally shed pounds, obviously. But like a weight's been lifted from my shoulders, from my chest, well, all over really.

"There was a lot of negative energy surrounding you. Maybe you've been taking lots of bad things on board for too long?"

I can only nod, as tears burst forth. Where did that come from?

Irene passes me a tissue. "It's OK. You cry all you want. It's good to release it. You've been holding it inside too long. It's nothing I've not seen before."

Well, that just makes me sob all the more. Permission to be a wuss? OK then. There's not much choice, as a surge of tears rips out of me along with inelegant wailing sounds.

"I'm sorry," I manage to spit out at last.

"It's fine. Let it go. This is a safe place, and you're free to release your emotions here."

Eventually, I pull myself together, and wipe the tears and snot from my face. Taking some deep breaths to steady my breathing.

"Better?" Irene queries.

"Yes, actually," I respond, realising I feel even lighter, "My head feels a bit spinny."

"Sit there and sip your water. You've released an awful lot. It's bound to make you a bit lightheaded."

"I'm not sure where all that came from," I tell her, sipping the cool liquid.

"You."

"Oh."

"You've been bottling all that up inside you, probably for years. Isn't it nice to get rid of it?"

"Yes. Surprising, but nice."

"Your solar plexus took the most energy. That's this one here," she explains, pointing below her ribcage.

"And that's good?"

"There is no good or bad. No right or wrong. The energy goes where it's needed most. At a guess, I'd say people have been critical of you and you've listened too much. It's affected your self-confidence."

That's just weird. How does she know that? It's spooky.

"Maybe," I admit with a shrug.

"Hopefully, today will begin your healing process. Maybe try meditating regularly or do some yoga. You need to start finding your inner confidence and take your power back."

"You make it sound so easy."

"Well, it's not easy, but it doesn't have to be too difficult either, and it'll be worth it. Sometimes we need to get out of our own way and break the learned behaviour of the past."

"Have you met my mother?"

"Ah."

"I'm not saying she's the source of all my problems."

"Of course not. But you know, how others treat you is their own karma, how you react is entirely yours."

My face scrunches up as the power of her words strikes me.

"What I mean is, you can choose how you react to her words. You can accept them and use them to beat yourself up with. Or, secret option number two is to ignore them. Let her words wash over your shield without striking you."
"Oh. Um," I murmur, at a loss what to say. I've never thought of it like that. It sounds so easy. I can choose how to react. Huh. She explains more about this energy shield and how to use it.
Finishing my appointment with Irene, I head home, quite frankly, in a bit of a daze. There's a lot to think about. And I still feel a bit odd, not in a bad way, just different.

Chapter 30 - Festivity

December disappears in a blur of fir. I've landed a couple of contracts with hotels who requested Christmas decorations after seeing my wedding flowers. There's trees to decorate and stunning festive brides to provide for.

Christmas weddings are lovely. It may be really cold, but there's something very romantic about them. The reds, golds and greens of the season lend themselves to the occasion. It's so sumptuous and almost regal.

My weight loss has continued nicely, by the way. I've got my two stone award; eep. In the nick of time for the gorging season. I know a little bit will go back on over Christmas, but I'm aiming for damage limitation.

There's still a long way to go, but I'm getting there. Wendy made me face some of my old photos the other day. There's not many, as I avoided the camera like the plague. The comparison is really quite dramatic already. If the evidence wasn't in front of me in the photographs, I don't think I'd believe it.

My health is still in jeopardy, but my doctor is happy with my progress. I'm in a much better position now than I was five months ago. It's really important to focus on that; how far I've come.

My mother is still pestering me to bring Nick to hers for dinner. I've been avoiding it. I don't think I can bear her opinion of my boyfriend. If she hates him it'll make my life harder, as they'll be this obstacle in the way. Another one, I should say. It's not as if my relationship with her is easy, is it?

On the other hand, she may like him. In which case I'll wonder what's wrong with him, and perhaps end the relationship. There must be something seriously wrong with someone she approves of. It's a no-win situation.

However, she's doing a big Christmas Day meal, and I've been forced into agreeing to take Nick. His own family live far away, lucky him. People don't stop dying just because it's Christmas. In fact, the mortality rate seems to go up. So it's tricky for him to visit his folks. So, the poor fool has agreed to meet my mother.

We've really been struggling to meet up, and it's becoming increasingly frustrating. I really like him. Is it so much to ask to spend time with my boyfriend? I do need to take some of the blame though, as Holly Molly work has taken up a great deal of my attention.

When I went back to Irene last week I decided to try the Emotional Freedom Technique. It was another fully clothed thing, and it sounded intriguing. Irene tapped points on my arms and head as she announced, "I deeply and completely accept myself." It sounded silly until she made me repeat the words. Amazingly, their meaning seemed to strike a chord deep within me, like a harp being played. It's difficult to explain, but it felt…hmm, it resonated with me.

We talked about some key issues, including ones from my childhood. No, you don't get details about what the issues were. Come on, I'm being really open here, but there's limits, you know.

Anyway, the tapping was repeated, and I was encouraged to let the hurt go. Irene had asked me how I felt about those issues before and after. Before, some had been an eight or nine (ten being the worst). Afterwards, they scored a zero. How can that be? Shouldn't these things take months of therapy? But as hard as I tried I could no longer feel upset about them.

My strides were more confident and my spirits soared as I walked to my van. I felt happy. It was incredible.

I also decided to take a Reiki level one course, to learn how to do it myself. Even if it's for my own personal use and I never go on to train to help others, this feels important.

So, a calmer, more confident me is now driving to my parents' house. Nick is going to meet me there as he was working last night. Not at all awkward (cough). But it's up to him. He's the one walking into the lion's den.

Father opens the door to me, as Mother is stressing, err, busy in the kitchen. He's wearing smart shirt and trousers as per the 'wear something nice' dress code. Foil decorations adorn the ceiling, and fake foliage is woven in between the banisters.

Father takes the opportunity to wrap his arms around me in a big hug.

"You look wonderful," he whispers with a proud smile as he steps back.

"Thank you," I reply, blushing.

I'm not used to compliments. How does one respond?

"I mean it. You always have been beautiful to me, but now you're even more so."

His stammering and sideward glances suggest he feels as awkward as I do.

"Alright, come on, don't keep me standing on the doorstep."

"Rightho."

He leads the way through to the sitting room, and hands me a glass of sherry. Well, it is Christmas.

"A bit of Dutch courage for the day," my father whispers with a cheeky wink.

I take a grateful sip of the sickly liquid just as my phone beeps with a text alert.

"Sorry, I'm running late. Trying to leave asap."

Of course it's Nick. But he's still at work? I thought he was heading home for sleep and having a rest before coming here?

Pushing myself up with my arms, I manage to eject myself from the very plush sofa, and make my way to the kitchen. Rubbing the base of my throat, I approach the mother-shaped tornado.

"He's running late."

"Pardon? Late? How late?" she asks, slamming trays in the oven and putting pans of water on the hob.

The kitchen is a disaster zone; bowls and pans are scattered on every available surface. She does know there's only four people dining, right?

"I'm not sure, he's caught at work. It's not a problem. We'll eat when dinner's ready, and can keep a plate warm for him if it comes to that. I just wanted to let you know."

"Most kind, thank you. Here, take these to share with your father," she commands in a clipped tone whilst shoving a plate of appetisers in my hand.

That's my cue to leave her alone. She hates other people in her kitchen when she's cooking.

I smile sweetly, but grit my teeth and roll my eyes as soon as my back's turned. She knows I'm on a diet, but there's pastry galore in my hands. I even reminded her I won't need much food, but still she has to go over the top.

My father notices my pained expression and spreads his hands in his 'there's no stopping her' way. I return the gesture with a weak smile, and only pop one treat in my mouth, then flump back down onto the sofa. I push the plate towards the lovely man sitting in the armchair near me, hoping to keep temptation out of my reach.

Bless him, he's already munching his way through a few of the delicious appetisers. My hand reaches out to one, but he gently swipes it away.

"You don't want to undo your hard work," he gently admonishes.

I smile gratefully at him, through slightly watery eyes. He's my hero. My heart sinks a little as the thought occurs to me that Nick should be here to help too. The man's a gannet, but doesn't seem to put much weight on.

We watch rubbish on TV, turning the sound up to drown out the clattering, grunting and colourful vocabulary coming from the kitchen. I wish she'd let me help, but Mother is master of her little catering world. Sweet cherub-like choir boys blare out carols, lending a far more wholesome atmosphere.

The lights on the Christmas tree are twinkling colourfully from the corner of the room, its baubles all gold and red. Tinsel in the same colour scheme adorns every shelf in here.

My father doesn't ask any awkward questions and says nothing of his own life. He's a very quiet man, and we sit in comfortable silence and let time pass by. It's wonderful. I'm enveloped in the squishy confines of the sofa and feel the homely relaxation warm my soul.

Nick still hasn't shown up when Mother calls us into the dining room. My parents are very traditional, and my father is called upon to carve the turkey at the table as we women help ourselves from bowls of 'trimmings'.

The place setting next to me is embarrassingly empty. Everything is ready for the vacant guest. My hand involuntarily rubs my arm as I stare into the void, but force myself to look away, and survey the feast.

There's enough food to feed an army, but I try not to overindulge. Only a couple of 'pigs in blankets' and roast potatoes find their way onto my plate, and a smidgen of stuffing. The vegetables get piled high, and I grab some beautifully carved turkey, oh, and a single Yorkshire pudding. It all gets drowned in gravy. I'm trying to be good but I have my limits. With tummies fit to bursting, we all sit back in our chairs a little, struggling to digest the plethora of food we managed to consume.

"I'll get it," my father announces as the doorbell chimes.

The conversation isn't quite audible, but the murmurs sound friendly. Then Nick is led into the dining room. He's had the good sense to bring some flowers for my mother and has a bag of presents in his other hand.

"I'm so sorry I'm late," he says to all of us as he bends down to kiss my cheek.

My mother stands and shakes his hand.

"You must be Nick," she says with a smile, but I see the speculation in her eyes.

"I am, and again, I'm so so sorry for my rude arrival."

He looks humble as he glances down at the floor and then to my father and I, unable to withstand the withering gaze of my mother.

"Sit down, and help yourself," Mother offers too sweetly.

"Anyone for seconds?" she asks Father and I, overly emphasising the last word.

Nick is hesitating, clearly feeling the tension he's created. So, despite my protesting stomach, I dish up some more turkey and veg. And you have to have some stuffing and gravy with that. Oh, how did that little piggy get onto my plate?

It's a lot smaller, but I basically eat another meal, just to make Nick feel better. Why? He was late, it's his own fault. But I took pity on him. It's not really his fault, and he looked so abashed.

My father is likewise forcing more food down, having momentarily disappeared to put the flowers in water. My mother is sitting with her arms folded, looking on with disdain. I pull Nick's cracker with him in a vain attempt to lighten the mood.

My mother only smiles once Nick thanks her and compliments the food.

"Oh, it was nothing really," she dismisses, but everyone knows better and appreciates her effort.

We sit sipping wine after we finish eating, and start talking, as my parents attempt to get to know Nick. But Mother clearly hasn't fully forgiven his late arrival, and my father isn't loud enough to take charge of the conversation.

"So, you were at work?" she quizzes.

"Yes. Sorry. I thought I'd be able to get away sooner than I did."

"Were you really cutting people up on Christmas Day?" she sneers.

"Actually no. I was analysing a sample of vitreous humor, but I suspect you don't really want to hear about that."

"That's the gooey eye bit," I add, hammering the point home.

It has the desired effect. Mother pales, and her hand goes to her mouth. Well, she started it. And I have to admit, it feels good to strike back. Maybe it shouldn't. Maybe that makes me a bad person. But my inner self is smirking. Take that.

Everyone is silent for a very uncomfortable few minutes of mild throat clearing and finger drumming. Well, what do you say after that?

Mother disappears, but returns, carrying a flaming Christmas pudding, just as I think a pocket of space may have emerged in my tummy. We're all forced to have some, and of course there's brandy butter to dollop on top of it.

A much more civil conversation ensues, thanks mainly to Nick's efforts.

Somehow, we manage to waddle into the sitting room afterwards, where Mother brings us coffee, and we begin to open our presents.

Nick bought my appreciative father a good bottle of whisky, and a very nice silk scarf for my now softening mother. His relentless charm and good nature seem to be winning her over.

I get perfume, chocolates and gift vouchers from my parents, as usual. Eurgh, chocolate. Thanks then. But my jaw falls open as I unwrap the beautiful bracelet from Nick. It's made of a rainbow of crystals, like the colours of the chakras Irene showed me. Tears prick my eyes as I hug him in gratitude. It's the most thoughtful gift anyone has ever given me.

Once we've stayed the socially acceptable amount of time, Nick and I make our excuses to leave.

"I like him," Father whispers as he hugs me goodbye.

We reach our vehicles, and Nick pulls me in for a quick kiss.

"I really need to go and get some sleep, gorgeous, but I'll dream of you."

Disappointment flitters across my face before I can conceal it.

"I'm sorry. Can I come over to do our own Christmas properly tomorrow?" he asks.

"Mmm," is all I can say with a nod, not trusting my voice.

I give him a quick hug and make a swift exit, only allowing the tears to fall as I drive away. How can he do this to me? I understand he's tired, I do. But I can't help feeling let down by him today.

He was embarrassingly late to an important meal with my parents, and now he's deserting me.

Couldn't he have come round my house, as we'd planned? I'm tired too, we could've napped together.

My house is empty and dark as I walk in, alone. I dump my presents in the lounge, and dash out into the garden for a much-needed cigarette. Today, I survived my mother's scrutiny. I was prepared for that, and was able to ignore the digs. Mostly.

Yes, she still pointed out my bad bits, and how I could do better. But I refused to let myself get hurt by her barbed words. I accept it's her warped way of showing she cares about me. She doesn't mean to offend, only to help.

No, today, the hurt was caused by my boyfriend. I wasn't prepared for that. Today of all days I expected him to put the effort into being on time, and making the best possible impression. Was this his best? More tears fall as I silently admit to myself that maybe it is, and his best just isn't good enough.

I'm worth more than this. Maybe it's taken me too long to realise it. But Wendy was right. There's ways of making things work if you want to. Nick and I aren't working, and maybe neither of us really want to. Neither of us seem to be putting in the effort required of a serious relationship.

Is this it? Is it time to call it quits?

Chapter 31 – Gifts

Just before lunchtime, Nick comes to my door with another gift-wrapped present in hand.

"I always seem to be apologising, but I truly am sorry about yesterday," he tells me before I can get a word in.

What do I do? Panicking, I decide to let him into my home. My heartstrings are being plucked again. My determination waivers, as I deliberate on my own reasonability. Maybe I was being too hasty. He's here now, isn't he?

Having planned on him being here after what was supposed to be a lovely cosy night together, there was food in the fridge in preparation. A healthy version of homity pie is in the oven, cooking to golden perfection.

"I'd be lying if I said I wasn't upset."

"And you have every right to be," he tells me softly.

Sure do!

"I need someone dependable," I tell him, putting my proverbial cards on the table.

"I don't want to lose you."

His hand brushes my cheek so tenderly, and his eyes are filled with remorse. Oh, what can I say to that? Full lips find mine, and the soft warmth of them makes me forget the sentence which was trying to form. Our mouths part, and I am lost in lust. Need takes over, and the heat melts what was left of my resolve.

"Am I forgiven then?" he asks.

In reply, my hands pull on his back to bring his body closer to mine and we deepen our kiss. Flames are licking my body from root to tip. I need Nick, need to feel him in me, to be together with him.

I turn off the oven before we head into my bedroom. Our clothes are rapidly discarded and I cling to his body, relishing the skin-to-skin contact. Our hands are all over each other, clawing for unity.

Our bodies join and I surrender to the overwhelming sensation. Friction builds and he fills me with bliss. We writhe and thrust, desperate for satisfaction.

My hips pump to match his rhythm, in time with the soundless drumbeats. The glorious push and pull drags me over and under the waves of desire. My nails dig into his butt cheeks, urging him on as I ride up the crest.

Pounding, thrusting, we move in harmony.

Grinding, pulling, we mount the summit.

His mouth sucks on the sweet spot on my neck and I come undone. My climax bursts into a thousand rainbow coloured bubbles, leaving me gasping for air.

As my back arches into him, Nick finds his own release, forcing moans of pleasure from his lips. We sink back into the mattress, feeling sated.

Regaining my breath, I roll over and cuddle into his side. His arm drapes across my waist, pulling me close for the sweet nipped kisses which make me feel cherished. I allow myself a few moments to linger in dreamy delight.

My stomach rumbles, and the spell is broken.

"Um, are you hungry?" I ask, looking up into his smiling eyes.

"Only for you, but come on, let's feed you."

I get up and dressed, immediately feeling remorse creep in. I'm supposed to be breaking up with this man, but somehow we ended up in bed. What was I thinking?

But as we make our way downstairs I can't seem to remember why I thought splitting up was a good idea. How can I leave a guy that makes me feel this way?

I turn the oven back on to finish cooking lunch. My back leans against Nick's front as I stand up. His arms wrap around me as he nuzzles my neck. A grin crosses my cheeks as he breathes deeply into my hair. If he carries on like this, we'll end up in bed again already.

It takes enormous self-control to dish up the food and not myself.

Ignoring my conflicting thoughts, I sit there eating humble, err, homity pie with my boyfriend. It's so annoying. He's so wonderful when he's like this. I wish this was more frequent, that's all. Just enjoy the moment, Molly. Go with the flow.

"This is delicious," he tells me.

"Thank you. And completely allowed on my diet. It's so nice when you find something that tastes naughty, but isn't."

"You're really getting into cooking, aren't you?"

"Maybe," I reply with a coy grin.

He pulls out the present he'd picked up from the hall on our way through, and hands it to me.

"Merry Christmas."

His accompanying grin is so boyishly joyous that it's infectious. I rip the paper off, and find a healthy eating cookery book.

"Thank you so much."

I go and hug him, and get pulled into his lap.

"You're welcome," he tells me with a kiss.

"I don't have anything else to give you," I apologise. I don't. I'd given him a leather-bound diary and a posh pen yesterday. They seem a bit pale in comparison to his thoughtful gifts.

"You've already given me enough," he says hoarsely before stealing another kiss.

The rest of the evening is wonderful, as we luxuriate in each other's company. But then he has to go and ruin it.

"I'd better head off."

"You're not staying?"

"As much as I'd love to, I have an early start tomorrow."

"Oh. I guess you'd better go then."

"I've had a lovely time with you. Please don't be like that and spoil it."

"Oh, I'm the one ruining it?"

The words are sulky and beneath me, but they're out before I can stop them. Besides, maybe he should hear how annoyed I am; how much it hurts when he runs away.

"I can't speak to you if you're going to be childish."

"Childish? Wanting to spend time with my boyfriend is childish?" I ask, my voice getting louder and higher.

"You're being petulant, and you know it. This is my job."

"And this is my life," I shout, rising out of the chair.

"I'm going before we both say something we regret," he announces, glowering as he stands.

He practically runs out the door. I watch in stunned silence as he drives away without even looking back. The door gets slammed shut and kicked as my frustration finds an escape route.

"Argh, how can I be so stupid?" I rant to the empty hall.

He's so annoying. It was all going so well, and now I'm right back where I started, thinking I'd be better off without him. It's Christmas, can't he stop thinking about work for five minutes? Can't we just be us for a whole day?

A few days pass and neither of us have broken the silence after our fight. I keep flipping between letting the relationship fizzle out, and wanting to try harder to make it work. Should it be this difficult? It is it worth it? What do I really want?

My doorbell rings, and I shlump my way over to answer it. There's a man standing there with a basket of fruit.

"Molly Wilkinson?"

"Yes."

"Sign here, please."

I do as requested, and take the basket from the delivery driver. Scurrying inside, I read the note:

"*Roses are red*

Violets are blue

Flowers are forbid

So here's some fruit for you.

Sorry we fought. Please forgive me."

Hmph, well, it's a sweet sentiment, but I don't know. Can I keep going through all this? He's constantly apologising, and that's not fair on either of us.

I send him a text, thanking him for the fruit.

"Can I come over to talk?" he sends back.

"Not yet. I think I need some time to think. Sorry."
"OK. Tell me as soon as you're ready. I'll be waiting."

So, no pressure then. I really need some head space. I can't keep yo-yoing. When he's away I know what should be done, but as soon as he's with me I'm so pathetically grateful and happy I can't let him go. And it's making my head spin. Maybe some time on my own will give me back some perspective.

Holly Molly is a hive of activity once more as more couples tie the knot, Christmas gets disassembled, and engagement flowers are ordered for the new year.

I'm too exhausted to attend any new year's eve parties, despite both Nick and Wendy trying to entice me. It's only another night. Nothing dramatic happens. A crowd of people gather in a venue to get drunk and cheer as the bells of Big Ben get played on a naff stereo. Not my idea of fun, sorry.

***

As the business quietens down once more, I attend my level one Reiki training. I've found someone close who teaches it, and my nerves are jangling as I make my way to her house. My mind tries to guess what the other students will be like, and whether I'll fit in. Part of me knows it's foolish, but I still fear others mocking me. Having been teased at school so often, I still half expect it now.

A lovely lady with blonde hair and blue eyes smiles as she lets me in. This is Moira, the Reiki Master. She immediately shows me the selection of tea I can help myself to as she welcomes another student. We're shown into the room where we'll be learning, and I instantly feel calmer. There's a tranquil feeling in here, a peace permeates the air.

Once everyone's arrived, we're talked through the basics, before being taken outside to perform the ritual which will align us to the level one energy. It feels a little odd, but humbling at the same time, as if I'm being given a great gift.

We get taught more details about what the energy is and how we interact with it before we're shown the symbols and how to connect. Moira uses me as the guinea pig student. We get to practise on each other afterwards. My hands feel warm as I concentrate on receiving the energy through my head and sending it out through my hands.

We break for lunch, and Moira takes me to one side. "I didn't want to say in front of the group. But sometimes when we channel Reiki our loved ones in spirit drop in. I felt a female presence near you, related to your dad, I think."

"Yes, that will be my grandmother," I inform her, astonished at this news.

"She said to tell you that you're doing really well, but can do better."

"Oh."

"She's been watching over you. She showed me a bee."

"Oh my God." My mouth drops open as she gives me this information.

Tears spring to my eyes and my hands spring to cover my gawping mouth as I acknowledge, "It *was* her."

"Does the message make sense? She wants you to be happier. To be more. Claim your power."

"Oh yes, thank you."

I excuse myself and have a cigarette in Moira's garden, tears trickling down my cheeks. My grandmother is watching over me. I feel elated and comforted by this revelation. But she has also confirmed my own feelings. The moment is bittersweet.

Pulling myself together, I rejoin the group for lunch and an afternoon of learning, feeling somewhat distracted.

Returning home, there's homework to go through, so I bury myself in studying. There's only time to grab a quick dinner as I immerse myself in this new world of knowledge.

As I sleepily climb the stairs for bed my feet stop in their tracks. There's a single white feather halfway up. Bending down to pick it up, a smile spreads across my face. I let myself feel my grandmother's loving presence.

"Thank you," I whisper, and go to bed happy.

The next day of training is really enjoyable, and we all sign up to the group's social media page. Once I get home I find some new friend invites. I made new friends!

***

Mother has summonsed me. Nick and I had a fight, but somehow even this is public knowledge. Not that she came out and said that, of course. She invited me to Sunday lunch, but there was no option of turning down the offer. I'm really not in the mood.

True to form, it starts as soon as she opens the door; the wave of warnings.

"I hope you're not cutting off your nose to spite your face. What have you done now? Don't be foolish and send him away in one of your miffs."

"Hello, Mother," I say pointedly, pushing past to enter the house.

Why? The easiest thing, the sensible thing is surely to turn around and seek the safety of my own home. It's baffling that I don't. It's with some bewilderment I find myself marching inside.

"Hello, sweetheart," Father greets me, standing up from his armchair to give me a hug.

I hold onto him a moment longer than normal, enjoying the brief moment of safety and love.

"I've done roast chicken. That's OK isn't it, for your diet? You are still dieting, aren't you? You don't want to go back to your old ways," Mother says in a flurry as I sit down.

"Thank you, Mother. Yes, I am still eating healthily." This is taking all my strength, but I sound remarkably calm.

How you react is your own karma. Do not rise to the bait. I can ignore her poisoned barbs. Deep breath; I have my auric shield up. Nothing gets in without my permission. Ommm.

"You look like you've put weight on. You're not comfort eating, are you?"

The rustling noise next to me signals my father's retrieval of his newspaper, which he uses as his own shield. It's held up high in front of his face but I'm sure he wouldn't be able to tell me what's in any of the articles if I asked.

"No, Mother. I am being very good. And my weight is actually still going down."

Not that it's any of her business anyway. What if I was stuffing my face with junk? I'm not. But so what? It's my body.

"I'm pleased to hear it. Now, what's all this about?" she asks, taking her place in an adjacent chair.

"You invited me for lunch."

"That is not what I meant, and you know it. Don't get smart with me, young lady."

"Oh, you mean why am I not speaking to Nick?" I ask, my mouth pinched, my eyes wide.

"Yes, of course. Really, I don't know where this attitude has come from."

"Well, Nick fucked me and kicked me out of his house straight away." Have that. Ding ding, round one.

Fine, so I just don't have the energy to face him yet. I have no idea if I want to turn to or from him forever. And until I know what I'm doing, I can't see him. He'll confuse me and I'll keep running around in circles. But she's not getting the full explanation.

Mother's eyebrows seem to be attempting to jump off her forehead. "Really. There's no need for such language. I was only asking."

"Were you? Just asking? Asking what? Why I look fat? Why I'm deciding whether to pursue my relationship? Why I'm having to answer to you, despite being a grown woman?"

Her mouth opens and shuts as she struggles for words, but she finds some. "I just want you to be happy."

"Really? How's that? With constant criticism? Reminding me every time we speak how I don't match up to your exacting standards?" Both my tone and pitch rise along with my temper.

"To help guide you to be your best."

"But that's just it. I am already my best. At any given time I am the best I can be. It may not be the best in your eyes, in the fairy princess ideal of a daughter you wish you had, but it's still my best." My voice cracks as I fight back angry tears.

"I...I..."

"You what? Want me to achieve unattainable greatness? Be with a man, because that's the only way to be happy? Well, I can be happy on my own."

"Of course. But wouldn't it be nice to find love?" she tries.

"Love? Yes. It'd be good to be loved. But I'm not even sure whether *you* love me. Do you?" I shoot my fury at her with my words and eyes.

There's an audible gasp from her corner. "What a question. Of course I love you. You're my daughter." I'm pretty sure I look like a hurt puppy as I gaze across. "Do you? You really love me? Not the daughter you think I should be. Not out of duty. But me. All of me. The good, the fat and the temperamental? Because all of that is who I am. I'm not perfect, but that's me."

"I do. I love you, Molly," she tells me through tears, and reaches forwards to hug me.

Big fat tears roll down my cheeks as I return the hug. "I love you too."

"Oh, my darling baby girl."

Sobs shake the both of us as we latch on to one another.

"You make me proud every day. You're beautiful, strong and independent. So independent it scares me. I worry you don't need me anymore," she says between bursts of breath and tears.

"I will always need you."

"I think some tea is in order," Father announces as he gets up to make said beverage.

As we pull ourselves together, wiping away our tears, catching our breath, I have to say it. "I'm sorry."

"Oh darling. I'm sorry. I never meant to hurt you."

"I know. Deep down, I know that."

"I'll try to be better. To not sound so critical. I had no idea you felt this way."

"Thank you. Some words of kind encouragement would be good."

"I'll try."

Lunch is somewhat subdued after that. But no harsh words are spoken.

Chapter 32 – Retreat

Still dithering over the Nick situation, I decide a walk
in the park may help clear my head. The rain's finally
stopped, for the first time this week, and I want to
make the most of this opportunity.

A sadness fills my heart as I tread the path Nick once
walked with me. I had hope then, but that seems to
have died. The expectation was we'd spend more
and more time together as a couple, but the opposite
has happened.

My steps get heavier but faster as my mind processes
the thoughts I've been battling with. Deep down, I
know there's no future with Nick. But my heart
doesn't want to let him go. He's so lovely when
we're actually together. I've been hoping to build
bridges, to reach him, to bring us closer. Is there a
way?

Maybe I'm giving up too easily. Perhaps I should be
more flexible. I always knew he worked anti-social
hours, so who's really to blame here?

One of the things we did on the Reiki course was a
guided meditation. That had a specific purpose, but I
asked Moira for more information on general ones.
She kindly sent me a link to an online tutorial on self-
meditation. As I reach the park I find a bench and sit
down.

Ensuring there's nobody nearby, I close my eyes and
take some long deep breaths. In my mind, there's a
stone staircase which I walk down, holding a golden
handrail. There's an ornate wooden door in front of
me, which opens to a green lawn. I walk down the
gentle slope, down to a meadow of wild flowers, and
down to a pond.

This is a safe haven. I kneel down by the stream and gaze into the still water. Images of my time with Nick appear. Our first meeting, romantic meals, bedroom athletics with rumpled duvets, but then his back is directed at me as he walks away, the door closing behind him, our increasing arguments, me alone and upset.

"You're being petulant," rings in my ears.

My vision self gets up, makes her way back up the slope, the lawn and the stairs. My actual body wriggles my fingers, and my eyes slowly open. I'm aware of the cold air chilling my cheeks and nose again.

I know what I must do.

***

Back at home, I make a tea, trying to summon the courage to make the call. The hot drink warms me, but my nerves are still jangling. There's never a good time, so it might as well be now.

I chew my lip and rub my throat as Nick's phone rings. Will he pick up? Don't make me leave a message and wait, please. It's going to go to voicemail, isn't it?

"Hello," he answers at last.

The sound of hope in his voice has my stomach butterflies fluttering like crazy.

"Hi," I begin quietly, "I've been thinking. Can you come over for dinner?"

"Uh oh," he murmurs.

"We need to talk."

"That's never a good phrase, but alright. I'll be there as soon as I finish work today. It's hard to give you an exact time."

"I understand. Thank you."

***

The wait seems eternal. My work sketches lie abandoned on the table as I realise there will be no progress made with them today.

The 'creation station' is infuriatingly tidy already, so I head back into the house again. I vacuum spotless floors and plump already fluffed up cushions. This is driving me crazy.

Phhw! The knife slices into my finger, missing the intended onion. Running over to the sink, I hold it under cold running water before wrapping a piece of kitchen towel around it to stem the flow of blood. Gingerly holding my finger up out of harm's way, I continue chopping and dicing the ingredients for a chilli con carne. It's healthy, warming, and it can bubble away until Nick makes an appearance.

Even with my injury, it doesn't take very long to prepare, and I find myself pacing around the house aimlessly. When is he going to get here?

My feet carry me up to the bathroom where I take a shower. Even this doesn't wash away my troubles. My wound reopens as I move my finger too quickly in my shampooing fury. Once I'm sud-free, I step out of the shower and wrap a large towel around myself and grab a plaster out of the cabinet. It gets tightly coiled around my finger, hopefully stopping any further mishaps.

Make up gets applied, despite my throbbing finger. And a brush gets dragged through my hair as I dry it. My mind is constantly fixed Nick. I'm doing the right thing, aren't I?

I squeeze into one of my smarter little black dresses, needing the confidence it offers, and walk downstairs. The bubbling pot of chilli gets a stir, and I pour myself a glass of wine. What? Caffeine's not helping, maybe this will?

Pacing around the kitchen, I sip my wine and wonder what Nick's reaction will be. Maybe this is a really bad idea. I'm being stupid. Foolhardy. Impulsive. Rash.

Sod's Law dictates that just as I'm thinking of backing out, the doorbell chimes.

"Hello gorgeous," he greets me with a peck on my cheek as I open the door.

"Hi Nick, come on in," I reply, squeezing his arm. Leading the way to the kitchen, I pour him a glass of wine and top mine up. I can't look him in the eyes, or find the right words at the moment, so busy myself with dishing up.

"Why don't you go and take a seat at the table? I won't be a moment," I suggest.

"Um, yeah, OK," he says, running his hand through his hair, frowning.

He may look unsure and confused, but he silently wanders off, leaving me to grab the rice which has been kept warm in the oven. Our meal gets dished up in a hurry in my eagerness to get this over and done with.

Placing the plates on the table, I catch Nick's gaze. His grey eyes are squinting at me in the low light as I take my seat.

"Nick. Look…" I start, but his hand holds mine to the table, halting me.

"Molly, please don't do this. I think we could really have something here. I know it's been difficult, but I'm willing to try harder. Please don't throw it away. Give us a chance."

I can't help breathe a sigh of relief. He's clearly got the wrong end of the stick, but it makes what I'm about to say a lot easier.

"No. You thought I was breaking up with you? No. Nick, I…I've been giving it a lot of thought. And yes, I did think maybe we should call things off, but my heart wouldn't let me."

Nick huffs out a long breath. "You're not breaking up with me?"

"No," I smile and shake my head, "Nick, I think I love you."

He beams back, and hoarsely tells me, "I know I love you."

Oh, my insides are turning into putty. He just said he loves me. Eep!

"The problem is we're not together enough."

"Yeah, I appreciate that. I don't know what to do. I've been trying to think about it, but I can't do much about my hours."

"No, I know. I'm not asking you to. It's your job, and I respect that. But, um, what if maybe you moved in with me?"

The world just stopped spinning, I'm sure of it. A deafening silence has descended as Nick gawps at me.

"Well?" I check.

"You mean it?" he asks, his eyes as wide as his grin.

I nod with a, "Mm hmm."

305

The world kicks into action again as he tells me, "I'd love to. If you're sure. This is your house, and I don't want to intrude on your territory."

"I've given it serious consideration. I need my workspace, and you're only renting your flat, so it's easier for you to leave there and join me."

"Well yes, but it's a huge step. Are you sure you're ready for me to be part of your life?"

"Yes. I want to spend more time with you, and this seems the best way of doing that. I don't know. You know when something just makes sense? When it feels right?"

He nods. "Yes, I certainly do."

He gets up from the table and holds my hands, encouraging me to my feet so he can wrap me in his strong arms. The reassuring hug is swiftly followed by a passionate kiss, and our dinner is left uneaten on the table as we make our way to my bedroom. Our bedroom.

Chapter 33 – New Beginnings

We didn't waste any time. Nick's lease still has a couple of months to go, but he's not having to pay me rent, so he vacated his flat within the week.
It's weird having someone else share my personal space. But he scores brownie points for not leaving the loo seat up. He does squeeze the toothpaste from the wrong place though, but that's not too bad in the great scheme of things, is it?
"I don't want to take over, or invade, but it'd be nice to have some of my own things here," he pointed out as he moved his few possessions in.
His flat came fully furnished, so there's really not many of his belongings. We've hung some of his pictures up. And I've agreed we can redecorate a couple of rooms, so our tastes blend. We've still got to agree on colours though; I favour muted, pastel tones, whilst he goes more for bold colours, but there will be a happy medium somewhere.
The bathroom door has to be closed whilst the toilet's used now. I keep forgetting, which is a bit embarrassing, but he's seen me naked, so it's not that big a deal. At least, it shouldn't be. Yeah, it's taking some getting used to.
He often has early starts, but not as early as mine, so I have to creep around in the dark, trying not to wake him up.
Only a couple of weeks have sped by. It's too soon to make judgements, but on the whole, his presence is a welcome if weird change. We're getting to see a bit more of each other, which was the whole point.

And tonight, Wendy and Gary are coming round for a mini housewarming dinner. Pots and pans are bubbling on the hob. Nick's helping chop and stir; very homely. And of course, hugs get mixed in whilst we cook.

The doorbell interrupts one such hug, and we both rush to the door to welcome our guests. Another odd thing. It's been my house for so long, and now it's ours, and we both open the door. Not that that's a complaint. It's lovely. Just new.

Wendy holds up a big bottle of champagne as she crosses the threshold, making her way in to hug me.

"Congratulations you two," she says as she squeezes us each in turn.

"Thank you," I struggle to reply from her vice-like grip.

The boys shake hands and nod; so macho.

"Come in," I tell them, ushering us all into the dining room.

Gary hands over two gift bags I'd not noticed.

"You didn't have to buy us anything," I gently admonish, glancing at them.

"Of course we did," Wendy dismisses with a wave of her hand.

I laugh as I unwrap the first present.

"Samurai kitchen knives," I exclaim.

They're very Nick. Not quite so me, but hey, I'm accommodating his stuff, right?

"Well, a pathologist needs something to slice and dice with at home," Wendy says with a smirk.

"There's something for you too," she tells me, still grinning.

"But I live here already."

"Shut up and open it," Wendy orders, rolling her eyes.

"Oh it's perfect. Thank you," I say through laughter as I unwrap a little bee house.

Dangling the wooden ornament in front of my face, I examine it closer. It's so cute, and my little bee friend should be most happy with it.

"I'd better go dish up," I announce, rising to my feet.

"I'll come and help," Wendy says, getting up too.

As we get to the kitchen, she grabs her opportunity.

"So, how's it really going? Are you playing house nicely?" she asks with a nudge and a smirk.

"It's OK."

"Only OK?" Her eyebrows rise.

"It's more than OK. It's great. But I'm still getting used to it."

"That's understandable. Maybe try being patient."

"Not like my usual self, you mean?" I ask, looking out the corner of my eye as I dollop some rice into a large serving bowl.

"I didn't mean it like that, and you know it," she tells me with a gentle nudge.

We carry bowls of curries and rice, and plates of poppadums, pickles and naan bread through to the boys. The main offerings are healthy, so I've snuck in a few treats and beer; this is a celebration, after all.

"This looks and smells delicious," Gary announces, helping himself to a bit from every dish.

We talk and laugh our way through the meal. I can't begin to tell you how wonderful this is. It just feels right, and fills me with a warm glow. Or maybe that's the beer? No, it's definitely the company.

"We have an announcement of our own," Wendy says.

I shoot her a querying glance.

"Gary's asked me to move in with him."

"Oh my God, that's amazing. Congratulations," I squeal, trying not to spill my drink as I hug her.

"I think Nick inspired him," she says with a wink.

"I do hope so," Nick says, grinning.

"To happy homes," he adds on a cheer, holding up his glass.

We all chink glasses together and chant, "To happy homes."

We sneak in another hug before clearing the table.

"Congratulations, mate," I hear Nick tell Gary.

But then he emerges in the kitchen behind me.

"Hello," I say, a little surprised as he pecks my cheek.

"I couldn't let you ladies have all the fun out here. Go on. Sit down. I'll bring in dessert."

Wendy raises her eyebrows in impressed amusement.

"What? This isn't the seventies," I remind her in what I thought was a hushed tone.

"It's certainly not," Nick says to our retreating backs.

Oops, the alcohol's getting to my head already. A giggle bursts from me, which has Wendy echoing it.

"What's so funny?" Gary asks as we rejoin him.

"Oh nothing," we both chime.

Poor Gary shakes his head at us. "If you say so."

Wendy smooches him as she sits back down by his side.

"Ooh, my favourite," Wendy admires, licking her lips as the Eton Mess is brought in by my live-in boyfriend.

It's my turn to get kissed, as Nick sits next to me.

Yes, I could definitely get used to this.

Chapter 34 - Bedding In

The months seem to fly by, and winter turns to spring. My happiness is blossoming along with my garden. Nick and I have been taking full advantage of our precious time together. Forgive me if this is too much information, but the term rabbit sex applies. Whenever time permits, we don't seem to be able to keep our hands off each other.

Aher, moving on. Communication seems key to the rest of our relationship. There's a calendar up on the wall, where we both mark the times we expect to be busy with work commitments. That way we can plan quality time together. It doesn't always work out that way, of course. Nick still gets called away, which is becoming easier to deal with. It's disappointing and frustrating, but at least I know he wants to be with me now.

It may be completely foolish, but my self-confidence really is growing. You shouldn't need a man for this, and I don't. But Nick does help. His love alone is a big boost. I feel desirable and cherished; worthy of someone's affection. And that someone is a good man; caring and supportive, and loves me just the way I am.

I would've got here on my own, but it may have taken me a little longer. The realisation that I am enough, the best version of myself, worthy of love from myself as much as others; yeah, that may have dawned a little later without Nick's support.

This all sounds plain sailing, doesn't it? Oh, my life is miraculously rosy and we live like a fairy tale prince and princess. Well, of course we don't. That's not what I'm trying to say. It's just a whole lot better than our previous situation.

If he's at home whilst I have client consultations he has to make himself scarce. Does this make me feel guilty? Yes. But it is necessary. Professionalism is important.

He often hides away in the kitchen during evening appointments, making dinner. Being able to eat straight after a late appointment is wonderful.

Being a bit of a genius, Nick's helped me find new ways of advertising. Holly Molly, the business, is now going from strength-to-strength. This is both a blessing and a curse, as it does tend to steal more time away from us, but helps fund our lifestyle.

When he's about, Nick joins me on my delivery rounds. It saves time and we often end up having a meal out together at the end of it.

Wendy and I thank our lucky stars that our partners get on as well as we do. We go round each other's houses quite often, even if one or two of us can't be there. We all have busy jobs, and it's really nice to have company if one of us is feeling lonely.

Nick and I are getting ready to go to their house now. Gary's apparently got a work thing to celebrate, so I've been told to dress nicely.

"I'm sure I can celebrate even better in jeans," I grumble for the umpteenth time at Nick.

"Mine is not to reason why. I only know Gary's really excited," he tells me, his hands held up in surrender.

With a quick check in the mirror, I'm ready. My weight is still on the way down, and an appreciative smile is reflected back at me.

"You look gorgeous, as always," Nick whispers in my ear as he hugs me from behind.

"You're looking pretty hot yourself."

He's so sexy in his smart shirt and trousers. And his aftershave is divine.

With a huge effort, I pull back from the ensuing kiss. It's very tempting to stay in the bedroom, and turn up late. But with Gary's big announcement, it'd be rude to keep him waiting.

We both sigh a little as we make our way downstairs and out to Nick's car.

My mouth starts watering as soon as Wendy opens the door.

"That smells scrumptious," I tell her.

"Thanks. Gary helped."

"Uh oh," I tease with a wink, approaching him in the hallway.

"Hey, you like my cooking," he reminds me.

"I do, and you know it."

They've been really busy. A host of Chinese dishes are brought out to the table, most of which are healthy choices, but no less tasty for that.

"So, what's the big news?" I ask, sipping my chicken and sweetcorn soup.

Gary does a very good impression of a fish as he works his mouth open and closed. Wendy scrunches her face up.

"What? Isn't it Nick with the news?" she asks.

"It's both of us, but you'll have to be patient," Nick interjects.

"What's going on?" I ask him, squinting.

"Nah uh, all in good time." He silences me with a brief kiss.

Wendy and I are left frowning and shrugging as if we were communicating in semaphore. After a few failed attempts of prompting the boys for more information, I take the hint and stop asking.

They can't both have work announcements, can they? I don't think they have any professional skills which would overlap enough for them to start a business together. Nick enjoys his job, and I don't think he'd give it up. Maybe I'm wrong.

Nick and Gary keep swapping furtive glances, whilst Wendy and I shoot each other querying ones. There's an uncomfortable silence as we try to eat the rest of the food.

"So, wedding season's picking up?" Gary asks me. Nick's glower at him doesn't escape me. What's his problem?

"Yes. The weather's finally beginning to warm up. Brides are coming out of hibernation," I quip, but nobody laughs.

Oh, this is horrible. We normally get on so well, but suddenly nobody has anything to say. I eat a little faster, hoping to bring an end to this awkward evening by escaping as soon as possible. Maybe we've all just had a bad day.

A mother and daughter quarrelled during their consultation today, and I was left playing peace keeper. But they were still bickering as they left. I was hoping tonight would help lift my spirits, not deflate them further.

The boys leap up to clear the table before I even have a chance to think about moving. Now, they're pretty good at doing their fair share, but this is enthusiastic, even for them.

"What's going on?" I whisper across to Wendy as we're left alone.

"I don't know."

"They wouldn't go into business together, would they?" I check my earlier hypothesis with her.

Wendy pulls a face like she's sucking a lemon. "No. They're too different. Aren't they?"

"I thought so. But I'm not so sure now. They're being very weird."

"What are you two whispering about?" Gary chides as he comes back in, carrying a plate of fortune cookies.

Well, at least that'll bring the meal to a close. I may politely skip coffee. Is feigning a headache too obvious?

We crack open our fortune cookies. It's a weird American tradition, so I'm not quite sure why we all insist on this every time we have a Chinese banquet. Just for fun, I suppose.

"What does yours say?" Nick asks me, leaning forwards and grinning.

"Will…you…marry me?" I slowly read aloud then shriek as I unravel the scroll.

Wendy is squealing too. We look at each other, our mouths hanging open.

"Are you serious?" we ask our partners in unison.

"Yes, deadly serious. So, what do you say?" Nick replies.

"Yes," I cry through my hands which are covering my mouth.

Tears roll down my cheeks as I'm pulled to my feet and wrapped in hugs and kisses. I manage to sneak a glance across at Wendy, who's in much the same position. Peeling away from our fiancés, we bound across and link arms, jumping up and down, making noises only dogs and bats would understand.

"I'm getting married," we scream at one another.

"Well, I think we can open the champagne now," Gary announces as he disappears to fetch said item.

"Oh my God, I can't believe you did this. This isn't a work thing," I say over to Nick.

"Well, we didn't want to ruin the surprise," he says, beaming.

My emotions are flying wildly around the room, my tummy butterflies have been released into the wild. I'm so relieved there was a good reason for the earlier awkwardness, and ecstatic I'm going to be married, and overjoyed for Wendy, and excited, and oh, my head is going a little dizzy.

"Cheers," we all chime as we clink glasses.

Chapter 35 – Dual

We've set a date for next June. None of us have big families, so it won't be a large affair. And it gives Wendy and me time to reach our target weight before our big day. Yes, the one day. She'll be my witness and then I'll be hers immediately after.

It's all going to take place at *the hotel*. It's a really beautiful venue, and as it's such a happy event, the wedding should wipe away any negative associations from the past. Turn a negative into a positive.

Needless to say, our mothers are horrified. It doesn't matter that others in our social circle have had small weddings, or not had a church ceremony. They expected better from us. And both getting married at once? Apparently this is vulgar. But you know what? We don't care. It's what we want to do. It was good enough for the sisters in Pride & Prejudice, after all.

As I meet with Holly Molly brides and their entourages, part of me is wondering what my own bouquet should be. Their excitement is even more infectious than normal.

I don't know how I'm going to wait over a year for my wedding, but at the same time, reality is still sinking in. Nick proposed. Can you believe it? It's all so sudden, but I know he's the one. Now we're living together, the way we fit is apparent.

Who would've thought it? I'm going to be a bride. It's happening.

My head is completely in the game. Getting into a stunning gown is a huge incentive to continue losing weight. Nick's brilliant at coming up with new recipes for us to try. And yoga is part of my routine now; another thing I never thought would happen. But it's actually enjoyable and seems to calm my temper.

Life has been turned upside down in my little world, but in the most marvellous way. My weight's going down, my happiness is going up. It makes me a little nervous. Is this real? Can it last? When life has given you nothing but lemons, but now you have lemonade, it does make one wonder. Do happy endings exist in real life?

"Come here," a masculine voice rumbles in my ear. My worry must've been showing, because I'm being beckoned into the arms of my fiancé as we sit on the sofa this evening. My eyes close as a contented sigh escapes me. Maybe this will be OK.

***

Becky, one of my new slimming group friends has invited me round for coffee. She told me at group last night that she was really struggling at the moment, and asked me for some advice. Yes, you heard correctly, someone asked me for advice. How amazing is that?

So, I'm on my way to hers, armed with pink wafer biscuits and a jar of chocolate hazelnut spread so we can have sugary treats but within our limits. She seemed really upset, so treats are essential.

"I just seem to not lose any weight," she tells me once we're sitting comfortably.

"Have you done your food diary?"

"Yes, look."

I glance down the list.

"Is that everything?" I ask.

"Oh yes, I was very honest."

"Don't you get hungry?"

"Well yes, but it's a diet, right?"

"I'm not an expert, but I'd say you're not eating enough."

"Not enough? But it's a diet."

"OK, we're going to stop using that word. It's a lifestyle change. A healthy one. Have you got your book?"

She passes it over, and I open it at the page I was seeking. "See these?"

She nods.

"It says you can have as much of these foods as you like, without limit."

"Really as much as I like? I thought that was more of an eat some of advisory."

"As much as you like. You should never be hungry. See these ones with the little symbol? They'll actually help you lose weight."

"It's so different from every diet I've ever been on. I was expecting to limit my food intake."

"Try it. Honestly, eat lots of these things for a week or two. If you don't lose weight you can try a different approach. But I'm pretty sure you'll see the difference."

She agrees to try, and we start to discuss some personal issues which had come up for her too. Sorry, you don't get to hear juicy details. Like so many of us, food has been an emotional crutch for her, and something used to beat herself up with too. She's yo-yoed from over eating to under eating. But hopefully she's now on the path to a happy medium. I'm honoured to be able to pass on some of the stuff I've learned.

***

Phew, Wendy and I have been having the time of our lives, planning the wedding. It's so much easier with two heads working on it.

Our tastes are similar, but we already knew that. The theme is set as 'country chic'. Nothing too ornate. Simple, clean, prettiness.

The months speed by in a frenzy of ideas. At one point I wonder whether a year is enough to put everything in place. The venue is booked, which allays my main fear. Everything else is just window dressing, right? As long as we turn up and say 'I do' that's what matters.

Summer is manic, and my attention is directed towards other people's events. Flowers come, they get arranged, they go; it's an endless conveyor of creation. The early mornings and late nights begin to take their toll though.

"Molly, stop, just stop," Nick shouts, grabbing my arms.

He tried the subtle approach, but I refused to listen, so he's trying the forceful alternative.

I struggle against his grip.

"I can't," I wail, avoiding his gaze.

"Just for five minutes."

"There's too much to do."

He pulls me by my hand, away from my workbench. I let myself get led up the garden path, literally, not figuratively. The only light in my dark garden is the solar lanterns. Looking at my watch, I notice it's gone midnight.

My arse gets plonked down at the table, and Nick brings me a bowl of fruit salad.

"You know what you're like when you're hungry."

"But there's no time."

"Make time. What sort of arrangements are you going to produce in your current state?"

He's right and I know it. Damn him.

"Did you eat dinner?" he asks, glaring at me.

My blush and downcast look tells him all he needs to know.

"Molly, just because I'm not here doesn't give you the excuse to neglect yourself."

He's been working late, and came home to a frazzled mess. It's the first time I've forgotten to eat in ages. But he wasn't here, and I got distracted. It's not like I did it on purpose.

"Sorry. Thank you," I say, taking the bowl and looking sheepish.

As I begin to eat so does he. Hypocrite, I bet he didn't eat dinner at work either.

"No, I didn't do any better myself."

"What? Did I say something?" Eek, I didn't, did I?

"No, you didn't have to. I know that scowl."

Maybe it's the sugar rush from the fruit, or maybe it's his intimate knowledge of me, but a grin creeps across my face.

"I love you," I tell him.

"Good. I love you too. Now come on, we can take mugs of coffee and instant pasta, and finish up together."

"But aren't you tired?"

"Yes. Aren't you?" he asks with that boyish grin of his.

"OK."

"Besides, it'll get done quicker with both of us working. Then maybe you can get some sleep."

"God, I hope so," I reply, dragging my hands down my face.

I love my job, and can't imagine doing anything else. But I do also love sleep. It's in short supply at this time of year though.

Nick gives me a 'friends again' hug before we head back to the 'creation station' together.

***

With the wedding season in full swing, time flashes by in an instant. Admittedly, the lack of sleep did make me a little prickly. But Saint Nick coped marvellously. He has a way of calming my inner beast better than I do myself. And without the aid of chocolate or biscuits.

If anything, it's proved our strength as a couple. If we can withstand that, we'll be able to cope with anything. More and more, I'm sure we're doing the right thing by getting married.

It's a bit difficult to reciprocate in the job assistance. I can't exactly help with his work. But he tells me that by just being there, and always being happy to see him, I supply all the support he needs.

Slowly, the manic period starts to fade. It's been my best summer yet, which I'm really grateful for. It's wonderful to see Holly Molly thriving; it's a complete success. But I'm also grateful for a brief respite, a chance to draw breath.

We're hiring the wedding co-ordinator at the venue, so thankfully, a lot of the pressure is off. Not that our mothers know, but we've chosen hessian bows for the chairs. I'm hoping to get a sash in the same material once I've chosen my gown too.

There's a standing joke between Nick and myself; in our early days, I commented that I looked like a sack of potatoes. He told me off, and corrected it to, "You'd look good, even in a sack." So the sack material is our little in-joke, as well as being suitable for the country chic theme. What? Of course Wendy's OK with it. She loves it, and has some funny little touches of her own too.

My birthday was a lot more fun this year. We all went out for a lovely meal, followed by a trip to the theatre. This may sound very middle aged, but I am, and this is what I wanted to do. Of course, I still had to celebrate with my parents, but Nick was by my side, and even that was almost enjoyable.

Leaves are turning to burned umber and gold as autumn arrives. We're all working together to finalise our guest list. Even combined, it's not a huge wedding with a mere eighty guests. Wendy and I are friends with mostly the same people, and Nick's not from around here, and doesn't have very many colleagues to invite.

To be honest, we're all a little glad of this. If it weren't for the mothers, I think the four of us would elope to a tropical island to perform our nuptials. But as critical as she is, I can't do that to my mother. Neither can Wendy. So, we're being good girls and having a moderately formal do.

The novelty of Nick living with me has worn off. Not in a bad way. He's part of the furniture now. Wait, that sounds bad. Not like that. Oh, he's just settled into my life comfortably and we're used to each other. Do you know what I mean? It's a good thing. We have some semblance of a routine going. I've been a little Nick deprived over the summer, due more to my own work than his. There's not been much chance for quality time together. But we're making up for it now. And we've even booked a holiday in November. It's only to Tenerife, but it's a welcome break away.

As the wedding's in June, we won't be able to go on honeymoon straight away. It may be slightly irresponsible for a florist to get married in a prime wedding month as it is. But that's when the flowers I want are growing, and I want the chance of warm weather for the big day. So, the compromise is to go on honeymoon later in the year.

However, neither Nick nor myself can wait that long to get some down time. And as work's been going so well we can treat ourselves to a little break. Just somewhere warm where we can lie like lizards, soaking up some rays. I can't wait. A whole week of Nick and me without any interruptions. Bliss.

The Bahamas are reserved for our honeymoon in the autumn. Wendy and Nick are lucky enough to be able to go on theirs straight after the wedding, and are heading to the Seychelles in June. It'll be the most exotic holiday either of us girls have ever had. It's almost as exciting as the wedding itself.

Chapter 36 – Plans

As winter approached, our countdown truly began. The entertainment, officiant, photographer and band have all been booked. I'm doing the flowers. I simply couldn't hand over control to anyone else. And we're keeping it simple. It's going to be an effort, but I'll cope. Most of the prep can be done before. It'll be fine. No, don't look at my face as I say that; it may be scrunching up, but that's no indication of my feelings. Nope.

The catering is being done in-house, so all we had to do was select the menu, which wasn't too much of an effort. It all looked good, and we actually selected the cheapest.

We've put it off as long as possible, but Wendy and I are finally dress shopping. I've been climbing the walls, stressing over this bit. But we wanted to be closer to our target weight before making this momentous decision. We should still need alterations closer to the day, but at least we're now close enough to judge style.

The shop assistant greets us with a smile and a glass of champagne as we arrive for our appointment. Wendy and I have done our homework and have armed ourselves with ideas of the best dress shape for our new figures. But our jaws still drop as we start walking along the rails of gowns. There's so many, and they're all squished together. I've no idea what type any of them are. It's a maze of ivory and white.

"What sort of style did you have in mind?" the assistant asks.

"I was thinking of a mermaid," Wendy says with a proud grin.

She's a little taller than me, and the figure hugging style should complement her gorgeous curves.

"And an A-line for me, please," I add.

We both sigh with relief as the lady pulls out a few options for us to look at, smiling all the while.

"And there's a few others for you to try, so you can select your favourite. They can be really quite different once they're on."

"Thank you," we chorus.

Feeling braver, we scour the racks, and find a few more which get taken into the changing rooms.

The able assistant is joined by another, and they help us do up the fastenings. There's a lot of giggling coming from the cubicle next to me, as well as from me.

Walking out, we giggle more.

"I *thought* I always wanted to be a princess," I state in mock glumness, fluffing out the huge skirt.

The large princess style swamps my short frame, as I knew it would. But I wanted to try it, just to see. My weight has decreased, but my height hasn't increased, obviously. I'm still short, and am left wishing I could grow so this beautiful dress would look right on me.

"Hm, maybe not," Wendy agrees.

She opted for a sexy silky number, which makes me frown a little as I shake my head. "Sorry. It's not really doing much for you, is it?"

Wendy clearly had already come to the same conclusion, judging by her downturned mouth.

"No. Next," she declares.

Back into the changing rooms we go. More wriggling and pulling ensue. I'm starting to feel out of puff. This dress malarkey is hard work.

Wendy convinced me to try on a mermaid gown. You know, all fitted before it flares out from the knee, like a fish tail. My steps are limited to a little waddle as I walk out to meet Wendy again.

"Oh, I love it," I gasp, looking at Wendy, my hands going to my mouth.

The mermaid style is definitely better on her. Tears spring to my eyes as I see them in hers.

"Molly, it's perfect. I think this is the one."

Our cheeks are moistened by our tears as we reach over for a hug.

"You're beautiful," I admire.

The assistants are on hand with tissues.

"What about you?" she asks as we wipe away our tears.

"Oh, it's much better on you," I snivel, "I'm still a work in progress."

"Are you still trying on your others?" I check, not wanting to drag this out for her if she's done.

"Oh yes. I know this is it, but I want to be really sure."

I shuffle back, and dress number three gets put on. It's my dream A-line one.

"Nothing suits me," I whimper as I shlump out to my friend.

"There's still more. We'll find something."

"But this was supposed to be the one." My lips are trembling as panic sets in.

"Well, that doesn't mean the right one's not here somewhere. Come on. Next!" she says, giving me a shove towards the changing room.

My heart sinks along with the fabric as it falls to the ground. This is supposed to be a magical experience, isn't it? But despite having lost all this weight, I feel as big as ever. I'm never going to look like a supermodel. Why can bridal magazines not advertise dresses using realistic women? My expectations have been set too high.

This dress is no better, and a tear trickles down my cheek.

"It really is useless," I tell Wendy.

"No it's not. This one's not that bad. There's still hope and other dresses to try."

"But nothing's right."

"So far."

She nudges me into the changing room again. I prefer the other dress she tried. The current one is nice, but not as good. The realisation halts my tears. Not all hers are winners either, but she's found the one.

My expectations are at an all-time low though as I try on a different A-line dress. It still feels too figure hugging as I get wedged in. It's got a dropped waist, so flares out near my hips, exposing the shape of my tummy. I can't withhold a sigh as the assistant seals me in and ties the sash.

My feet shuffle me out to Wendy, my eyes fixed towards the floor.

"Molly! Oh, Molly, look at yourself in the mirror. Oooohhh," she ends in sobs.

Obeying her command, I look up.

"Is that me?" I gasp.

My friend silently nods.

"Oh. Really? It can't be. I'm…I'm…"

"Beautiful," she finishes for me.

We're both in bits, and grab more tissues, blowing our noses and wiping our eyes.

It's a miracle. The reflection is stunning. My hands touch the fabric then my face as I try to believe the bride in the mirror is really me.

The wide, ivory, lace shoulder straps hold 'the girls' securely in place whilst flattering them in a v-neckline. My waist is pulled in, highlighted by the sash, which incidentally, is at least the colour of hessian. The lace bodice holds in any wobbly bits, and flares out in soft netted gorgeousness. The chapel train disguises my bum beautifully, I notice whilst turning around.

Wendy joins me in the mirror, as she looks at herself too. She's back in her favourite dress.

"We're really going to be brides," Wendy whispers.

"We're really going to be brides," I confirm, grabbing a hug.

***

After that, all the rest of the planning has been relatively straight forward. I'm alarmingly calm. There's seven months to go, and there's no panic. Everything's going smoothly. Too smoothly. I'm waiting for something dreadful to happen.

Even our mothers behaved when we took them to view our dress choices. Neither Wendy nor I wanted to be put off by judgement before we'd made our minds up. There was some mild muttering, but they seem happy enough that we're being respectable. Mother really is trying hard, bless her.

Before I know it, Nick and I are taking off on our holiday to Tenerife. Up, up and away. The contrast of the warm heat which greets us as we get off the plane with the chilly, grey drizzle when we boarded is astonishing.

To the others on the coach, we must appear to be that sickeningly in love couple, but I couldn't care less. I'm happily snuggling into my fiancé's side, and make no apologies for that. There's a stag party on our coach, roaring their excitement, so maybe nobody actually notices us.

"Have you sorted out your stag do?" I ask Nick, my voice thick with sleepiness.

"Nothing to sort. I'm just going out for drinks with a few of the guys. Nothing like those guys," he tells me quietly, indicating our boisterous coach companions.

"Is that it? Is that what you want?" I ask through a yawn.

"Yes. Now, get some sleep. I'll wake you up when we get there."

The action of the coach rolling along soon sends me to sleep, despite the noise, with my head resting against my Nick pillow.

A kiss on the top of my head has me stirring from my slumber.

"We're here."

How did that happen? My aching limbs are forced out of my seat, and my feet shuffle down and out of the coach. Nick collects our luggage and leads the way to the hotel reception. I prop myself up against a wall as he checks us in.

"Come on Sleeping Beauty," he calls, holding out the room keys.

In a daze, I follow him. What is it about travelling that is so tiring? It's not like I'm not used to early starts, but I'm shattered.

After a quick look round the room, I flump down on the bed and take a nap. So romantic, aren't I? But when I'm woken up, it's time for dinner, and my stomach is rumbling its displeasure at being neglected.

We're staying all inclusive, and there's a large selection at the buffet. Keeping my beautiful wedding gown in mind, I make the healthiest choices possible.

The following days are filled with strolls, a fair bit of swimming, and plenty of bedroom antics. Sun lounging intersperses our activity. Utter bliss! It's all I hoped for and more. Wall-to-wall Nick. I don't think it's possible to be happier. But that may be the cocktails talking. There's a fair few of those too.

But you know what? As I make my way down to the pool, I strut. My body's barely hidden by my bikini, and I'm owning it, proud of my tremendous success. I may not look like some of the super skinny girls around here, but I'm me, and that's good enough. So, my head's held high as we search for a spare sunbed.

Our luxurious time disappears in a haze. And all too soon it's time to head home. I wish our whole life could be this way, but that's only possible for lottery winners, isn't it?

The holiday blues are hitting hard as I work through the cold and the damp of home. But my spirits are lifted at my next weigh-in. Thanks to my increased exercise, and careful choices, I've actually still lost weight this week.

***

Christmas arrives in the blink of an eye. Nick and I have been invited to spend it with his parents, who I've not met yet, and probably ought to, seeing as I'm marrying their son. It's only good manners, really. This of course upsets my own mother. As Nick's family live so far away, we can't see everyone on Christmas Day. We have promised to visit my parents the day after Boxing Day, but Mother is still upset with me. We went to hers last year, and poor Nick's not been to see his folks on the day itself for five years. It's only fair he does now.

"You're fussing. Come on, we need to leave," Nick gently chastises me.

At least three different outfits have been tried on and discarded, and my hair's not staying in place, no matter how much hairspray's applied.

"I just want to look nice."

He pulls my hips to his.

"You look beautiful, as always, Gorgeous," he tells me before planting a kiss on the end of my nose.

"Thank you," I whisper, allowing myself a moment to nestle in his arms.

Pulling away and taking a few deep breaths, I nod at Nick. "OK. I'm ready."

"They're going to love you."

"I hope so."

They live near Nottingham, so I have over three hours to worry away. Nick insisted on driving, bless him. As I fidget and rearrange my hair in the mirror, I appreciate this was probably for the best. My attention's all over the place, and my mind insists on playing out all the potential outcomes.

Nick's younger sister is with her boyfriend's family. Apparently, she's devastated she's going to miss us, but had already agreed. But it means I'm under even closer scrutiny. It's just us and his parents.

Music. I'll concentrate on the radio. I start singing along to the Christmas tunes the station is insisting on playing. Which is fine until they play "Driving Home for Christmas". Eurgh, home, his home. What if his parents don't like me?

Every so often, Nick's hand gives mine a squeeze before he returns it to the steering wheel. And he keeps trying to say all the right things. But I still don't feel good enough.

My lipstick's been bitten off by my nervous actions, so I quickly apply some more as Nick informs me we're nearly there.

The car comes to a stop outside a nice semi-detached Victorian house.

"You're going to be fine," he tells me for the hundredth time, kissing my cheek.

Sucking in more air, I undo my seatbelt and climb out of the car on shaky legs.

We're halfway up the path when the front door opens.

"There you are. Hello," his mum cheers.

Nick rushes into her open arms and gets plastered with kisses.

"I've missed you. How are you? How was the traffic?"

Wrestling his way out of her arms, he replies, "I missed you too. We're good. Sorry it took us longer than expected. Traffic was a nightmare."

"Never mind. You're here now. And this must be Molly," she cheers, holding out her arms to me.

My feet appear to be glued to the ground.

"Hello," I say with a small wave.

"Don't be shy. I'm so happy to meet you at last." She beckons me forward.

She must've sensed my discomfort and settles for a hand hold whilst inspecting me.

"Nick, she's every bit as beautiful as you said," she tells him, leading the way inside.

Over her shoulder, she adds with a wink, "I thought he might've stolen a celebrity photo off the internet." I blush wildly, realising he must've told her about that long ago first conversation in the coffee shop.

"I'm sorry it's been so long before we could meet, Mrs Harding," I apologise.

"Please call me Alison. And I didn't mean it that way. It's hard for you, living all that way away. I'm surprised you managed now. And we've not been able to come down either, so it's as much our fault anyway."

"Is that them?" a voice calls from the back of the house.

"Who else would it be? Come and say hello," Alison yells back.

"Right with you."

A tall, slim, older man emerges, wiping his hands on a tea towel. One of those hands gets extended to me.

"Hello, you must be Molly. I'm Barry. Glad you could make it to these northern lands," he says with a laugh.

"Hi," is all I manage in response.

To be honest, I'm taken aback by all this enthusiasm, and am still waiting for a raised eyebrow or an acerbic comment. I'm to be their daughter-in-law, surely there's something that means I'm not worthy of their boy?

But nothing horrible passes all day. Alison shows me to the guest room so I can freshen up after our journey. We're staying here overnight, and there's guest towels neatly piled on the end of the bed, and cushions at the head. She's clearly gone to a lot of effort. It's like she's trying to impress me, not the other way round.

Barry's the main chef apparently, but is being assisted by his wife. We're given orders to relax in the lounge. Drinks and snacks are brought in from time-to-time.

Nick's grinning at me.

"What?" I ask him, squinting.

"Told you so."

"Told me what?"

"That they'd love you."

"Alright smart arse," I tell him, lightly tapping him with a cushion.

Pulling me into a hug, he asks, "Do you believe me now?"

"About what?"

"That you're gorgeous and a lovely person."

"Maybe I'm starting to."

Our ensuing kiss is interrupted by a call of, "Lunch is ready."

"This looks wonderful," I admire as we walk into the dining room.

Candles are lit, tasteful decorations hang across the ceiling, the place settings are all laid out with colour coordinated precision, and the plates are piled high, with extra helpings waiting in serving bowls.

"I won't be hurt if you don't eat it all. But it's Christmas, and we wanted to spoil you two. We may have got a bit carried away," Alison says, smiling.

"I'll do my best," I say, returning her grin, taking my place at the table.

Christmas songs play softly in the background as we eat and talk. Questions fly around, but none are obtrusive, merely curious. And my answers are met with smiles and nods, not a single scowl in sight. Sitting back in my chair, rubbing my stomach, I have to admit defeat.

"That was delicious. Thank you so much," I tell Barry.

"You're welcome. I was glad to have the excuse. Taught Nick everything he knows," he says with a head bob in his son's direction.

The routine is reminiscent of my own family's. We decamp to the lounge, heaving ourselves onto the sofas whilst we digest the copious quantity of food. The TV is on quietly, but gets turned up for the Queen's Speech, which we all have an opinion on. As similar as the actions are, the atmosphere is a million miles away. We're relaxed and informal. There's free-flowing conversation and plenty of laughter. This only increases as the board games come out in the evening. I've lost count of the glasses of wine that've been poured into me, but I'm sure there's a slight slur in my voice.

Somehow, we manage to eat a small plate from the buffet his parents spread out at dinner time.

Nick is so happy here. His boyish grin has barely left his cheeks all day. It's clear this was a loving home, and still is. He's been supported and cherished his whole life.

"You've had a long day. Don't stay up on our account," Alison gently encourages me.

My eyes are trying to close, so I smile and thank them both, and let Nick pull me upstairs to our room for the night. My clothes are barely off my back before I flollop down on the bed and instantly fall asleep.

I'm only vaguely aware of a whispered, "I'm so proud of you. I love you."

Chapter 37 - Oh My Days

Buoyed by the success of Christmas, the new year starts on a positive footing. The six month countdown clock has started ticking. Eep! So, amidst dismantling Christmas, we all start to look at the invitations, and have set up a website, or wedsite if you will.

We're trying to include the boys in our decisions, but they keep waving us on, telling us they're happy as long as we're happy. We've actually booked our honeymoons, which they did have an opinion on. It's all really happening, isn't it? Pinch me.

The registrar has met us all, and we've now registered our intent to marry. And Wendy's told me which flowers she wants. I really hope I've not bitten off more than I can chew here. Maybe we should've booked another florist, but the idea had my stomach twisting itself in knots.

Each new month seems to bring a new task, but I'm still trying to desperately lose my last bit of weight and run a business and spend time with my fiancé. As the big day approaches, my stress levels increase. The cake gets ordered, shoes and underwear purchased, dress fittings conducted, hair and makeup trials are performed, music is selected, invitations are sent, readings are organised, vows are confirmed, rings are bought, bookings firmed up, deposits paid, a small hen day at a spa is enjoyed (and much needed), the license is obtained, seating plans are formed, oh the list has been seemingly endless.

The first half of the year has disappeared in the blink of an eye. I barely noticed the seasons changing, yet planning seems to have lasted an eternity. But finally the day is almost upon us.

Wendy has come to my house, and the boys are in her place. Being careful not to chip my manicured nails, I'm arranging my own wedding flowers with Wendy supervising. I say supervising, but she's standing there, happily watching whilst sipping her wine.

We've chatted the evening away.

"Go on. Off you go. You need your beauty sleep," I say with a chuckle, shooing Wendy with my hands.

"You need it more. And you're not finished yet," she retorts, laughing.

"I'm nearly done. Go on."

"No. I'm going to stay until you're done, otherwise it's not fair." Her voice is ever so slightly slurred.

"Fine. But don't blame me if your eye bags are like suitcases in the morning."

"I won't," she tells me with a dopey grin.

I really hope she doesn't wake up with a hangover. We're both nervous excited, but I've deliberately not had much to drink, as I wanted to be sober so the flowers didn't end up in a mess. Wendy seems to have taken it upon herself to have my share.

Right now, I'm happy I decided to do our flowers. It's almost distracting my mind and calming my nerves. My fingers are only slightly trembling as I poke flowers into arrangements, trying to do as much as I can tonight, so tomorrow it's just me to get ready.

Jan really outdid himself. He was glowing with pride as he delivered these magnificent blooms. There's Victorian Blush Peonies for each of our bouquets. I've got Quicksand Roses, Chocolate Cosmos and Wax Flower for mine. And Wendy has succulents, Dusty Miller and Ivory Garden Roses in hers. A combination of these are going into the table displays. The grooms are getting a small rose with a little of our selected foliage for their buttonholes.

It's getting late, but I don't think I'd be able to sleep anyway.

"Come on, you're done," Wendy finally whines.

"I'm not. But you go up if you want to."

"I may not be an expert, but even I can see you're fussing. Come on, before you get overly perfectionist."

"I am not—"

"Molly, don't even think of finishing that sentence. I love you. And your professionalism is admirable, but come on. You are a perfectionist and you know it. Put...the...flowers...down," she finishes firmly.

My eyes roll, but I have to concede. I know she's right. "Fine. Come on."

Looking over my shoulder for a final glance, I turn out the lights in the 'creation station'.

"See you in the morning," I whisper to the flowers, and sigh deeply.

Only I seem to notice the little buzz of my late night striped friend.

Wendy squeezes my shoulders. "We're going to be fine."

"I know. I just want it to be perfect."

My friend plonks herself in front of me, halting my progress through the garden.

343

Looking me straight in the eyes, she tells me, "Nothing in life is ever perfect. We're human, perfectly imperfect. And that's OK. We're us. Now deal with it."

She wobbles slightly as she finishes her little speech, sounding like a positive quote meme. But something hits home. I inwardly accept all of me; every part. The good and the not so good.

I'm at my target weight, so am finally healthy, I've been primped and preened to within an inch of my life. Tomorrow I'll be the best ever version of me, at least so far. Am I perfect? Hell no. But you know what? I'm pretty bloody happy with who and what I am.

Thirty-six years old, thinner, still short, successful florist, home owner, bride-to-be. Redhead with a fiery temper, but a kind soul and big heart. That's not bad going, is it?

As we make our way up the garden, I take slow wide strides like a bride. Wendy links arms with me and we sing the tum tum te tum of "The Bridal Chorus", giggling madly on our way to our beds.

***

The sun has barely risen when my alarm goes off. Today's the day. I'm getting married. Eep.

Silently creeping downstairs, I grab a coffee and take it with me to the 'creation station' to check on our flowers. Surprisingly, they're still there. I know, shocker, right? They shine like beacons of love through the glimmer of the overhead lights. I can't resist a final zhush before heading back inside.

As quietly as possible, I make breakfast. Wendy pads downstairs in her dressing gown and slippers. We beam massive grins at each other.

"Good morning Mrs to be," I chime.

"Morning, fellow bride," she returns.

"Eggs and bacon OK?" I check.

"I think so. I'm so nervous, I'm not sure I can eat anything."

"I know what you mean, but let's give it a go, shall we?" I ask, dishing up said food.

We manage to eat, and wash breakfast down with cups of tea, before heading up to have a quick shower, Wendy first. Well, she's a guest here, so it's polite.

I sneak back to the 'creation station' as she's getting ready, eager to check one more time.

Once we're both changed, it's time to make our way to the venue. She helps me load the van, our happiness flowing out in laughter all the while. Our bags and gowns are also piled into the back.

"Ready?" I ask.

"Ready," she replies with a firm nod.

"Then let's do this."

We make our merry way to our venue, unusually silent. My head is ticking off things on the list, and I'm taking deep breaths, trying to reassure myself that everything's all sorted. It's slightly grey overhead. Rain may still fall yet.

Antonio comes out to greet us as we pull up.

"Ciao bella. How are our beautiful brides?"

"Oh, fine. You know, nervous happy."

"Ah, a little nerves is a good thing. I am here, at your service," he declares, holding out his hands.

"Thank you," I say as I pass him one of the displays.

"Anything for our most important VIPs ever."
Presumably, he's here to make sure the brides don't fall arse over tit, but I'm grateful for his help. The three of us get the flowers inside in record time. Karen met us in the wedding breakfast room, and has made a start on placing the centrepieces for us. And has kept the buttonholes to give to the boys. She's our wedding coordinator, and the one who came to my aid that fateful day.

Coming with us on the last trip, Karen takes our bouquets, and carries them to our rooms whilst a porter helps with our bags.

"Right. Do you have everything you need?" Karen asks.

"Yes, I think so for now. Thank you."

"Everything's in place as arranged. I'll send up your hair and makeup ladies once they arrive. And some champagne will accompany them. I'll leave you to start getting ready. Call down if you need anything."

As she leaves, I turn to Wendy who's in my room with me. "I don't know about you, but I need another shower."

"Good idea. I'll nip into my room, and be back in a jiffy."

"Take the spare key," I tell her, pointing to the one on the desk.

We made it. The flowers are here safely. I didn't fall down the steps. It's going well. These are the thoughts buzzing through my mind as the hot water cascades over me.

Putting on my robe and slippers I begin to get nervous again.

Staring at myself in the enormous bathroom mirror I tell myself, "There's nothing to be nervous about. You're marrying Nick. We know Nick. He's lovely. This is the happiest day of your life. Just think calm thoughts."

It doesn't help. My tummy butterflies are out of control. This is ridiculous. Seriously, what do I have to be nervous about? It's not like I can get stuck in traffic. Wendy and I are here. Our dresses are here, hanging up. We just have to wait for the boys and guests to turn up.

A knock raps at my door.

"Are you decent?" a familiar voice calls.

"Only in so much as I'm dressed," I reply.

A similarly enrobed Wendy slowly emerges.

"Why am I so nervous?" she asks.

"No idea. Why am I?"

"Oh, that's easy. Because you're as daft as a brush," she giggles.

"Thanks," I tell her with a mock unamused look before laughing.

"Honestly. What are we like? It's a happy day," she says, grabbing me for a hug.

There's another knock at the door.

"Hair and makeup," a lady hollers.

We race over to let the two ladies in. As promised, a waiter is on hand with a tray of champagne filled glasses and snacks.

"Oh, I'm even happier to see you," I tell him, leading us all into the room.

The waiter beats a hasty retreat once he places the tray down. I waste no time in grabbing a glass and offering the others around.

"OK, who's first?" the hairdresser asks brightly.

It starts. She works on pulling and combing my hair into submission whilst the makeup artist makes Wendy even prettier, before we swap seats. The ladies are very good at chatting away our nerves, and we're happily laughing as the transformation into bride takes place.

The hairdresser stops and kindly answers the door for us. Our mothers are here, looking very smart in dresses and hats. They start buzzing around, but the girls are brilliant at continuing their styling as planned.

The photographer arrives, and starts snapping our 'getting ready' shots. Shoes and rings are lined up and have their photos taken too.

There's a hive of activity as we buzz around, posing. The hairdresser checks her watch. "OK, do you need help getting into your dresses, ladies?"

"Oh, would you? That would be marvellous, please," I reply.

"Yes please. I need all the help I can get," Wendy adds.

"Oh, that saves my nails. Thank you," Mother chips in.

"That's my cue to leave. I'll go and take photos of the venue, and will be back in about twenty minutes," the photographer informs us as he heads towards the door.

My dress has been taken in quite a lot, and it requires some fine wiggling to get into, but with the hairdresser holding it, we manage to get me in. The makeup artist is assisting Wendy.

"It's so lovely having two brides in all their finery," she admires once we're both dressed.

"Are either of you wearing a veil?" the hairdresser asks.

We nod in unison, and she helps secure them in place.

"No, no—," Mother starts, but stops whatever criticism was about to come out of her mouth.

"You're both beautiful. I think our work here is done," the hairdresser admires.

"Thank you so much," Wendy and I chorus.

"Our pleasure," she says, packing up.

The ladies leave us, and the slow wait starts. The room's suddenly quiet after all the manic preparations.

I hold Wendy's hands and tell her, "You really do look beautiful."

"Thanks. So do you. This is it. We're brides, Molly."

"We really are, aren't we?" I ask, touching my veil as I turn to gaze in the mirror.

It still feels surreal.

"You look radiant," Mother tells me.

It's still a struggle to tell if she's being critical or complimentary sometimes. She could mean I look hot and sweaty, but I choose to take this comment as a good one. It's my wedding day; there's no room for anything buy happy thoughts.

"Knock knock, only me," cries the photographer as he taps on our door.

Wendy goes to let him in.

"Don't you both look gorgeous? I think we have time for some more photos before we go down."

"Have the boys arrived?"

"Yes, they're downstairs, looking handsome."

I breathe out a sigh of relief. Thank goodness. Now anything else really doesn't matter. The people saying 'I do' are on the premises. So why is my stomach tightening?

The makeup artist didn't touch her champagne, so I wander across and start sipping, leaving Wendy to have her photos taken. Mother casts a disapproving glance in my direction, but I ignore her.

"Are you OK?" Wendy asks me quietly as she wanders over.

"Yeah. I think so. I don't know."

"It's all a bit real, isn't it?"

"There's going to be so many people down there."

"All people we know, and who will be looking at the beautiful brides. And your Nick will be at the end of that aisle. Just focus on him."

"You're right. I know you are. Just focus on Nick. Sure. I can do that," I say, taking another sip.

"They're both lovely boys. You'll be fine," Wendy's mother adds with a nod which makes the feather on her hat bounce.

"I think a shot of you both by the window here," the photographer announces.

He's still snapping away as Karen knocks and enters with our fathers.

"How are we doing, ladies?" Karen asks.

"Fine, I think," I reply.

"We're good," Wendy affirms.

"You look beautiful," my father tells me, wiping at his eyes.

"Don't. You'll start me off," I warn him, fanning my face with my hands.

"I'm so proud of you."

More fanning happens as I blink back tears.

Wendy's getting hugged by her father as mine hugs me.

"Here, quick," Mother says, passing me a tissue, "Dab, don't wipe."

"The guests are all seated, and your gorgeous men are waiting for you," Karen announces once we all get ourselves back under control.

A thrill runs through me at her words.

"I'll see you down there," the photographer tells us as he leaves.

We take a minute to steady ourselves again. Phew! Up, down, up, down, this is becoming a bit of a rollercoaster, isn't it?

"Ready?" Karen asks, and receives head nods from us both.

Deep breaths, deep breaths. Phhhhw. Nick. Think of Nick.

With sweaty palms gripping onto my bouquet, I follow Karen out of the room, with Wendy behind. Down the stairs we step, dresses gathered up a little to ensure we don't trip, our mothers holding our trains up. Down the corridor, and past reception.

"Ciao bella, beautiful ladies, you all look beautiful," Antonio calls as we pass.

Really? Does he ever turn off? Oh, to hell with it, this is a happy day.

"Grazie, Antonio," I coo before blowing him a kiss and sending him a playful wink.

Giggling, we proceed to the room. Karen and the mothers ensure our attire is all perfect, before disappearing through a side door.

A few minutes later, music greets us as she opens the main doors from the inside, and the guests rise to their feet. The thrum of the action makes me jump a little, but I begin my walk down the aisle, "The Butterfly Waltz" measuring my steps. I grasp onto my father's arm for support, grinning through shaking lips.

Amelia looks tired as she bounces her little boy in her arms.

Further along I go. Sharon is grinning at me in amongst the ex colleague crowd. No Paul, mercifully. Tum tum tum, the music carries me along. Jan comes into view, looking very dashing next to his boyfriend. I knew I was right about him. It's lovely to see him looking so happy.

Another step. My eyes travel upwards, towards the front. I see him. Nick is smiling at me. Relief flows through my veins, carrying a surge of excitement. It's as much as I can do not to run the rest of the way into his arms. Father has a firm hold though, and we continue serenely until he can pass me over to my fiancé. We're both grinning like the proverbial cat with the cream.

Wendy and her father follow closely behind, and she takes her place next to Gary. The fathers join our mothers.

"Gorgeous, you've outdone yourself," Nick whispers as he plants a kiss on my cheek.

I smile at him, but am struggling to hold back my tears. My cheeks, lips and, well, possibly everything are trembling. Does it show?

As the registrar speaks, I look up at Nick next to me, and nothing else matters. His hand squeezes mine, and it dawns on me, as my voice tremors across my vows, that this was never about nerves. It was love. A love which now bursts forth from my lips and eyes; having been contained all morning, building up its intensity until it had no option but to erupt.

Cheers erupt as we have our kiss after making our vows, my eyes glistening all the while. We sign the register, along with our witnesses. And then we return the favour. More tears flow down my face as my friend completes her nuptials.

With "The Waltz of the Flowers" serenading us, we're led outside where many more photos are taken.

"Molly, you look beautiful," Mother tells me with a wide smile, her eyes dewy as we have our photograph taken.

Well, there's no mistaking that one. Definitely a compliment. From Mother. Who would've ever thought that would happen? I decide on the spot that it's the best wedding gift I could ever wish for.

My cheeks are hurting by the time Karen leads us to a room as the guests are seated for their feast. My grin may be stuck this way forever now.

Then she announces us, "Ladies and gentlemen, please be upstanding for your brides and grooms. Dr & Mrs Harding, and Mr & Mrs Phillips."

Another thrill runs through me, as I hear my new name. I'm really Mrs Harding now. My eyes are wet again when I look at my husband as we enter the room as man and wife.

Epilogue

It's been over a year. I'm sorry I went quiet. It's been hectic.

My post wedding blues were somewhat numbed by the many brides coming through my doors. I still had weddings to plan for, even if a part of me did wish it was me all over again. Our day was so wonderful. You know one of those that you wish you could just freeze in time and relive forever?

The Bahamas were glorious, and we were spoiled on our honeymoon. We managed to get an upgrade on the plane. The hotel was a paradise; picture postcard perfect.

Gary's parents decided it was time to retire down south, so have moved a lot closer. That made Christmas a lot easier. We all piled round their house, so my mother didn't have to cook, with the promise it's her turn next year.

Nick finally has a new team member, as the budget was increased after much nagging, so he's around a lot more now. Which will come in very handy.

You see, I'm sitting here, holding our brand new daughter in my arms as she sleeps. Yep, I just gave birth to baby Alice. She's so tiny but is making my heart burst. I know instantly I'll do anything to make her happy and safe.

Tears are glistening in Nick's eyes as he stands by my side, the very model of a proud father.

There were times during the pregnancy where I was sick, that I panicked as the number on the scales went up and up, where I hurt all over, when I couldn't sleep. But they were all worth it. Alice wiggles in her sleep as if to prove the point. She's here.

Wendy gave birth to Olivia last month. I hope they grow up to be as firm friends as their mothers.

I never thought I'd get here, to this happy place, but I have. It's been a tough journey, but once I started respecting myself it got easier.

Some things I've learned through all of this:

What's on the inside really is as important as the outside. Weight loss alone will not make you happy, it has to be a holistic approach.

It's a lifestyle, not a diet. My healthy ways are here to stay. I had to find food I enjoyed, not torture myself with, so it can stay on my menu forever.

I am worthy of love and affection.

I will live every day of the rest of my life with a grateful heart, counting my many blessings.

Self-love is not selfish, it's essential.

And...

The most important love is the one you have for yourself.

It opened up the door to the greatest love of my life.

Thank you for reading Self Love.

Please do leave a review, they are more valuable to me than you can imagine.

About the Author

TL Clark is a British author who stumbles through life as if it were a gauntlet of catastrophes.

Rather than playing the victim she uses these unfortunate events to fuel her passion for writing, for reaching out to help others.

Her dream is to buy a farmhouse, so she can run a retreat for those who are feeling frazzled by the stresses of the modern world.

She writes about different kinds of love in the hope that she'll uncover its mysteries.

Her loving husband (and very spoiled cat) have proven to her that true love really does exist.
Writing has shown her that coffee may well be the source of life.

If you would like to follow TL or just drop in for a chat online, you can do so on Twitter, Facebook, Goodreads or Instagram

@tlclarkauthor will find her across most social media

She also has a blog where she shares random thoughts and book reviews. She's very kind and supportive, so often reviews other indie authors.

You can also sign up for her newsletter on her blog, to ensure you don't miss any exciting news (about new releases or special offers).

http://tlclarkauthor.blogspot.co.uk

Other Books by TL Clark

<u>Young's Love</u> – One woman's fight for independence, and a holiday in Tuscany

Samantha Young is a British, downtrodden thirty-something woman. Her life is controlled by others, particularly her overbearing, abusive husband. This is the story of her voyage to independence.

Will she ever find true love?
Well, there will always be gelato, at least.

<u>Trues Love</u> – Suspense and suspended reality in Ibiza.

Mild admin by day, wild clubber by night, Amanda travels to Ibiza for fun in the sun.

A captivating Russian bodyguard challenges her defences when he saves her whilst protecting his rich client.

Danger lurks around the corner as spies and assassins zero in on their target.

Can they or their love survive?

<u>Dark Love</u> – A romance novel with BDSM in it too.

This book follows Jonathan, a male Submissive. His attention is grabbed by another woman, but can he bear to turn his back on the life he's always known and loved? Is it even possible?

This book investigates the love that exists in a BDSM relationship and beyond.

<u>Broken & Damaged Love</u> – a book with an important message.

This one comes with a trigger warning, as it features a sexually abused girl.

It was written to give hope to CSA survivors. They too can go on to have healthy, happy relationships.

Profits are regularly donated to charity from the sale of this book.

<u>Rekindled Love</u> – Hatches, matches and dispatches.

We join Sophie just in time for her first 'experience', but she gets torn away from her first love.

We go on to follow her life, through marriage, birth and death. Hers is not an easy life, but hold her hand through the bumpy bits to get to the good times.

There's a rollercoaster of emotions waiting for you.

<u>The Darkness & Light Duology</u> - The paranormal romance
– formed by Love Bites & Love Bites Harder

Shakira didn't fit in. The reason why is tragic…
…the solution is unbelievable.
A rich tale of witchcraft, sorcery, elinefae and a dragon.

Shakira struggles to balance darkness and light.

That's it for now. Don't forget to write that review.
Happy reading.

Love and light,
TL Clark

Size/Weight Conversions

Approx. ladies dress size

US	0	2	4	6	8	10	12	14	16
UK	2	4	6	8	10	12	14	16	18
EU	30	32	34	36	38	40	42	44	46

Weight (approx.)

stone	10	11	12	13	14	15	16
lbs	140	154	168	182	196	210	224
kg	63	71	76	83	89	95	102

Lightning Source UK Ltd.
Milton Keynes UK
UKHW010005130922
408733UK00001B/300